Mid-Century Murder

Edited by Andrew MacRae

DARKHOUSE
BOOKS

Anthology copyright © 2020 by Darkhouse Books
ISBN 978-1-945467-25-7
Published February, 2020
Published in the United States of America

Darkhouse Books
160 J Street, #2223
Niles, California 94539

Coming soon from
Darkhouse Books

Fearrington Road

A collection of Lovecraft-inspired
tales of mystery and horror.

*What We Talk about
When We Talk About It*

Poetry and Prose

Table of Contents

9   Scallops with a Side of Death
    by William J. O'Connor III and Arthur Vidro

27 Roadside Attraction
    by Kenneth Gwin

43 Lorna
    by Camille Minichino

53 Where's Sara Jane?
    by Michael Bracken and Sandra Murphy

73 Clara's Helper
    by John M. Floyd

87 Nothing But the Sleuth
    by Diane Arrelle

95 A Dish Best Served
    by M.M. Elmendorf

111 A Desperate Act
    by Herschel Cozine

127 4BR/3.5BA Contemporary
    by Margaret S. Hamilton

143 The Hitler Heist
    by Michele Bazan Reed

155 Agent Provocateur
    by Michael Allan Mallory

171 The Corpse Flower
    by Adam Beau McFarlane

183 Ashes to Ashes, Dust to Dust
    by Mel Goldberg

201 Year of the Pig
    by Karen Keeley

Table of Contents

219 The Tango Queen
by Albert Tucher

235 Trouble at Lunatic Lake
by DG Critchley

253 Life and Death on the Road
by Kaye George

265 Also Available from Darkhouse Books

Introduction
by Andrew MacRae

Mid-century America is rapidly receding in our rearview mirrors as we careen in our two-tone convertibles down time's highway and into the future. It was a time when television was the latest shiny object to occupy our attention, the threat of global nuclear war cast a nihilistic shadow, and the thin veneer that masked long-standing societal classist, racist, and chauvinist conventions started to be stripped away.

It was an era whose occupants pleaded for a return to normalcy, as the carnage and turbulence of World War II and Korea wove their way into stories and novels, movies and television. Rough, tough crime stories told tales of death and despair in a dark world lurking below the soft belly of what passed for normal, everyday life.

On television, Clarabell the Clown spoke for the first and last time as he said goodnight, and we watched the Howdy Doody Show fade away to a single dot. On radio, stalwart shows of long duration either successfully metamorphosed to television or became lost to the static of time. In the theaters, on stage and screen, a new generation of actors took the stage and brought a burst of intensity and vitality that forever changed that ethereal world.

Upbeat, sophisticated jazz filled the airwaves and fanciful cartoon characters populated the commercial art of the day, in capitalistic recognition of the image our nation wished to see in the mirror, while the writers, artists, and musicians of the age reflected the way we were really were.

Return with us now to those thrilling days of yesteryear!

Andrew MacRae
February, 2020
Niles, California

We begin our anthology with a slam-bang, action-filled story from William J. O'Connor III and Arthur Vidro that harkens back to the world of private investigators in post-war America. A quick stop one evening for a drink ensnares PI Bill Mooney in murder.

Scallops with a Side of Death
by *William J. O'Connor III and Arthur Vidro*

It was a hot July evening. My shirt was sticking to me like a floozy to a sailor with money remaining in his cracker jacks.

I was listening on the car radio to Curt Gowdy announcing a Sox game. Lou Boudreau had the team poised to take its annual dive into the depths of the American League basement. They had plenty of hitting with Ted, Dom, and Bobby, but Mel Parnell couldn't carry the pitching alone.

I was driving through Sterling, the kind of hick burg where the one weekly train stops only upon signal. My eye caught the word *Grille* on a raggedy sidewalk sign in front of a low building. I reined in the LaSalle and entered the joint. Immediately my eyes were drawn to a tall drink of water behind the bar.

She wasn't pretty in the cover of *Photoplay* sense, but she was easy enough on the eyes. She had a certain presence.

"Cold beer, Mister?" She had a lilting voice that would shame a Carolina warbler.

"Yeah, but pour it from an Old Overholt bottle."

She reached in back of her, grabbed a shot glass, slapped it in front of me, and poured the rye.

I grabbed her wrist with my left hand before she could withdraw the bottle, while with my right I flushed down the first of what I could see was going to be a long parade of its brothers.

She put her face into mine and said, "If you're going to drink like that, you're going to eat."

"How about a couple dogs, mustard and chili, Stretch?"

"My name is Jane. And we don't sell hot dogs."

"What grill doesn't sell hot dogs?"

"This one. If you want more to drink, you'll have scallops and like them."

I did, and I did. I've never been a seafood guy. Probably too many Gorton's cod fish cakes on Friday nights growing up. But I could easily become a seafood guy here.

Many drinks later, Stretch tried to steer me away from her by introducing me to a blonde dwarf who had slid up on the stool next to me.

"You'll like Trixie," she encouraged me. "She used to be an acrobat with Cole Brothers Circus."

Trixie asked me to walk her home. Out we stumbled onto the street. She dragged me up a flight. What luck, she lived over the bar. She threw me onto the bed and proved her being an acrobat was no lie. I vaguely remember feeling drained and falling asleep.

Suddenly, I felt some idiot whacking my head with a board. I opened my eyes and saw nothing but the inert form of Trixie. Pretty as she was, the picture was flawed by the fact that she snored and drooled. I climbed over her and grabbed my clothes.

Looking at my Benrus, I saw it was 7:30. I went home to shower and change. I had to go far out of town to collect a big payday from a slow-paying client. It took me all day.

That evening I returned to the grill in Sterling. A Statie's bluebird was parked in front of the door to Trixie's apartment.

I slid into the grill. Stretch nodded me over to the side. "No talk. Leave now."

"This is sudden. Didn't Trixie give me a good recommendation?"

She took a step back. "You'll have to look elsewhere for a reference. Trixie was found murdered around noon."

"Who killed her?"

"Everybody saw you leave the joint with her. Nobody saw her alive again."

"You could have sauntered over to the cops when I came in and done your civic duty."

"She was stabbed to death and the weapon wasn't found. None of her knives were missing. I don't figure you for carrying a knife. Plus, there's something about you I like."

"No doubt my Irish wit and charm."

"That and a dime will get you a coffee. I don't want to know anything about you. The Staties have no clue; they look at Trixie as trash and don't care. But our local chief, Tom Lewis, is no dope. He took my vague statement with a grain of salt."

"Want to try your luck running off with me, Stretch?"

"Don't read more into this than my desire to see Trixie's killer caught. You'll be arrested unless you can find the killer first."

"Give me something to go on."

"Trixie's story was about some accident at the circus. A guy fell to his death during a trapeze rehearsal. Trixie was suspected of messing with the rigging because she had just dumped him for somebody else and he wasn't taking it well. She jumped the show and got as far as Sterling. She spent her last bucks tanking up at the Grille and I let her stay in an apartment in my building."

She shoved me out the door.

"Don't underestimate Chief Lewis." She returned to her customers.

I stood there feeling empty as a keg two hours into a frat party. I took her word that the Sterling Police weren't duffers and decided to lam it. I figured some folks had seen my car parked overnight by Trixie's, so my safest bet was to call a cab. Going home for clothes or my gun would be too dangerous.

I traveled by taxi, changing cabs once. At a payphone in Worcester, I dialed my secretary at her home.

"Bill, did you really kill that girl?"

"How many women have I killed in the ten years you've worked for me?"

"None that I know of, but you wouldn't tell me anyway."

"How is it you know all about the jackpot I'm in?"

"The cops came to the office looking for you this afternoon."

"Ha! They knew I killed her before I knew she was dead."

"Five cents for three additional minutes."

"Here's a quarter." BONG.

"Bill, you've got to solve this before the cops get you."

"Sweetheart, you're the second dame to tell me that today. You can help. Find out where the Cole Brothers Circus is playing for the next three weeks. What do the cops know?"

"They're looking for your LaSalle. The town cop was the only guy who asked good questions. I didn't tell them anything. I don't know anything to tell."

"The office phone might be tapped. So when you get the info I need, give it by hand to Paul Cushing. I'll get it from him. I'll be in touch."

I hung up warmed by gratitude for having such a good girl Friday.

I bought an Evening Gazette from the coin-box on the corner. There I was on the front page looking back at me. Swell picture, from when I cracked the car-barn murder case. Well, yesterday's hero, today's fugitive.

I found a hovel to spend the night cheaply and read the paper.

I learned Trixie's name was Nicole LaFlamme. She was "believed to be a prostitute." Sure, why not slam her. No mention of her circus career.

I lingered over one paragraph: "The State Police learned of the identity of the suspect through his fingerprints, found in the victim's apartment, and the license plate of his car parked overnight nearby."

I could see the Sterling chief patrolling each night, writing down license plate numbers of cars that didn't belong. The car registry must have given him my name, which he sent to State Police headquarters along with the prints he found in Trixie's. The Commonwealth had my prints on record from my PI license. No need to send it to the FBI and wait weeks for a reply.

All I could do was wait for Joanne to come up with something.

Morning came late. I slunk out with my collar up and found a grocery store where I stocked up on cold cuts and Nissen rye bread and a liquor store for other necessities. I also grabbed the Worcester Telegram.

I spent the day reading the Telegram. They had found the LaSalle and were going over it for clues. The sports page showed the Sox in fourth place, half a game ahead of the Indians. I did the crosswords of both papers and kept wetting my whistle. About 3:30, I chanced walking to a drugstore where I called Paul Cushing's office, which is down the hall from my own.

"Law office."

I recognized the voice. "Sharon? Is the fat boy in?"

"No, but I have a message for you."

"Shoot, Shorty."

"I'm not that short. The Cole Brothers Circus is playing in Buffalo. They last played in Manchester, New Hampshire; Burlington, Vermont; Brattleboro, Vermont; and Syracuse, New York. They're next engaged in Erie, Pennsylvania, then to Ohio for Cleveland, Elyria, Sandusky, and Toledo; and then Elkhart, Indiana. Joanne wants to know your plans."

"Tell her I'm running away to join the circus."

I bought a razor and shaving soap and returned to the hovel. My clothes were grimy, but at least I could shave. I checked out, carrying just a paper bag with the remainder of the rye bread and a bottle.

Three taxi rides later, I was dropped off past midnight in Springfield. At the train station I slapped my hand on the counter to wake the ticket agent on duty.

"Ticket to Cleveland."

I handed him a twenty and got thirty-three cents and a ticket.

The train pulled in and I stumbled forward three cars until I found the Pullman conductor.

"We have units open," he said. "I'll assign you one with a longitudinal bed. This car comes off in Buffalo at 7:10 in the morning. You'll have to move to a coach then. I'll have the porter get your bags."

"This is it." I lifted my paper bag and paid for the sleeping accommodation.

The porter made down my bed. I put my shoes in the locker and drifted off instantly.

When we pulled into Cleveland, I hailed a cab and asked to be taken to a used clothing store. He drove me to a seedy part of town.

"You won't find a cab around here. Want I should wait?"

"Yeah. I'll be ten minutes, tops."

I walked in to the fanfare of a bell tinkling over the door. Ten minutes later I walked out with a canvas grip containing shirts, slacks, socks, and shorts. Best of all, I had on a sturdy pair of boots even more comfortable than my Nunn Bushes. I was carrying a cardboard carton, sealed with tape, containing the clothes I had arrived in.

"Where to now?" asked the hack.

"Post office and wait again."

I sent my dirty clothes to Paul Cushing and bought a few stamped envelopes.

Returning to the cab I said, "Find me a flophouse near the freight yard."

He stopped at the Randall Arms, a five-story unadorned building in Hoover gothic style. It didn't even have a neon sign that could go on the fritz.

"Two dollars a day or ten-fifty a week," said the geezer with the arm garters and eye shade behind the counter.

I counted out ten dollars and fifty cents. He spun the register around. I wrote, G. Saunders. He gave me a key.

The room was dreck. It was time to check in at home. There was a payphone in the hall, but I wanted privacy so I walked to a drugstore.

I called Cushing's office and got Sharon. I told her where I was and warned her to expect a box but not to open it. She reported the Staties were watching the building and had a tail on Joanne. I bought a Plain Dealer and returned to my room.

The paper had ads ballyhooing the circus' upcoming three-day visit. I needed to shake info out of the circus. The hardest task for a PI is interviewing people under a pretext, feigning interest in what they feel like telling you, waiting until they let slip the information you were really after.

I had two days until the circus arrived to cook up a plan. Thinking is thirsty work. I found a place a few blocks away called the Erie Grille, slipped my ass on a barstool, and ordered Stroh's Draft.

The barkeep drew the beer, making sure he sold me a lot of foam. They didn't have scallops, so I settled for a rare steak. You could still see the Neolight mark on it, but maybe my jaw needed the exercise.

After my repast, I chatted up some guys while shooting pool and swapping rounds. They were railroad men killing time before they were called to go out again.

My second night in Cleveland, a group of us sauntered to the yard to watch the circus train pull in. It was long and pulled by two steamers. Next to the engine was a string of old passenger cars, then old baggage cars, some modified inside to house animals. At the end were flatcars carrying wagons and equipment trucks. Each car was painted in gaudy colors and emblazoned with "Cole Bros. Shows." It was meant to look exciting and cheerful, but the paint was faded and peeling. It was as depressing as an old hooker trying to paint herself up to get in another year's work before packing it in. I walked back to the Randall.

Sitting on the edge of my bed, I took stock of my situation. I was wanted for murder in my own bailiwick. My only clue was the victim supposedly was mixed up in a death at the circus where she'd worked. Based on that slim lead, I was 635 miles from home in a flophouse hoping to get a job in the circus, without any idea how.

The next day, I headed out for brunch at the Erie. I found Otis alone at the bar. I'd played pool with him and he seemed like a good egg. I sat two stools from him and ordered eggs and hash.

"Let me buy a round for the house."

"You ever do that when there are more than two customers?" grumbled the bar man.

"Not if I'm sober."

"Thanks, buddy," said Otis.

"Day off today?" I inquired.

"No, I worked last night. Just stopped off on my way home."

"Is Otis your first or last name?"

"Neither. My name is Stan Thompson. They call me Otis because of my job."

"I thought you worked for the railroad."

"I do, but I'm a bridge tender on the New York Central drawbridge over the Cuyahoga River. It's a vertical-lift span bridge, and the control room is on the lift. I go up and down all day like an elevator operator, so the guys here call me Otis."

"Sounds like an easy job. Can't be more than five or six ships a day to raise the bridge for."

"Except the boats have the right of way and the normal position is up. I have to lower the span for trains. Each train has to stop and blow for the bridge, I then lower the bridge, interlock the tracks, and signal the train. Hobos use this stop to hop on trains. It's a nuisance."

"Otis, you have inspired me. Let me buy you another."

I left the Erie Grille whistling. I went to the river and confirmed what Otis had said. Then I hurried back to the drugstore near the Randall Arms and called Cushing's office. No news, except the box had arrived.

I bought a crossword book, a Plain Dealer, and a couple pencils. In my room I started thinking about six-letter words starting with M. The next two days were boring. I saw the Indians play the Browns and caught a movie.

The circus had its last show and struck their tents. I packed and checked out.

Some hobos waited a bit away from the track where a couple freight trains were stopped for the bridge. The span came down, the light changed to green, an engine chuffed, and half a dozen would-be passengers ran from cover and hopped it. I studied their technique. The light went red, and the span rose.

Eventually, the circus train ground to a halt at the light. It had to wait as a barge was pushed down the river. When the train started I jumped from the bushes and stood by the track. There were no other gratuitous customers for this train. I started running when the last baggage car passed. I tossed my bag onto a flatcar and then grabbed an iron, pulled myself off the ground, and got my foot in a step. I once saw Gene Autry do this from horseback in a movie. As I lay on the deck panting, I had to give Gene credit.

I went forward and climbed over the coupler into the vestibule at the end of the baggage car. The door was open. As I stepped through, an elephant wrapped a trunk around my arm. Maybe he was trying to tell me something. With my free arm I pulled a hay bale down from a stack. It split open when it hit the floor. I picked up a couple flakes and held them up. The trunk forsook my arm for the hay.

Then I spotted a surly looking guy in gray coveralls standing at the end of the car holding a vicious-looking club. He advanced. His eyes questioned me.

"I just want a job," I murmured, picking loose hay off my neck.

"Here's your audition: each elephant gets two bales of hay and a pail of water. The pails are in the closet. Fill the pails. See the tap under the cistern? Do not take any bags of grain out of the closet. An elephant will grab it and eat it all, then founder, and we'll never get it up in this car. If they finish the water they can have a second. I'll go wake the road manager."

As I was humping the last pail of water, the door opened and another guy came in. He was dressed in brown clothes, an Ike jacket, and riding boots.

"Carl said a job applicant just dropped in. That you?"

"You the guy can give me a job?"

"I need performers. Can you work a trapeze or do acrobatics?"

"In my youth I could do handstands and cartwheels but I was thinner then. I grew up on a dairy farm, so I can handle horses and cows."

"You can work as a roustabout. Five dollars a day, food and shelter, and we do your laundry. Or else get off in Elyria."

"I'll take the job."

"Pull up some hay and grab some sleep. Tomorrow Carl will tell you what to do."

It was hot and smelly in the car. The door was open, but I didn't sleep near it because I was afraid of falling out.

In the morning, Carl woke me and handed me two sets of coveralls emblazoned with the Cole Brothers name. Carl was in charge of elephants, horses, zebras, a donkey, a giraffe, and now me. In each town a local farmer picked up all the manure and gave us hay and green vegetables and fruits for the elephants and giraffe.

The story of my plopping onto the moving train got around fast. By the time we got to Ann Arbor I was accepted but none the wiser. I had played up to Half Ton Trudy Hart the fat lady who was also bearded, providing two attractions for the cost of one. She weighed 360 pounds.

We sat together at lunch. While she ate my dessert, I ventured, "Do the performers do well? I can't live forever on five dollars a day."

"That's why positions like yours are always turning over. Some think you're running from the law."

"What do you think?"

"You're running from a wife and family."

"Wrong. I'm a desperado wanted for murder."

"G'wan," she laughed, and slapped me on the back, rattling my teeth.

"I almost didn't get this job, because I'm not a flier or acrobat."

"Usually those are family acts that stay together. Mostly Europeans working for small circuses hoping to get called up to Ringling Brothers. We need acrobats and fliers because of jealousy and sex."

"Sounds interesting. I always like a little sex, but in your case a lot."

Thus flattered she disclosed, "We had a cute little acrobat not of the family. This Trixie was a cheerleader in high school, too cute not to hire.

"Then the Flying Vigliottis trapeze act needed to replace a gal so Trixie started training with them. A lot of sparks flew between her and Guido Vigliotti. Everybody knew Guido was sneaking into Trixie's berth. That didn't sit well with Guido's wife Maria, so Trixie was sent back to the acrobat act, and Guido made up with Maria and dumped Trixie. Trixie didn't take it well. She made threats against Maria and called her an old cow.

"One day during practice in Manchester the rigging broke and Maria fell to her death. Trixie was suspected and ran away. Guido was very upset. He vowed vengeance and was never seen again.

"The circus is split whether Guido went off looking for Trixie to get revenge or because they'd arranged to be together.

"Funny thing is, the cops and safety inspectors swarmed all over us, and they found the equipment was worn out and it was only an accident.

"So that's why we need an acrobat and trapeze artists. Funny, huh?"

"Yeah, Trudy. A barrel of laughs."

Stretch had gotten the story a little wrong, but had given me enough to start me on the killer's trail.

We closed that night in Ann Arbor and headed for Lansing. In the middle of the night the train stopped for water. I slipped off, rode locals to Detroit, and booked a room on the Wolverine. It didn't leave until 8:30 p.m. To kill time, I went to the Fort Shelby Hotel and got a room. I put in a call to Paul Cushing.

"Hey, short stuff, walk down the hall and tell Joanne I'm okay but still have to lay doggo for a couple days."

"Hang on. Paul will be right with you."

A man's voice came on. "Hey, big guy, is the prodigal son coming home?"

"Yeah, counselor, but it's too soon to kill the fatted calf. Can you get me a cold car and a colder gun?"

"Will the '40 Ford pickup from my dad's farm do?"

"Perfect. Leave it on Summer Street near Sis's Silver Dollar. Can it be there by tomorrow night?"

"The key will be over the passenger's visor and the gun will be under the seat. Hope to see you soon and not in the corpse house."

"Thanks."

I drew a hot bath and soaked until the water got cold, then I took a shower. The smell of the elephant dung swirled down the drain. It would be Lake St. Claire's problem now.

I was certain Guido was my man. To find him, I should start where I suspected he'd gone—Sterling. But I didn't want to show my mug there. Strangers stick out there. Good for finding Guido, but bad for me schlepping about.

I called the main desk and asked them to send up a typewriter and phone book.

I wrote a brief note to Joanne on hotel stationery telling her about Guido and asking her to nose around Sterling. When the bellhop appeared, I found the name and address of a local collection agency and typed that as the return address on one of my stamped envelopes and addressed it to my office. If the Staties were monitoring my mail, this would not look out of the ordinary. I went down the hall and dropped it in the mail chute. It would probably hit Worcester about the same time as me.

At Woolworth's I purchased lunch and a Detroit Free Press. The sports page said the Tigers were hosting the White Sox that afternoon. I took a cab to Briggs Stadium and got a seat close enough to the action that I could see Nellie Fox's cheek puffed out by his wad of chew. I forget who won.

That night I boarded the Wolverine. It pulled into Worcester at 10:13 a.m. I trudged up Front Street to a hock shop across from the common, bought a suit and shoes, and a Knox fedora. Denholm and McKay provided me with white shirts and a tie.

As I walked to the Mayflower Hotel, I passed Frank E. Sessions Casket Company. I figured they were building one for me if I couldn't carry this off.

The Mayflower was a mediocre joint that didn't ask you many questions. I signed in as John H. Watson, M.D. The room wasn't much, but neither was I.

At 3:30 I strolled over to my old buddy Eddy, who runs a newsstand at the out-of-town bus depot in Trumble Square. I'd helped him out of a pickle once without asking for a fee. Since then Eddy would do anything for me.

I grabbed a Gazette and whispered, "Don't look up."

Eddy handled a couple customers and then said quietly, "You must have had a powerful reason to kill that girl."

"Don't believe what you read in your merchandise; can you run an errand for me?"

"Sure."

"Go to my office and speak to my girl. Tell her I want to meet with her. I need your place for the meet. Have her figure out how and when; I'll be by tomorrow morning to pick up the Telegram."

I started to walk away. "Hey, you gonna pay for that paper?" I produced a dime.

I walked over to Summer Street and saw a worn but not beat-up Ford pickup parked near Sis's Silver Dollar. I climbed in, found the key and flipped the ignition. I drove to the Mayflower, pulled into a lot behind it, and turned off the truck. I reached over the transmission hump and under the passenger side of the bench. After shoving the gat in my waistband, I reached again and pocketed a box of cartridges.

Back in my room, I examined the piece. A Beretta, probably a war trophy smuggled home. I put one into the chamber and replaced it in the clip.

I don't hold much store by guns—they're uncomfortable to carry and a general pain. Plus, too many clowns who carry guns lack the sense not to use them; they're unable or too lazy to think, and the short-cut to thinking is to draw a gun.

I went to the Sherwood Diner and had Yankee pot roast. Back at the Mayflower I stopped for a couple at the El Rocco Room. A fat Jewish comedian with bulging eyes told jokes, mostly at his own expense; but he was funny, and I laughed for the first time since I'd met Trixie.

Next morning I was up before the rooster crows or whatever the urban equivalent is. I slid around the corner to Eddy's news-stand. He was breaking open bundles of papers.

"Meet your girl at my house at 2 p.m.," said Eddy as he folded his key into a Telegram. "Leave it under the doormat." I handed him a twenty and went back to the room to learn the Sox had slipped to fifth place. There was nothing about my case.

At 1:30 I got in the truck, went to Eddy's modest home and entered. Presently a strange car pulled in behind the truck. A guy got out, approached the door and knocked. I pulled out the Beretta.

"Do I have to stand here all day?" came a voice I recognized.

I let Joanne in. "Nice ensemble," I cracked.

"I went to work and a cop followed me. So I phoned my husband. He came to the office but went in the back way, left me some of his clothes, and took a cab to his shop. Later I changed and took his car here."

"Goofy, but effective. What have you got for me?"

"I went to Sterling and visited this Jane your letter mentioned. I sat at the counter, ordered chowder, and slipped her your card. She said 'the ladies room is this way. Here, I'll show you.'

"She led me to a small office. I told her you were returning to look for Guido. She said the only foreigners in Sterling were migrant workers hired seasonally at the orchards. She said she'd ask around. She left the office and after a minute I went back to the counter. She handed me a round cardboard container and I paid up. Certain I was being followed, I detoured to City Hall and the library and then back to Worcester.

"Late this a.m. a woman who didn't identify herself called, but I recognized Jane's voice. She said she'd bring you scallops at 9 tonight at a corner two blocks east from where you met her, and hung up fast so the call couldn't be traced. That's all I have."

"Sounds promising. You're a good man, kid." I kissed her on the cheek and she left.

I drove back to the Mayflower with time to kill. I would need my wits about me so I couldn't tank up. When it was time, I drove the truck to the rendezvous. It was an elementary school closed for the night. A solitary figure stood in the murky shadows on the walkway out front.

I cautiously approached.

She handed me a bag. "Have the last scallops you'll get from me."

"Why am I here other than I love you and scallops?"

"Probably not in that order. I asked around. Bart Smith has migrant workers and one is an Italian with vineyard experience from the old country. Bart's been trying to grow enough grapes to make a little wine for friends. This guy said he had worked in Asti growing Moscato grapes for La Serra vineyards—whatever that means. He's still working for Bart. So if he's Guido, he's around. The immigrants drink at Gay's on Route 140 every night."

"Thanks, Jane. After I'm cleared, we should get together."

"No. I have a guy at home who loves me and I'm lucky to have him."

She walked away.

I drove over to Gay's. It was a roadhouse with a neon Bud sign and a picture window showcasing chickens riding a rotisserie. I entered, sat at the bar, and ordered.

I looked around and saw farmers, a bunch of black guys, and a swarthy guy with a muscular build sitting alone at the end of the bar.

The bartender poured from a Three Feathers bottle, then brought me some tender chicken.

"Who's the guy at the end of the bar? I think I know him."

"He's a dago. Comes in with the Jamaicans. They all work on the orchards in town, but he doesn't hang out with them."

"My mistake. This chicken is great. I'll have another."

"You can eat two chickens?"

"No," I laughed, "another rye."

I kept an eye on the presumed Guido. When he got up and headed to the john, I put a five on the bar and followed him in. I took out the Beretta.

"Finish your piss, then button up and stick your hands in your pockets, Guido."

"What's for this?" he asked in a thick Italian accent. "I'm not a Guido, I'm Gianni."

"You're dead is who you are if you don't do what you're told. Gonna walk out of here in front of me and do what I tell you. If you talk to anybody, I'll shoot you. Capisch?"

I pocketed the gun, marched him to the truck, opened the passenger door, told him to slide in and keep his hands in his pockets. I trained the gun on him with my left hand as I started the truck.

"I'm not Guido, so let me go. Why you want me?"

"I want to introduce you to the police chief, who doesn't take kindly to acrobats being killed in his town. You killed Trixie and you're gonna fry."

Big talk from a guy who didn't know where the cop shop was. My hope was to get downtown and find somebody who could call the cops. I still had no plan. As we took off he looked scared.

"She killed my *bello* Maria. The *puttana* had it coming," he cried, giving up his pretense.

"Trixie didn't kill Maria. It was your rotten equipment."

"Liar!" He pulled a knife from his pocket and lunged at me.

The Beretta went off deafeningly and the truck went off the road. I turned off the engine and sat there dazed. Guido had a big hole in his chest. There was blood all over me and the inside of the cab. The driver's door I was leaning against opened and I fell out. I was grabbed by the collar and pulled to my feet.

"Go around and pull the stiff out of the truck," said a large guy with a military mustache. His green work shirt boasted a gold badge that proclaimed him Chief.

"This stiff killed the girl above the Grille, Chief Lewis," I said.

He nodded. "I know. I took a lot of prints in her apartment. Yours were identified first. Eventually one set was identified from a passport as Vigliotti's. He had a visa to work as a trapeze guy. I learned he had left Cole Brothers unexpectedly just before LaFlamme's death. Jane told me the decedent had worked as an acrobat, so he looked like our man. But I didn't know where he was."

"You were Johnny on the spot."

He nodded again. "Jane called and told me what she'd told your female detective. Jane thought Vigliotti would be at Gay's and you might find trouble. I arrived just in time to see you taking Guido out. I followed and was about to pull you over when you shot him. You handled this poorly. I'll fix things for you after the body is discovered. Wait a few days, then resume your life. Next time you have business in Sterling check in with me first. Forget you saw me tonight."

"We've never met," I agreed.

"Oh, I have a message from Jane. She says to buy your scallops elsewhere from now on, and her name's not Stretch."

We left Guido there and went our separate ways.

Routes 12 and 140 join at a causeway over the Wachusett Reservoir. I stopped where the water ran under it and tossed the gun.

Next morning, I stashed the truck with a pal who does body work. For three hundred dollars he would clean what he could, sand and repaint the metal, and reupholster the bloodied seats, armrests and visors.

Three days later I trudged into my office. Joanne was there.

"Hello, Stranger. Your friend Mahoney called and asked you to pick up a truck." She handed me the newspaper. "Page 3."

I sat down. The article reported a body discovered in Sterling two days ago was that of Guido Vigliotti, who had murdered Nicole LaFlamme; the two had worked together as circus performers and were romantically involved; and a knife found on Vigliotti fit the bill as the LaFlamme murder weapon.

A state police spokesman acknowledged although William Mooney had been the suspect in the LaFlamme murder, "We are no longer convinced he was involved."

"Not exactly a ringing endorsement," I muttered.

"Well, Bill, fame is fleeting. Let's hope infamy is also."

Paul's father was delighted with his truck's new interior. When I offered money for the gun, Paul declined but hinted he wouldn't mind one of those new devices, like a radio but with pictures.

Me? Business is back to normal. I still drink too much, but my real thirst is for a tall drink of water. I won't be ordering scallops from any other restaurant.

We travel now from the grimy streets of an eastern big city to a remote gas station in the American Southwest, where a geezer named Virgil is about to have an interesting, and very dangerous afternoon, under a merciless sun.

Roadside Attraction

by Kenneth Gwin

Wildwood Springs Beer-Gas-&-Snacks
There hadn't been a car on the road for hours. Only two stopped by that morning and not a one that afternoon. Those that did bought gas, used the can. Still piss poor business, anyway you look at it. Not much comes out in this kind of heat. Nothing with any sense, at least.

Too damn hot.

Even the flies were asleep, resting in whatever shade could be had in the middle of that god-forsaken desert. But this was Virgil's spot, his place in the shade—except for those fucking flies, spiders, ants, burrowing bugs, and a rat that started a turf war.

It's enough to drive a man to drink.

Virgil rolled out of his chair, just far enough to reach the refrigerator and grab a cold one off the bottom shelf.

Damn, this heat was killin' him.

He pried the beer open.

And all the while there's all that sand and dust constantly on the move, finding its evil way into every crack, window, door—

open or closed, it didn't matter. The heat was one thing, for sure, but a man couldn't never get used to sand and dust. It got in your eyes, your hair, your food, your teeth. It was everywhere, blown in from miles of sunbaked wasteland. 'Course dirt's all that was left since the copper mine went bust—dirt, dust, sand, and the constant wind bringing with it all those failed hopes, dried up dreams and emptiness.

Virgil looked out the window to see if anything else was on the move. Strange. Nothing. Not a spec of wind. Not even a leaf was moving on that scraggly tree out front. Just that buzzing sound in the air. Probably from the heat, or the noise inside his head.

He mostly didn't mind the isolation. Eventually somebody'd wander in. They'd run out of gas, blown a tire, or their car just up and quit. He'd fill 'em up, add some oil, sell 'em soda, beer, even ammunition. But if was anything more, then they were shit out of luck 'cause it was at least forty miles to the next human being, and two days out 'til parts could come in from the city.

He knew Kansas was the middle of America, but Wildwood Springs Beer-Gas-&-Snacks had to be smack dab in the middle of nowhere. There was a time it was in the middle of somewhere, a friendly oasis on the only road through this whole damn desert. Then the new highway came through. Now it was nowhere, all used up and pushed aside. The old road wasn't that far from the new one, but it might as well have been up on Mars. He could see the interstate over there as it sliced its way straight across the desert. If the winds were blowing right, he could sometimes even hear it.

He took a sip of beer. He hated to drink up all his profits.

Of course there was always the occasional vagrant, or some dry, lost, beat-down traveler in search of food, water, desperate for shelter, or lookin' for a way out of some kind of trouble.

The desert sure brought out the strangeness in folks.

Virgil'd been looking for a way out too.

He took another sip of beer, settled back in his chair.

He must have fallen asleep and hadn't heard them coming up the road. The sign outside said *OPEN*, so they'd walked right in the door.

"Hey, mister."

Startled awake, Virgil almost fell off his chair.

"Our car broke down." A woman's voice.

He rolled his eyes.

Well howdy-do.

Pretty young thing she was, a regular Daisy Mae stuffed into tiny shorts, a sleeveless shirt, dragging behind some tired-assed ten-year old—mama's little angel. The kid was dressed pretty much the same, right down to sunglasses, a fancy handbag, dainty sandals, and those little painted toenails.

"Water," she croaked. "Me and my kid here are dry as hell."

She clanked an empty container on the counter.

"We walked."

He could tell.

"It's hot as hell out here."

He knew that too.

"You're not much of a talker are you. How the hell do you stand the heat?"

That was a question he couldn't answer.

"Water's free. Help yourself. There's a spigot outside." He pointed.

Virgil stumbled behind just to watch and stood by the pumps as she bent to fill her thermos.

Entertainment like that was rare in the desert.

The kid eyed him with suspicion.

"So what's the problem, ma'am?" he addressed the mother as she stood up. "Run out of gas?" He motioned to the pumps behind him.

"The car died." She drank from the thermos, swished it around, spit the water out. "The piece of shit. Can you get it towed? It's just down the road. Not very far, but in this heat it felt like thirty miles." She took another drink, handed the thermos to the thirsty kid.

Her little darling looked the worse from walking in that blazing sun. Fidgety too. They both looked nervous, like someone was on their tail. He wasn't surprised. He got all kinds out there.

Hoisting with both hands, the kid gulped the water, a good portion running down the front of her cotton shirt.

"Picked a fine time to cross the desert. Where you headed?" He did his best to sound concerned. He even smiled, checking her over head to toe.

"Anywhere but here. Planning on getting to Kansas City." She reached in her bag and pulled out a cigarette.

"You got a long way to go." He looked at the woman. "You headin' home?"

She didn't answer, lit a match. She sure acted nervous and didn't look a thing like she belonged in any Kansas City.

"You got a phone?" she finally asked, exhaling a cloud of smoke that lingered lazy in the quiet air.

"Sure. Right inside, hangin' on the wall. You just missed it."

She seemed to think about calling somebody. Picked a loose piece of tobacco off her lip.

"Can you help me get my car off the road? I don't want it left out there."

"Afraid someone will steal it?"

"It's all I got."

He wasn't sure about that.

"If you want it moved, a tow truck's hours away. Cost you a pretty penny. All I got's my pickup and a length of chain. I might be able to help if you give me time to gather a few things. Cost you ten bucks—labor and loss of business."

"Seems fair," she noted.

"Cash."

"Fine. Didn't expect you'd take a check." She reached in her bag. The cigarette dangled from her lip. "Can you figure out what's wrong?" She handed him a crisp new bill.

"Ain't no real mechanic, but I'll give 'er a look." He gave her a wink.

She looked at him. She dropped an ash on the concrete slab.

Virgil went inside. "This won't take long," he called out. "Be right there." He finished the beer he'd left next to his chair, shut the door to his back room and made sure to turn the sign to *SORRY CLOSED*. He closed the door behind him.

His truck was parked around back under a lean-to shed where he could do a little repair work sheltered from the sun. Tires were stacked on the ground. Tools hung on the wall. He grabbed a rusty chain from a wooden crate stashed in a corner.

"Door's unlocked. Hop inside." He tossed the chain in the back of his truck.

The little girl seemed unsure.

"Come on." He wiped a layer of dust off the seat with the palm of his hand. "Slide right over. I won't bite."

"Get in the truck, Lea Ann," the mother demanded. "We're not staying here forever."

The kid stepped on the running board, eyed the shotgun hanging across the back window, then cautiously crawled to the middle where she sat with her hands held tight between her knees.

"That's better." Virgil slid behind the wheel. "How old are you young lady?"

She stuck her lip out, her mouth clamped tight.

He tried another approach. "You in the third grade?"

She looked at him as if he had no clue about little girls. "Why don't you shave?" she finally asked.

Virgil smiled. "I guess 'cause I don't have to."

"You look like Gabby Hayes." The little girl gave him another disapproving look.

Snotty little shit, he thought.

The mother scooted next to the child, her bare legs squeaking as she moved across the seat.

Closeness pressed in as the door clanked shut. Animal perspiration and a morning's dab of perfume filled the stuffy cab, her fragrance rising like a breath of spring air above the smells of dust and oil and gasoline.

She rolled down her window.

"Too stuffy in here."

Virgil turned to this wonder the saints had delivered to his door.

"Not much of a breeze," she complained.

He watched her, entranced by the beads of perspiration on her forehead, the small drops that gathered on the edges of her hair and trickled invitingly past her ear to rest in that hollow spot along her collar before sliding down to that promised land inside her loosely fastened shirt.

Women like this don't come by often.

The kid's eyes bored right through him.

He turned the key and pushed the starter. "Here we go," he proclaimed cheerfully. "Hold on to your hats."

The truck lurched forward, ground its way across the gravel, crawled up on the asphalt and whined its way down the road. He shifted gears. The kid shrank from the movement of his arm and edged her knees over to avoid the gear shift lever.

"The car's up a ways." The mother watched him closely. "Just in front of the sign that said your place is up ahead."

"Yep, beer, gas and snacks. Lucky for you, you found this place." He kept practicing his smile. "You could a died out here." Virgil took a furtive glance in her direction. "Where you comin' from anyway?"

The mother looked back at him. "Out west," she answered without explanation.

This *is* out west, he thought.

"How'd you happen to turn down this road? Everybody else takes the new highway over there." He pointed toward a line across the desert. "Straight as a goddam arrow."

"We thought we could see the sights." The woman looked out the window at the empty scenery passing by.

Tight lipped, she was. Virgil drove along in silence.

There was her car, up ahead, a fancy new Ford painted coral pink and white.

"That's your car?" he asked, surprised. He was expecting some old junker.

"Yeah. You'd think it'd make it across this place. It's hardly broken in."

"Well, we'll see."

Virgil made a U-turn on the narrow roadway and backed in front of the woman's car.

They all got out and stood around surveying the damage. The stench of burnt oil and rubber was everywhere. Virgil opened the hood.

"Smells bad, lady. What happened?"

"I don't know. First it started smoking. Then it just died. I don't need this shit. I gotta be somewhere."

We all gotta be somewhere, he figured.

Virgil reached under the hood and pulled out the dipstick. "You ever put oil in it lady?"

"Oil? It's not even a year old."

"Well, you're not going anywhere with this car. These things need oil."

"Well, put some in it."

"Too late now."

"What do you mean?"

"These things need lubrication and don't run without it. This thing's got no oil and your engine's turned it's last."

"Can't you fix it?"

"Time and money, lady. You need new parts and a real mechanic, one who knows what's what." He stood up stiffly. "I can fix some stuff, but taking an engine apart and putting it all back together, well, that's beyond me." He dusted his hands off, wiped them on his pants. "Might be better just get a new engine."

"Damn it!" The woman started screaming and that precious little kid began to cry.

He stood back in admiration. A fiery woman can be a fierce and beautiful thing.

Virgil closed the hood gently and waited for the storm to pass.

"What am I going to do?" She stood with her hands on her hips, searching the horizon, looking for any answer. The goddamned kid blubbered quietly to herself.

"We gotta get going. We can't be stranded out here."

"Well, you're stuck here now. Your car ain't goin' nowhere." She paced in circles.

"I can call ahead and get you towed to the next town. Cost you real money and take some time to get it fixed. Maybe a week, who knows?" He waited for an answer. "Or I could drive you over to the highway. You could hitch a ride from there. Or catch a bus. Send for your car later."

"Can you still tow it back to your place 'til I figure this out?"

"Sure. You already paid."

Virgil seldom got this kind of excitement. Still it was hard for him to feel sorry for anyone who didn't plan for the unexpected. Mother Nature don't take much to ignorance or much to foolish strangers.

"Damn," she muttered, still fuming.

Virgil dragged the chain out of the back and hooked one end to the frame under her car. He looped the other end around his bumper, gave it a few good tugs.

"Get in. I'll pull ahead and add a little tension. You steer just like regular." He hoisted himself into his truck.

The woman got in her car. The kid climbed in on the passenger side.

Virgil could see the mother in his rear view mirror. She was sitting behind the wheel, her expression hidden behind pointy dark glasses. The kid was just a bump where her head stuck up above the dash.

"Make sure it's out of gear and release the parking brake. I'll go real slow," he called out the window, loud enough for her to hear.

The truck began to move. The chain made groaning sounds under the strain as it pulled tight. He eased ahead. The car rolled onto the pavement.

"Everything okay?"

He could see her wave, steering dutifully behind him.

Steady as she goes.

Eddie saw the car.

There was barely a rise, but he could see it—something on a side road caught his eye—a glint of light flaring like a beacon in the afternoon sun. Something shiny don't usually mean a thing, but a flash of chrome and a touch of pink, now that could be her car. He knew she couldn't have gotten much of a head start and he'd been driving like the devil.

He pulled to the side, parked his car, walked across the road for a better look. He was in a foul mood. That bitch ran off with all his money and he wasn't about to take any chances. And damn this heat. She could have picked a better place to run.

He shaded his eyes. Now what was that? Off in the distance…

Through the shimmering heat he squinted.

The image came and went in watery waves.

There it was. Sure as hell. No chance there'd be another Crown Victoria like hers in the middle of nowhere. She must be trying to keep off the main highway—trying to trick him once again.

Strange too, by the looks of things, the car didn't seem to be moving. Why would she stop out there? he wondered. Maybe she's taking a nap. The idea floated in his imagination, the picture of her laid out in the backseat, sweating like a pig in this baking oven. And her kid too, cooked like a little meat pie. What bothered him more, the mother or that fucking kid? One just as bad as the other. He'd get them both—good as in the bag. That sneaky bitch. She should have never stopped. Now it was all just a matter of time.

A moment of panic hit him as a sudden realization crashed his thoughts. She'd ditched the car! The lousy bitch! There must be an accomplice, some other guy, some other sucker helping her steal his money.

Damn! That bitch is treachery running on two nice lookin' legs.

Blinding flashes of anger ripped through his head.

He waited for a truck to pass before he crossed the road. The blast of hot air that followed nearly knocked him off his feet.

Eddie grabbed two boxes of ammo out of the trunk, pulled out his rifle, his pistol, and slammed the trunk down hard. He piled the weapons on the seat beside him, turned the car around and drove back several miles looking for the turnoff.

Goddamn.

Goddamn.

Goddamn.

Beguiled. That's what it was. Those tits and ass and that fancy hair—he should have seen it coming. Pure hate and vengeance filled his soul. He swore he'd see her rotting bones dry to powder in this goddamn heat.

Women.

Can't live without 'em; he swore he'd be more careful after this.

And her? He'd see the birds pick her rotting guts out when he was finally done with her.

And the same for her goddamn kid.

———

Whistling with satisfaction, Virgil looked across the desert, across the miles of low brush, rocky outcroppings, to the grey mountains in the distance. He searched the sky for any bird or plane, then turned to the pockmarked road ahead, lulled by the putter of his engine, the hypnotic squeaking of the springs beneath his truck, the strumming and groaning of the chain that stretched behind him as they slowly motored down the road.

There was Wildwood Springs Beer-Gas-&-Snacks, falling apart on a road to nowhere, a lonesome wind-blown oasis for anybody dry and thirsty and tired of watching mirages float above the colorless sand. It had seen some better days, he knew.

Now it wass just a sad and lonely outpost the march of progress left behind. It wasn't much to look at—that's for sure—one sad tree and a sagging roof loosing shingles; a sign on top, the awning cursed by a plague of falling, peeling paint; the gas pumps sandblasted by desert winds and faded by the scorching sun. It was only a rest stop now for people passing through, most he'd never see again.

What's left for him? Time seems to last forever in the desert.

He looked in the rear view mirror. Sad as they were in their broke down car, it was hard to feel sorry for those two fools. It was pure luck they found him. The desert's a dry and lonely place. Hardly a car comes by on any given day. Fair enough she wanted something to drink and her car dragged off the road, but he wasn't buying much of her story. And sure as hell, those two were runnin' away from something.

None of that was his concern. Still he needed to decide what to do with them. Doubtful they'd be gone before sunset, and there was nowhere else to go without a car. He'd be stuck with the both of them 'til after dark. Maybe 'til the morning.

He didn't get many overnight guests these days, 'specially pretty ones who smelled so good.

Then there was that goddamned kid.

Virgil turned off the roadway, crunching across the gravel as he pulled alongside his shed. The rhythmic squeak of springs and the groaning chain fell silent as they idled to a stop.

He opened the door and stepped to the ground. There wasn't a wisp of dust in this dead-still air. A man could sweat to death in this heat.

"I'll unhook the chain. Then we'll go inside and you can call ahead when you figure out what to do with that car." He looked up.

She was pointing a little black pistol right at his head.

Well that was unexpected.

"Just finish what you're doing," she demanded. "Unhook that chain and we'll be on our way."

Looks like he'd been underestimating.

"Lucky me. Soon we're getting' outta here—down the road like a cool breeze." She wasn't smiling. "I can't wait."

He guessed she wouldn't be staying over.

"Come on! Now!"

"All right. All right." He stumbled back. "No need to be unfriendly."

And there was her little angel standing behind her, gloating like she'd just won a stack of chips in Vegas.

"Get on with it." The woman moved away, waving the gun toward the back of his truck. "Over there. We don't have all day."

Sometimes it don't pay to argue with a woman.

"Anything you say, lady." Virgil held out his hands, shuffling slowly, biding his time. "Anything you say." He started to reach under the front of her car to unhook the chain.

"No, dimwit, the truck." She waved the gun again, pointing toward his rear bumper. "That car's not going nowhere."

"Okay." He stooped and untangled the chain from the back of his truck instead.

"Now give me the key."

"Key's in the ignition." Virgil turned to look her straight in the eye. "We don't expect much crime out here."

"Stand back then. Move away."

He took a few steps.

"Lea Ann, get inside."

The kid looked at Virgil.

"And don't get near him. He's a crazy man. Climb in on this side." She indicated the open driver's door.

The kid hopped on the running board and scrambled into the cab.

Like in a dream, Virgil could hear the sound of a speeding car in the distance. Company? A customer? He was hoping for a state trooper, guns blazing, but any car would do. He knew it was like that sometimes in the movies.

A black car came into view and slowed on the road behind her. He could tell it wasn't the police.

The car stopped.

The woman turned to look.

There was always hope, but she was still pointing that gun right at him.

Virgil could hear the car's engine rev and his hopes begin to fade. Maybe the car would drive away and leave him here with this crazy woman and a bullet in his head.

The car turned and drove straight toward them.

The woman started shooting at the driver.

The car swerved away from the rain of bullets, sliding to a stop. The door on the other side flew open. A man's voice called out from the swirl of dust.

"Mona, you bitch, put down the goddamn gun. Just give my money and you can walk away."

"Not a chance, Eddie. You won't need it where you're going."

He stood up and fired in her direction.

She ducked behind her car.

Virgil ran toward his shed. Hopefully, they'd work things out and leave him here in peace.

Eddie fired another shot.

Mona peeked around the fender and fired two more.

"Just give me my goddamn money! You're never going to get away," Eddie called again.

Virgil could see everything from where he was hiding. He wished he had a gun.

Mona took another shot.

Eddie held his fire, waiting.

Virgil couldn't see the kid. Now both truck doors were wide open.

Mona fired two more. He could hear the thunk of lead against the other car.

Eddie fired back.

Then everything was quiet.

An eternity passed.

"I don't hear anything," Eddie taunted.

More silence.

"Run out of bullets?"

Virgil could see Mona crouched behind the car. There was panic in her eyes.

"Time to pay the piper." Eddie stood up and walked toward the pink and white car.

"Fuck you Eddie!" She tossed the useless firearm at Eddie and started to run.

"You had your chance." He calmly leveled at the fleeing figure.

She stumbled as the shot rang out and fell forward.

Eddie stepped between the Ford and Virgil's truck, careful to avoid the chain. He held his gun out steady.

There was a shotgun blast from behind the truck, spinning Eddie around.

Eddie fired back, and then fell in a heap.

The shooting stopped.

Virgil waited a good long time to make sure there wasn't any more gun play. The desert was strangely quiet.

He walked over.

There was Eddie rolled up in a ball with most of his face gone. The pistol, a sharp lookin' Browning Hi-Power, still held tightly in his grip. The little angel was sprawled out with a bullet through her chest. Virgil's shotgun was several feet away. She must have dragged it out of his truck and tried her best to stop Eddie. Pretty big gun for such a little girl. Mona was twenty feet out, face down in the dust. She'd never even tried to save her kid. So much for motherly love.

He looked at this mess of bodies scattered about. What was all the fuss? Eddie kept yelling about his money. So where was the money?

He looked on the front seat of Mona's car, found her fancy bag and turned it inside out. All that female stuff spilled across the upholstery—lipstick, mirror, nickels, pennies, hair pins, cig-arettes, chewing gum. Inside her wallet was a good amount of cash—ones, fives, twenties, better than a hundred bucks—still not enough to fight over, unless you were just plain crazy. Of course, you meet all kinds in the desert.

He looked in the back seat. He could see a few comic books, a pillow. Nothing close to any kind of treasure.

He took the woman's car keys and opened the trunk. Not the fancy luggage he'd expected, but one suitcase was locked up tight.

Virgil went to the shed, brought back a screwdriver, and pried the latches loose and looked inside.

Oh, my, oh, my. His eyes grew wide. Here was a suitcase full of hundred dollar bills. Now that was some real money.

He closed the suitcase, closed the trunk, and carried his new-found riches into the backroom of Wildwood Springs Beer-Gas-&-Snacks. Better there for safe keeping.

Tidiness wasn't one of his strengths, but he'd have to get rid of those bodies. The heat wouldn't be kind to them come morning.

First things first. He gathered up all the weapons, even the rifle in Eddie's car, and stashed them in his back room. Then he loaded the bodies in the back of his truck. Living near an abandoned mine in the middle of nowhere meant dumping a few dead strangers was pretty easy. Afterwards, he pushed the two cars behind his shed. He knew the folks at a midnight auto back in town could take care of any abandoned cars. A few bullet holes wouldn't matter to them. They were in the reclamation business, with no questions asked. Anyway, by then the sun was going down and he couldn't wait to count his money. He'd finish with the cars in the morning.

He went inside, locked the door to the back room and in-dulged himself by shuffling through the pile of crisp new bills. Sure enough, he was rich. Very rich. He'd never seen so damn much money. Better yet, nobody knew it was here.

Surprised and satisfied with this turn of events, he went out front, pulled a Carling's off the top shelf, and sat in his chair for a relaxing sit as nighttime closed around him. Resting quietly, beer in hand, he considered what to do with all that cash, a thought deserving some careful consideration. It was a lot of money. He was rich. It felt good to say it over again.

He took a sip of beer and looked out the windows into the silver-blue of desert night. He started thinking. It was so damn quiet here, so peaceful. But what does it mean in the world, he wondered, where crime and virtue both exist? There must be a balance somewhere in life, a natural give and take. So it only seemed right; the scales of justice must sometimes tip in his direction.

First thing in the morning, he decided, damn this desert heat, he'd order that air conditioner he'd always wanted. Sometimes these things just happen for the best.

*We travel down the road to Los Alamos, New Mexico
where engineers and scientists work to develop ever bigger
and better atomic bombs. It's a long way from Brooklyn
Heights, and Lorna is willing to do anything to return home.*

Lorna

by Camille Minichino

I can't believe I agreed to live here. There's nothing to recommend this parched, blazing hot New Mexican desert. How did I let my husband talk me into it?

"It's the best move for my career," Mickey had said. "I'll be working on the site of the Manhattan Project. Where all the greats worked only a few years ago. Oppenheimer, Teller, Fermi—"

I continued to wipe down my new aqua kitchen chairs, wondering if I'd be able to take them with me. Would I have to buy all new furniture? I was used to reading in *Life* and the women's magazines at my hairdresser's that everything was "slightly higher on the West Coast." What if we couldn't afford the new regency chiffonier I wanted for our bedroom? I had my eye on a rosewood sideboard in Gimbel's.

"Why is it called the Manhattan project if it's not in Manhattan?" I asked, pointing out the window at the Brooklyn Bridge, our bridge into Gotham.

Mickey shrugged. "I'm not sure. I think some of the supplies are stored in Manhattan, but the, uh, lab work has to be done in a more open area."

"You mean bomb work. You said we wouldn't need any more bomb work."

"That was five years ago. And it's a *gadget*. We call it a gadget, and we have a lot more testing to do."

"What testing? It worked, didn't it?" I shut my eyes against images of Hiroshima that still appeared in the movie newsreels.

"Look, Carmina, I can't say any more, and I can't say no to this opportunity. When the project's over, we can come back. By then I'll have it made in the shade. I'll be able to get any job I want."

I thought of my friend Nina, who used to live downstairs. Her husband's company moved to some square state in the middle of the country. Only for a year, they told him, just to train the new guys. That was five years ago and they were still AWOL. When Nina came back for our tenth high school reunion, we all asked, "When are you coming home?"

Nina shrugged and said, "It's not so bad out there."

Hmph.

"Do you realize how many guys would kill to work where Oppenheimer used to work?" Mickey is still talking.

"And I might kill myself being there. Why can't we stay here, where Ed Sullivan still works?"

Mickey had walked out of the kitchen, toward our suitcases. That was a year ago. I'd given it my best shot. A lot of arguing, but no dice. I lost. We moved to Los Alamos so my engineer husband, an expert with wires, could be on the same page of history as General Groves and E. O. Lawrence, he said. So he could play a key role in the testing of really powerful explosives, he said. I supposed that was better than testing bombs in Central Park.

I found out there's no shortage of space once you get past the Hudson River. Our home in New Mexico is big and sprawling. Ranch style, they call it, with three bedrooms and as many baths. Out here, every person has a toilet of his own. A few steps up from our flat in Brooklyn Heights—one-bedroom, all of five hundred and fifty square feet, including the bathroom that we shared.

But all I see out the windows of my spacious living room here is scrappy desert and boring stucco houses. No pretty window boxes, only sand and cactus for a front yard. Makes it hard to find a stoop to sit on.

I miss being able to buy pastries half a block away, then yell up the fire escape to Annie. "Come on down for coffee." Annie has three rug rats, so I usually go upstairs instead, and we complain about the food at Woolworth's counter and how the movie tickets have gone up to thirty-five cents.

I miss all the griping.

I try to fit in with the other wives here. It's tough, because I don't know how to sew or make jam and I don't want to learn. I bought a shirtwaist dress like they wear around the house. When I put it on, I feel like a television crew is on the way for an episode of the new show with George Burns and Gracie Allen.

Nobody drops in around here, either. You have to invite people for coffee or a meal. "Come at six o'clock," they'll say, and you better not be a minute early.

And all the wives are dull, even the ones who call themselves "steno girls," whatever that means. They can't even pronounce my name. What's so hard about Carmina? But they say, Carmine-ah. Some of the women work, but the work is dull, too, like sitting at a switchboard all day without even knowing who's on the line or what they're saying because everything is secret. We have secrets up the wazoo. No gossip like the kind that sailed across the lines back home:

"Poor Joey. I hear he got a knuckle sandwich when Nick caught him eyeing his girl."

"Yeah, poor Joey. That Nick's a thug."

Extra good gossip spiced up my day at home, since I had my own shift at the dry cleaners—all kinds of people coming and going. Lawyers, plumbers, teachers, auto mechanics. I was the first one to know whether a telltale stain would come out, or who was borrowing whose dress, and sometimes what they did while they had it on.

The big thrill in Los Alamos is when one of the scientists comes for dinner (they call it dinner, not supper). The wives spend all day cooking and baking. They have to, because there's no fish market, no bakery or deli handy. You can't get black-and-whites at the snap of your fingers or even a good slice of pastrami. Compared to good old-fashioned Brooklyn food, the recipes of the southwest are so spicy the flavor is drowned out. The chilis could bring on ulcers.

No buses rumble past our home; no El rattles the china and tilts the pictures on the walls. No trolleys or subway. And to get a taxi you have to make a phone call, then wait at least a half hour.

"You should learn to drive a car," Mickey tells me.

"I don't want to drive a car. I hate traffic. Oh, wait. There's no traffic."

Mickey, of course, is happy. Walking where Oppenheimer walked. Eating in the cafeteria where Fermi ate. My husband is considered a patriot and he can buy as many wires as he wants with government money. He works late a lot, comes home with sand in his pants and strange stains on his shirt. I wonder about the stains, but I don't have any way of figuring them out since I don't have my dry-cleaning supplies. And I can't ask any questions. If I do, Mickey comes back with, "What? Are you writing a book?"

Did I mention, everything is secret? Not that I'm suspicious of my husband or anything. Mickey is quiet and reserved. He isn't the kind of a guy who has a roving eye. At least I didn't think so. But who knows what a year in the desert can do to a person? Could it turn a wet rag into a daddy-O?

I have to admit, he does what he can to please me. He brings me nylons and cartons of cigarettes from a store that I'm not allowed to visit. That's something, but I could buy my own cigarettes in Brooklyn and how many pairs of nylons did I need sitting around the house?

You'd think it would be exciting, married to a guy who knows national secrets. He has a special badge, and a secret code word to get past the gate. Mickey was becoming famous in his own right. Not Einstein-famous, but he got a patent for some kind of instrument that measures the damage the bombs do. I can't pronounce the name of the thing—a something-meter—but it sounds sexy. Not that Mickey is that sexy, with his straight, slick-backed hair and the pocket protector that he cleans off every night. I wondered why I hadn't needed sexy in Brooklyn, but in New Mexico it seems necessary.

Day after day, night after night, I sit and watch the tube. "Queen for a Day" and "The Milton Berle Show." "What's My Line?" when I'm in the mood for a quiz show. All the while, I can't help questioning whether Mickey really is working. Now and then I hear what sounds like an explosion, and I think, okay, that must be Mickey at work. But who knows?

Some nights I wander into the bedroom closet and smell his clothes. No perfume. I inspect his collars. No lipstick or pancake makeup. No proof that Mickey is fooling around with anything but different colored wires and his something-meter.

A little before our second Christmas, I start to get really suspicious. Mickey is staying out later and later, and he's preoccupied when he's at home. He eats his supper in silence, gives me a quick peck on the cheek, and goes back to the field.

"Lots to do," he says.

When I press for more information, he offers, "We heard rumors that new rules are coming down, so we have to do it while we can."

"Do what 'it'?"

"You know I can't tell you what."

"Right."

Finally, one evening he screws up and leaves the key to his desk drawer hanging there, in the keyhole, for all to see. I see it, all right. It's what I've been waiting for. One slip up like this. I know it's not right, but how can I resist?

Besides it's his fault, isn't it? How did such an idiot get a top secret clearance in the first place? They probably only give him the lowest level jobs. On the other hand, how hard can it be to wire up a bomb? *A gadget.* It's just a case of the red wire and the green wire, isn't it? Even I know: never cut the red wire. Or is it the green? I'm giddy with the idea of breaking through the wall of secrets.

Mickey has gone back to work, so he says, and I have his office and desk key all to myself. I open the drawer and immediately see the little book, the one he always keeps in the back pocket of his work pants. Except for tonight. The book is small, with a marbled cover like the ones we used to have in school, but inside is a weekly calendar, with space to write notes.

I sit at Mickey's desk, in his chair, the gray set issued by the government. I flip through the pages of his book, week by week, hardly believing what I'm reading. As far back as I can read, there are different girls' names written down. Donna on Monday, Edith on Tuesday, Francie on Wednesday, Gert on Thursday. And on and on. Most of the girls are crossed out after only one date. *Didn't go well, Mickey? Heat getting to you? Or is it the altitude? Seven thousand feet above sea level can make all kinds of things go wrong.* I seethe as I run through the louse's schedule for the last few weeks. Only one name comes up over and over, with no cross-outs, but a record of how many dates: Lorna1 on Friday and then Lorna2 and Lorna3 over the weekend. The hussy.

Lorna. Imagine naming a girl after a cookie. And not a very good one at that. A plain shortbread cookie, not the luscious chocolate covered marshmallow ones with the sweet streak of jelly in the middle. That was me, Carmina. Luscious. Not like Lorna, which is just frigging butter and sugar.

He drags me all the way to the desert so he can work at a famous lab and then he cheats on me with a woman who sounds like a Girl Scout cookie? I think about taking a match to the little black book. Then I think about taking a match to myself. I yell, then I cry. I'm glad I'm right about Mickey; I hate that I'm right.

I consider packing up and going home. Right now. I could call a cab to take me to the airport. They'll all be glad to have me back. Josephine, Rose, Annie—they all feel sorry for me in the middle of nowhere and would welcome me home in a minute. Vinnie Impellittieri is still mayor, and he's Josephine's cousin's uncle-through-marriage, so it's not out of the question that a modest parade could be arranged.

But I don't want to lose my share of Mickey's money. When he got that patent, I tried to find out how much it was worth, but Mickey lied, like he's been lying about working late.

"There's no money," he told me. "The patent belongs to the government." As if I'd be dumb enough to believe that.

I know I have to do something.

And I do.

It turns out the desert is lethal. Poisonous plants everywhere. All I need is one. Those stuffy wives were good for something. I finally got some benefit out of the book club they talked me into. One of the books is a gold mine of information about these natural weapons.

I read about jimsonweed, castor bean, peyote, and water hemlock. Happy reading.

I settle on oleander. Its lovely pink flowers are misleading. A cluster of three leathery leaves, crushed and carefully buried in meatloaf—left in the fridge with a love note to my hubby—does the trick. Too bad I can't tell the ladies of the book club that it works.

So sad, the desert husbands and wives said, as they filed into my home after Mickey's funeral. They came bearing tuna noodle casseroles with crushed chips on top, celery stuffed with peanut butter and raisins, and green Jello loaded with canned fruit cocktail. Not a bad menu, until the corn chips with squashed avocado dip (yuck) arrived.

Though no one was crass enough to ask me exactly how Mickey died, I overheard a guess or two from his coworkers.

"A heart attack, and so young."

"Makes you want to exercise more."

"I heard he went into some kind of seizure."

"No one was home. Carmina was shopping with my wife, so who knows?"

"Tsk-tsk," I said, but not so anyone would hear.

Upstairs my bags were packed. One large suitcase with a matching hat box that I'd never opened. I was ready to beat it out of the Southwest.

I left the gathering for a minute to work up some tears and fondle my airline ticket out. *Brooklyn, here I come. Genuine cheesecake, here I come.* I knew I could get the girls together for a trip to the Botanic Garden. And a Dodgers game. *Pee Wee Reese, here I come.* Mickey's insurance money would go a long way toward a new wardrobe. *Bonwit Teller, here I come.* I planned to toss my year-round khakis in the trash on the way out.

Chuckling, hidden behind a curtain, I overheard a snippet of conversation.

"We'll sure miss Mickey on Lorna," one guy said.

"Sure will," said another.

On Lorna? Pretty crude, wasn't it? Befitting a hussy.

"Who do you think will take over?"

"They'll probably give her to Jack. Or Eddie; he's young, and done with Katie, I think."

What? Was Lorna a paying gig? The lab's official prossy? Couldn't my dumb, cheating husband even get a mistress of his own?

I came out of hiding and joined the group, unable to resist a shot. "So, you all knew about Lorna?" I asked, swirling my Manhattan. Giving my best imitation of Ingrid Bergman in *Casablanca.*

"Of course. We were all on it at one time or another," Mickey's best pal said.

Now Lorna was an *it*? Was she really a cookie?

"I always thought Lorna was too pretty a name for an explosion," one of the wives said.

"I've never understood why they give all the test shots girls' names," another said.

"Yeah, Carl was on Julie for a while. Then Katie. I guess they go alphabetically."

"Silly, isn't it? Why not numbers or something?"

All the wives nodded—yes, numbers would have made much more sense.

"I hope they don't use Patricia when they get to P," said Patricia, and everyone chuckled. Not too loudly, because it was a sad occasion, after all.

I fell onto the chair behind me. Mickey really was working late. On Lorna, the test shot.

Oh, well. One road back to Brooklyn was as good as another.

Police Sergeant Clark Gruenwald is assigned the task of looking into a cold case, seven years after teenage Sarah Jane Wilson goes missing from Crystal Springs. It's an annual task, performed each year on the anniversary of her disappearance.

Where's Sara Jane?

by Michael Bracken and Sandra Murphy

At ten o'clock on a cool Friday evening, blue-eyed, blond-haired, eighteen-year-old high school senior Sara Jane Wilson clocked out of work and walked out the back door of Woolworth's on her way to the 1948 Ford four-door sedan she had purchased two weeks earlier from Honest Abe's Used Car Emporium.

She never made it.

Her seven-year-old sedan remained untouched in the parking lot behind Woolworth's until the following morning, when Sara Jane's co-workers commented to one another about it. Sara Jane had been so proud of the car that she had taken every one of them for a ride during the first week she'd owned it.

That morning the store manager, Myron Threadgill, received a telephone call from Sara Jane's father and learned that she had not made it home the previous evening. Myron confirmed that the young woman's sedan remained in the parking lot behind the store, and soon he was repeating to a police officer everything he told Sara Jane's father.

"She clocked out precisely at ten p.m.," Myron said as he handed Sara Jane's timecard to the officer. "I saw her put on her sweater and grab her purse, but I didn't actually see her leave."

"Did anyone?"

"I don't know," Myron said. "I'm the only one working this morning who was here at closing time."

"I need the names, addresses, and phone numbers of everyone working last night."

Myron was quick to oblige, and by mid-afternoon all the employees, whether working or not the evening Sara Jane disappeared, had met with the police officer investigating the young woman's disappearance. Only Ethel Abernathy, the gray-haired spinster who worked in sundries, acknowledged wishing Sara Jane a good evening as the young woman pushed open the rear door.

"I wouldn't be surprised if she went off with some young man," Ethel sniffed during her conversation with the investigating officer.

"Why's that?"

"The way she's always flashing her legs, making sure the boys get a good look at her stockings, why I just—"

The officer didn't let Ethel finish her sentence. He thanked her for her time and was about to leave when she added, "When she opened the door, I heard a dog barking. Not a big dog, a little dog. More of a yapping than a bark, I'd say."

"There was someone walking a dog behind the store?"

"I didn't see anyone, but there might have been."

Sara Jane's picture was published on the front page of the next morning's newspaper. Her parents—Ethel and Wilber Wilson—had given the paper a copy of her senior class portrait, and the accompanying news story described her attire the night of her disappearance: a long-sleeved white blouse, a red four-button waistcoat, and a matching red, ballerina-length, full-circle skirt with staggered pleats, made from a Simplicity pattern as a Home Economics IV assignment. Her dishwater blond hair was in a loose ponytail, and she wore gold-plated clip-on earrings and just a hint of make-up. Though her co-workers didn't remember it, her parents insisted she wore a gold cross on a gold chain around her neck, a gift from her mother's parents on her sixteenth birthday.

When asked why they waited until the following morning to report their daughter's disappearance, Mrs. Wilson told the newspaper reporter that she and her husband were in bed by nine-thirty each evening, and that Sara Jane knew not to wake them when she arrived home. Mrs. Wilson also told the reporter she suspected something was wrong when Sara Jane didn't have breakfast prepared when they awoke that morning.

A day passed before the investigating officer met with Anton Hussman, a prissy man wearing pince-nez glasses, who admitted to walking his toy poodle, Gloria, near the Woolworth's the evening Sara Jane disappeared.

"Did you see a young woman exit the store about that time?"

"You mean the girl in the newspaper?"

"Yes," the investigating officer said, "that young woman."

"I can't say for certain that it was her," Hussman said, "but I did see a young woman crossing the parking lot while Gloria was doing her business."

"Going to her car?"

"Her car?" Hussman shook his head. "No, I don't think so. The woman I saw was walking away from the parking lot."

———

Police Sergeant Clark Gruenwald closed the file folder over the top of the two-inch-thick stack of reports he'd spent much of the day reading. Peeking out from beneath it was that morning's newspaper, and he stared at the headline—the same headline that topped the front page of the local newspaper each year on the anniversary of Sara Jane Wilson's disappearance: "Where's Sara Jane?"

Gruenwald was no closer to answering than the investigating officer had been prior to retirement five years earlier. He had retrieved the file only because it was his turn to review Crystal

Springs' notorious unsolved case. He rubbed the palm of his hand across his bald pate and then flipped the newspaper over so he could not see the headline taunting him.

"Anything?"

Gruenwald looked up at his lieutenant. "Houdini couldn't have done a better disappearing act."

"It's been seven years," Lieutenant Washington said. "Too long for this case to be hanging over us."

"Before I read through all this," Gruenwald said, "I called Osborne down in Florida. He remembered the case and said he wishes he didn't. Everything he knew about the missing girl should be in the file. And he said to tell you the fishing is good."

"Good for him, maybe. Not so good for us," Washington said. "Police work is a lot like fishing. You bait the hook, toss it in the water, and see what you catch."

Gruenwald waved his hand at the folder on his desk. "Looks like we've been fishing with dry hooks."

"Find something," the lieutenant insisted. "Find anything."

As Washington exited his office, Gruenwald grabbed his jacket. Fifteen minutes later he stood on the porch of the Wilson home and introduced himself to the old man who answered the door. "You know why I'm here?"

"Your lot shows up every year," Wilber Wilson said. "And every year the damned newspaper asks the same damn question. Fat lot of good any of it does. She ain't coming back."

"Mind if I come in?"

The old man stepped aside, and Gruenwald followed him into the living room. The house had the musty smell of a tomb and Gruenwald saw no evidence that the place had been cleaned in the recent past. That morning's newspaper lay folded open on the coffee table, and a local grocery store's ad had several prices circled in blue ink. As Wilson settled into a wingback chair, Gruenwald settled onto the couch and asked, "Your wife? Is she home?"

"Ethel passed three months ago. You should already know that. She died never knowing what happened to her baby."

Gruenwald noted the old man's turn of phrase. "Her baby? Sara Jane?"

"I guess she was as much mine as she was Ethel's," Wilson said, "but I never thought of her that way. Ethel's the one who brought her home."

"You didn't want children?"

"Couldn't have 'em," he said. "Measles. I'm sterile as a mule."

"That information's not in the case file," Gruenwald said as he leaned forward. "Why's that?"

Wilson shrugged. "No one ever asked."

"So, your wife—?" Gruenwald was unsure how to ask a man about his cuckolding. "Who was the—?"

"I'll not have you disparage my Ethel," Wilson said as he stood. "She did what she thought was right."

Gruenwald stopped at the Dairy Queen for a Dilly Bar, vanilla soft serve coated in chocolate. As he re-read the Sara Jane file, a shard of chocolate dropped onto the backside of a report. He reached for a napkin to wipe the page and noticed something new—a woman's first name and a phone number, written lightly in pencil. After cleaning up the mess and finishing his Dilly Bar, Gruenwald fished a coin out of his pocket and approached the pay phone outside.

"Hello." The answering voice belonged to a young boy. When Gruenwald asked to speak to Patty, the boy said, "Patty don't live here."

"I need to—" Gruenwald realized he was talking to a dial tone. The kid had hung up. He found another dime and called back. "If Patty's not there, can I talk to your mom?"

"You're supposed to say, 'may I,' not 'can I.' My mom says so. You ask for the lady of the house."

"Okay, son, may I talk to the lady of the house?"

"No, she's laying out in the sun, getting a tan and drinking orange juice. She said to leave her alone."

The phone went dead.

Gruenwald dialed the operator, gave her his badge number, and asked her to use the reverse directory to provide him with the name and address matching the phone number he provided.

A moment later the operator said, "That's the Johnson residence."

"Patty Johnson? Patricia Johnson?"

"You trying to find Patty?" she asked, reminding him that Crystal Springs, despite recent growth, was still a small town. "This time of day, you'd be better off calling her at the State Farm office. Let me connect you."

A moment later a woman answered. "State Farm, how may I help you?"

Gruenwald confirmed he was speaking with Patty Johnson and then identified himself. "I need to talk to you about Sara Jane Wilson."

"Finally."

Her response caught him off guard but when he tried to press, she said she couldn't talk. They agreed to meet later that afternoon at a diner across the street from the State Farm office.

<hr>

"Sara Jane was, I don't know, nervous, excited, the afternoon she disappeared," Patty said. She was less than half Gruenwald's age and had what his wife would call a generous figure. She wore her black hair cut in a bob, and her dark eyes peered at the world through thick lenses. "I went by Woolworth's during her break and we shared a chocolate malted."

"It didn't say anything about that in her file." Gruenwald laid the file on the table. "In fact, you weren't even mentioned. Not directly."

"That might be because that cop wasn't paying attention to me. He was trying to flirt with Donna, the cosmetics manager." Patty sipped her soda. "I only talked to him the one time. He told me he thought she ran away with a boy, and he wouldn't listen when I told him she wasn't like that."

"We revisit this investigation every year," Gruenwald. "Have any other detectives ever talked to you about Sara Jane?"

"You're the first."

"So tell me what you would have told the original investigator if he'd asked."

Patty gazed out the window as if thinking. When she returned her attention to Gruenwald, she asked, "I heard you called my mother's house. Did you talk to Bobby?"

"He hung up on me after correcting my grammar." Gruenwald laughed. "Made me ask 'may I' talk to you instead of 'can I,' said his mom told him to say that."

"That's because I wanted to be an English major. Words are important."

"Bobby isn't your brother?"

"No, he's my son, the result of a fast-talking soldier on leave and me falling for his line. I left town a few weeks after Sara Jane disappeared, though not by choice. Couldn't bring the shame down on my father. He was a deacon at his church."

"Did you go to one of those homes for—"

"Unwed mothers? No. When I told Sara Jane that day that I was in a family way, she made me promise, no matter what happened, to never go near one of them. She said they weren't safe."

Gruenwald nodded encouragingly.

"I was showing by then, and when that cop talked to me a few days after Sara Jane disappeared, I'm certain he could tell. I think that's why he wouldn't listen to what I said. If Sara Jane was friends with a girl like me, what kind of a girl did that make her?"

"So, what happened?"

"Within a week, I went to live with my aunt—my mother's sister because my father's family would have nothing to do with me. When I came back, I was toting a baby."

Gruenwald returned to the station and dumped the files on his desk. He had already learned two things none of the other detectives had, and he considered that a good day's work. He signed out and went home to find his wife pulling a meat loaf from the oven.

Over dinner, Gruenwald told her that he had been assigned the Wilson case to review. Ginger knew what that meant, and she parroted that morning's newspaper headline when she asked, "Where's Sara Jane?"

He shrugged in response, and then he told her about his meeting with Wilber Wilson and his later meeting with Patty Johnson. By the time they were drinking after-dinner coffee, he and his wife were deep into a discussion about premarital relationships that made Gruenwald uncomfortable.

His wife, on the other hand, was not. "Unmarried girls have been getting pregnant since the Garden of Eden, Clark, and they've never had many options: an abortionist or a home for unwed mothers. Heck, we even had one of those here."

That caught Gruenwald's attention and allowed him to change the subject. "Where?"

"You don't remember Holiday House?"

Gruenwald shook his head—unlike his wife, he was not a life-long resident of Crystal Springs—and he listened while she explained. "Before the war, Holiday House was a home for unwed mothers. The girls came from all over the state, and once their babies were born the mothers went back to whatever small town they came from."

"What happened to it?"

"Oh, it's still there, but it's a nursing home now, filled with geriatric patients. You know the place. Resthaven? Out by the old highway?"

Gruenwald knew the place.

The next morning, Gruenwald drove to Resthaven and asked to speak to the administrator. After waiting several minutes, he was ushered into the office of a pinch-faced woman wearing a brown tweed skirt suit over a white blouse.

He identified himself, displayed his badge, and was in turn directed to sit in a hardbacked chair on the visitor side of Wanda Firestone's desk.

Sensing that she was uncomfortable with his visit, he dispensed with the usual pleasantries and came to the point. "I understand Resthaven was once a home for unwed mothers."

"Holiday House," she corrected.

"Why the change?"

"The war," she explained, "gave cover to many pregnant women. Slip on a cheap ring and tell everyone your husband died during Pearl Harbor or D-Day and you could keep your baby and your dignity."

"So you lost business?"

"I wasn't here then," Firestone said, "but, yes, the home lost business and was sold about ten years ago to the current owners. I was hired shortly after they took over, and I must say we're doing a booming business in doddering grannies."

The slight upturn at the corner of her mouth let Gruenwald know the director was trying to tell a joke, so he chuckled appreciatively. Then he said, "I suppose the new owners disposed of the old records."

"Actually, no. We moved them to the basement when we took over, and everything's still there." She hesitated. "Well, almost everything."

"Come again?"

"About seven years ago—maybe closer to eight—someone broke in and ransacked the old Holiday House files."

"What were they looking for?"

"I have no clue. They didn't take anything of value that we know of, so your department wrote it off as an act of vandalism."

"What about employees? Are any of your current employees holdovers from—"

Firestone looked aghast. "Heavens no! They weren't medical professionals. They were zealots, convinced they were saving the souls of young girls and their progeny."

Gruenwald asked to see the old records, so Firestone called in her secretary and had her escort Gruenwald to the basement. There he found himself staring at more than a dozen filing cabinets, a bookshelf crammed with ledgers, and an old desk. He turned to Firestone's secretary. "Were you here when this was vandalized?"

"Who do you think put everything back in order?" she said. "And without overtime!"

"Did the vandals tear everything up?"

She shook her head and pointed to the third filing cabinet from the left. "They seemed most interested in this one."

Gruenwald watched as she pulled open the bottom drawer and pulled out an empty file folder with *Marsha Eckmann* typed on the tab. "After I matched up all the paperwork, I was left with this empty folder."

"Who was Marsha Eckmann?"

She walked to the bookcase, pulled out a ledger, and began thumbing through the pages. She stopped and pointed to a single entry. "I think this is her."

In a neat script, someone had written *Eckmann, baby girl, 6 lbs. 4 oz., March 12, 1937. DOA.*

Gruenwald copied the information into his notebook and then asked, "Do you have a list of all the employees of Holiday House working around that time?"

She pulled open another filing cabinet drawer stuffed with file folders. "Knock yourself out," she said. "They're filed by name, not by date of employment."

He pulled out a handful of folders, the first for *Abrams, Clara,* and carried them to the desk.

A few hours later he had a list of seven women employed at Holiday House the day Marsha Eckmann gave birth. One of them was Ethel Wilson, whose last date of employment was March 12, 1937.

——————

Gruenwald called the retired detective in Florida who first caught the missing person case he had spent the previous few days reinvestigating, and he waited through eleven rings before Jerry Osborn picked up the phone. He identified himself but, before he could ask his questions, found himself listening to Osborn tell him about the catch-and-release bass fishing competition in which he had participated the previous week.

"Second place," the retired detective said. "I put in all that work and didn't get to bring home a fish."

"Still," Gruenwald said. "Must have been fun. I haven't been fishing in ages."

"You should go. Get some fresh air. Get a new perspective on life."

"Perspective," Gruenwald said. "I need a little of that."

"You still working the missing girl case?" Osborn said. "The last couple of detectives who caught the annual review of unsolved cases—"

"Case," Gruenwald corrected. "There's only the one."

"They gave up after a day or two," Osborn said, "told me all they did was duplicate what I had done."

"None of them ever spoke with Patty Johnson."

"Why would they? She didn't know anything."

"Teenage girl, friend of the missing girl, and she's not even mentioned in any of your reports."

"Why would she be? The little tramp gave me nothing," Osborn said. "How'd you tumble to her?"

"Her name and number were penciled on the back of one of the forms in the file. I only saw it by accident."

"And?"

"And I talked to her. She told me what she told you. She said you thought Sara Jane had run off with a boy, and Patty told me Sara Jane wasn't like that. She said she told you the same thing."

"Still think that's what happened," Osborn said. "I talked to one of her co-workers who said the girl was a flirt. She's probably barefoot, pregnant, and in somebody's kitchen right now."

Gruenwald realized the retired detective's attitude had likely colored the direction of his investigation, and that he would have to find a new perspective on his own. He thanked Osborn for his time and wished him luck the next time he went fishing.

Lieutenant Washington's office door stood open, and Gruenwald rapped once on the door frame. When the lieutenant looked up from the papers atop his desk, Gruenwald said, "Have a minute? I tossed in a dry hook and caught something off the bottom in the Sara Jane case."

Washington motioned him in. "What've you got?"

Gruenwald settled into the chair across from the lieutenant. "The girl wasn't theirs. Not biologically. Wilson said he was shooting blanks, became upset when I asked how the wife got pregnant, and threw me out of the house. Ginger put me on to Holiday House, a home for unwed mothers out by the old highway. Ethel Wilson worked there until a young woman named Marsha Eckmann gave birth. Wilson quit her job the same day, which coincides with the missing girl's birthday. I think she took the Eckmann baby, named her Sara Jane, and told everyone she was theirs."

The lieutenant shook his head. "Rules were different then and I remember hearing about those homes. They made the girls miserable, telling them they were sinners, like there weren't two people involved in a situation like that."

Lieutenant Washington had children and Gruenwald didn't, so the lieutenant gave him a quick lesson in parenthood. "I like to think I taught my daughter better than to get herself in trouble like that, but if she did, I certainly wouldn't treat her like some parents treat their daughters." He paused for a moment of reflection. "I might shoot the boy, though."

After the lieutenant left his office, Gruenwald began working the phone. He located three of Edith Wilson's former co-workers. Of the other four, one had died, two had relocated, and one was a resident of Resthaven and unable to remember much of anything. The three he spoke with remembered Edith, none of them favorably, but only one remembered her sudden departure from Holiday House.

"Edith was the midwife on duty that morning," explained Gladys Becker, "and experienced her first stillbirth. That must have shook her up something awful because she quit the same day. The baby's mother, though, insisted her child wasn't still-born. She said she heard her baby cry."

"Did she?"

"I wouldn't know. The baby arrived around three in the morning and Edith was the only one working."

"Anyone else see the baby?"

"We had a process for disposal of non-viable remains. I'm sure she must have followed procedures."

"What happened to the mother?"

"Some as all the others, I suppose. We sent her home."

After making extensive notes about his telephone conversations, Gruenwald headed home, where his wife fried a slice of leftover meatloaf and served it to him slathered in mayonnaise between two slices of Wonder Bread. Between bites, he told her about his day. He concluded with, "I don't think the baby was stillborn."

"You think Mrs. Wilson stole it?"

"Even if she did, that doesn't explain how Sara Jane disappeared a second time."

"One baby, two mothers," Ginger said. "Maybe the birth mother came back for her."

"After eighteen years?"

"Regret does not have an expiration date."

During Patty's lunch break the next day, Gruenwald met her again at the diner near the State Farm office. After exchanging pleasantries, he asked, "Did Sara Jane ever tell you she was adopted?"

Patty shook her head.

"But she told you not to go to a home for unwed mothers. When did she tell you that?"

"The day she disappeared."

"And why do you think she told you that?"

Patty shrugged. "You can't imagine the fight I had with my father when he wanted to send me away."

"I think I can," Gruenwald said. "But Sara Jane—"

"If you knew how she lived," Patty said, "if you knew how her parents treated her, you might not be surprised to learn that she dreamed she was a princess and that someday she would be rescued."

"Rescued? How she was treated?"

"Ever read Cinderella? Sara Jane was Cinderella in that house. They made her do everything. Cook. Clean. Care for them. And all of it on top of school and the part-time job she held at the Woolworth's. If Prince Charming showed up with a glass slipper, she'd have been gone in an instant."

"You said she wasn't the type to go off with a boy."

"Not for that reason. Not like me."

"What if her mother showed up?"

"Her mother?"

"What if she was adopted and her mother showed up?" He avoided telling her exactly how he thought Sara Jane had come into the Wilson household. "What would she do?"

"You really think she was adopted?"

"Looks like it."

"I wouldn't ever give up my baby, and if he was taken, I'd fight tooth-and-nail to get him back."

<hr>

Gruenwald went from the diner to the Wilson home. After knocking three times, the old man finally answered the door.

"There's no need to beat the door down, give a man a chance to get some pants on." Wilson could have also used a few minutes to comb his hair and find his upper teeth.

Gruenwald stepped forward, forcing Wilson back into the house. "I don't think you want your neighbors hearing what I have to say."

They sat at the kitchen table, old, worn out, and wobbly on one leg. Gruenwald turned down the offer of coffee when he saw the dirty cups on the counter.

He opened the file folder. "Your wife worked at Holiday House but abruptly quit."

"She had a new baby to care for. She couldn't work and care for a baby at the same time." The old man clanked a spoon in his coffee cup. The coffee smelled burnt and days old.

"You told me Sara Jane was as much yours as she was your wife's. If that's true, then she wasn't really either of yours. Your wife was never pregnant, was she?" Gruenwald said. "She never gave birth. So where did you get the baby? Holiday House?"

Wilson wouldn't meet Gruenwald's gaze. Instead, he stared at his coffee cup. "Ethel wanted a baby, somebody to take care of us when we got old. The girl's mama didn't want her, so what was the harm? People bring stuff home from work all the time. What was the harm?"

"How'd you get away with it?"

"My wife was—" Wilson hesitated as if thinking of the correct word. "Stout. Ethel was stout, so she could have been pregnant without showing. There wasn't a hospital within fifty miles, so we told everyone she had the baby at home. She was a midwife, so she took care of things herself. Ethel certainly wasn't the only woman to give birth at home back then."

"And you led everyone to believe Sara Jane was yours, even after she disappeared seven years ago."

"She *was* ours. We raised her. We gave her everything."

"Everything but the truth about her parents."

After a moment of silence, Wilson said, "I did it for Ethel. I did everything for Ethel."

"And the baby's mother? What did you know about her?"

"Ethel always told me the mother was from St. Louis."

Finding Marsha Eckmann from St. Louis took several phone calls, and he finally located her under her married name in a town sixty miles from Crystal Springs, a round trip he could make in an afternoon.

So he did, and he found himself sitting in the kitchen of Mrs. Marsha Hobson, a slender blonde only days past her fortieth birthday.

She readily admitted to her time at Holiday House.

"How old were you when you were sent there? Fourteen? Fifteen?"

"Fifteen," she said. "Just turned. I was three months along by then, and I spent six months living in that hellhole before my daughter was born."

"And what happened to your daughter?"

Marsha hesitated before she answered. "I don't know. I never saw her. They wouldn't even let me hold her."

"You wanted to, though, didn't you?"

"Of course. I never wanted to give up my baby."

"So why were you planning to?"

"My parents consented to adoption."

"And then your daughter was stillborn."

"She wasn't," Marsha said. "The midwife lied. I know she did, and Holiday House covered it up."

"If you thought you daughter was alive, did you ever look for her? You ever try to find her?"

"I—no." She shook her head and looked away.

"You ever return to Crystal Springs, to Holiday House?"

"Of course not."

"Holiday House closed," Gruenwald said. "It's a nursing home now, but all the Holiday House records are still in the basement. Your file, though, there's nothing in it."

"I just wanted to know what happened to my baby," she said. "You going to arrest me for that?"

"The break-in? The statute of limitations has expired on that. But kidnapping—"

"Kidnapping?"

Where's Sara Jane?

"You contacted your daughter, didn't you? Met her one night after work and took her away."

Marsha stared at Gruenwald.

"So, where is your daughter now, Miss Eckmann?"

———————

That afternoon, Gruenwald asked to use two of his unscheduled vacation days.

Lieutenant Washington asked, "What about Sara Jane?"

"It's been seven years, Lieutenant. What difference will it make if I take a few days off to go fishing?"

The next day, Gruenwald crossed two state lines before he reached his destination. He had to stop at a service station on the edge of town to ask directions to the address Marsha Hobson née Eckmann had given him.

Gruenwald rapped on the apartment door and waited until a brunette with blond roots answered. In her mid-twenties, she was dressed in black Capri pants and a cherry-red button-front blouse. She wore neither shoes nor jewelry, and her hair was pulled back in a loose ponytail.

Gruenwald identified himself and displayed his badge before he said, "I'm looking for Sara Jane Wilson."

"She's dead," the woman said. "I killed her."

"Your mother phoned ahead, didn't she?" Without invitation, Gruenwald stepped past the young woman into the apartment. The living room was sparsely decorated, and the furniture appeared well-used. He turned back to her. "Seven years is a long time to pretend to be someone else, Miss Eckmann."

"Not as long as the eighteen years I spent with people who pretended to be my parents."

"You've made a life for yourself as Elizabeth Eckmann."

"And it's a life I'd like to keep."

There was a stack of a paper half an inch thick on her coffee table, and she handed it to Gruenwald. He quickly thumbed through it, recognizing the Holiday House stationery. "Your mother give this to you?"

"My entire life was a lie," the dead woman said, "and the people who pretended to be my parents didn't love me. Not really. They treated me like a servant girl. Made me clean the house, do the cooking, everything. When you're a kid, you don't know any better, but as I grew up, I realized other people's parents weren't like mine. I dreamed I was adopted. I dreamed my real parents were out there and that they would come for me some day. I was right, but not the way I expected. I never thought I might have been stolen from my mother and that she would—"

"—come back for you?" Gruenwald said, completing her sentence.

Elizabeth nodded. "So, what now?" she asked. "You take me back to those people and—?"

"Ethel Wilson passed away a few months ago," Gruenwald said. "Wilber Wilson has resigned himself to your loss. There's no one to take you back to, but we've been looking for you for seven years. I need to take you back to close the investigation."

"You can't take back a dead woman."

"Oh, but—"

"It wouldn't be the first time I died without leaving behind a body."

Gruenwald glanced at the stack of paper from Holiday House. If Ethel Wilson could make the Eckmann baby disappear, maybe he could make the Eckmann adult do the same.

Upon his return to Crystal Springs, Gruenwald stopped at Wilber Wilson's home, gave him the news about the death of his daughter, and had the old man identify a single possession of Sara Jane's he had brought back with him. Then he drove to the police station and walked into Lieutenant Washington's office without knocking.

"You catch anything?"

Gruenwald admitted that he had not gone fishing and that he'd been tracking a lead on the Sara Jane Wilson case.

"You find her?" the lieutenant asked.

"Not exactly."

Washington looked a question at him.

"She's dead."

"Who identified the body?"

"I think this is proof enough." He opened the handkerchief in which he had wrapped the gold cross and gold chain Sara Jane had received from Ethel Wilson's parents on her sixteenth birthday. "I met the woman who buried her, and I have this. Mr. Wilson identified it as his daughter's. He didn't seem broken up about the news of Sara Jane's passing. I think he resigned himself to it a long time ago."

The lieutenant examined Gruenwald for a moment. "Something you're not telling me, Clark?"

Gruenwald had reeled in his catch and then thrown it back, and he needed time to concoct a whopper. He shook his head and said, "I'll put everything in my report."

But he didn't. Not exactly.

So an old case became a closed case, and no one ever looked for Sara Jane Wilson again.

The death of a reclusive old woman turns into a classic who-done-it mystery in our next story by John M. Floyd. This story originally appeared in Thema, spring 2006, Midnight, Dogwood Press, 2008

Clara's Helper

by John M. Floyd

The doorbell chimed. Somewhere in the house there was the sharp clocking of footsteps on a wooden floor, then the release of a latch and the creak of a door as it opened wide. Sunlight flashed off the long blade of a butcher knife.

Jim Holliman took a step back, almost to the edge of the porch. "Miss Vanetti?" he asked.

"Mrs.," she said. "I'm a widow." With two quick swipes of her dishtowel the lady in the doorway finished drying the knife, then pointed it off to her right. "That newfangled lawnmower's around back, if that's what you're here for."

"Excuse me?"

She studied him a moment. "Didn't you come for the mower?"

"No ma'am." He flashed his badge. "I'm Inspector Holliman, from downtown. I wanted to ask you some questions about Mrs. Endicott."

"Oh." The knife drooped. "My mistake." She took a long look at his outfit, which included a cowboy hat and boots and a brown leather jacket. "You're not… what I expected."

"Neither are you," he said, pocketing his badge and removing his hat. It was the name, for one thing. The yellow-aproned woman in the doorway was pretty and blond and blue-eyed, like a housewife you might see in one of those Frigidaire commercials on television. She didn't look like a Vanetti. Also, she seemed too young to have been Clara Endicott's housekeeper for thirty years, which was what he'd been told by one of the neighbors. Holliman asked her about it as he followed her down the dark hallway toward the rear of the house.

"I started here when I was twelve," she said. It sounded like the kind of joking remark often heard when the subject is age and the number of years on the job, but Holliman saw that she was serious. "I came over on afternoons and weekends until I got done with school," she added, "and by that time my folks were gone and I was married and I needed the money even more than before."

The hallway led to a large kitchen with a shiny Linoleum floor and tall white cabinets, where Ruth Vanetti tucked the knife away in a drawer, draped the towel over the rest of the waiting dishes, and waved her visitor toward a chair at the table. A wringer washing machine stood in one corner, looking out of place. On the counter, a radio was playing "Unforgettable." Nat King Cole. Mrs. Vanetti switched it off. "How about a glass of ice tea?" she asked.

"No, thanks." Holliman shrugged out of his coat and sat down, taking a quick glance around the room. "You were saying…?"

"Oh. Yes." She took a seat across the table from him. "By that time I was married, but I just stayed on the payroll, so to speak. Every day I came over and did the laundry and cooked her meals and swept the floors and so on." She paused and adjusted the tablecloth. "A few years later, when my husband died, I more or less moved in with her."

"You moved in here, you mean? In this house?"

"That's right. Clara was getting pretty frail even then, and needed me more than just part-time." Mrs. Vanetti paused again, as if remembering happier days. During the silence Holliman took a pencil stub and notepad from his pocket and flipped to a clean page.

"Were you her only housekeeper, during all that time?"

She blinked and looked at him. "Yes. I was."

"So you were close, the two of you?"

"I'm not sure anyone was very close to Clara Endicott. We got along, I guess you'd say."

He licked the point of his pencil and made a note in the pad. "So there were disagreements, then?"

"We were both women, Inspector Holliman. Of course there were disagreements. But as I said, we got along most of the time."

Holliman stopped what he was writing and studied the result as if regarding a rare piece of artwork. "How did your husband die, Mrs. Vanetti?"

She didn't reply right away. Finally he raised his head, and their eyes met. "An accident at work," she said. "The sawmill."

"I see. And afterward, you said you moved in here."

She shrugged, and for an instant Holliman saw the sadness underneath the composed outer shell. "I had no choice. Creditors took our trailer, and Paulie wasn't much on the idea of life insurance."

"And you've been here ever since?"

"Going on eighteen years."

"Were you with her the night she died?"

She sat there and stared at him for a long time.

"Is something wrong?" he said.

"Inspector, you said you wanted to ask me some questions about Mrs. Endicott."

He leaned back in his chair. "I thought that's what I was doing."

"All your questions so far have been about me."

He sighed. "I'm a detective, Mrs. Vanetti. I just like to get all my facts strai—"

"The doctor said she died of natural causes, Inspector. Isn't that right?"

"That's what he said, yes."

Neither of them spoke for a moment. Outside the kitchen window, the branches of an old cedar tree nodded in the breeze.

"Why did you ask me how my husband died?" she said.

"I told you, I only wanted—"

"Inspector, I'll be direct." Her expression was no longer composed, or even sad. There was a challenge in her eyes now. "It doesn't sound to me like you're investigating what you think is a death from natural causes. It sounds like you're investigating what you think is a murder."

Slowly Holliman closed his notepad and held it flat between the palms of his hands. "I'm not sure it was a murder," he said. "It might have been suicide. But it was one or the other."

She stared back at him in disbelief. The defiance in her eyes had disappeared as quickly as it had come. Her round face had gone slack, her cheeks pale. Even her bright blond hair seemed to have lost its color. It was as if someone had waved a wand and rendered her Old.

"But… she died in her sleep."

"She died, yes. In her sleep? Possibly. But not of old age." He paused, then said, "She was poisoned."

This time Mrs. Vanetti just blinked. Otherwise her face remained frozen with shock. Holliman watched her closely. If she was faking, she was the best actress he'd ever seen.

"Poisoned," she repeated.

He nodded.

"But the doctor said—"

"He didn't know. The coroner noticed it later. Smelled it on her breath."

Ruth Vanetti gaped at him.

"Sorry," he said. "Bad choice of words. He smelled it on her mouth. The poison was something called strophanthus, and he had run across it before, in an overseas post in the military. It's an arrow poison, like curare. The effects are blurred vision, then circulatory failure, then death." He rubbed his forehead. "At any rate, the coroner caught it, and did an autopsy. Definitely strophanthus. Taken orally, in this case."

Mrs. Vanetti swallowed hard, as if demonstrating the procedure in question. She looked dazed. "I... don't quite know what to say."

Holliman opened his pad once more and raised his pen. "Were you with her," he asked again, "the night she died?"

"I was here in the house, yes."

"But not with her?"

"I... found her. Afterward."

"In her bedroom?"

"That's right."

The inspector flipped back through notes he had made when talking to the other officers. "That was on the twelfth? Two nights ago?"

"Yes." Her face had regained some of its color now, but she was still shaken. She seemed to be having trouble focusing her thoughts.

"What time would that have been?"

"What time?"

"When did you find the body, exactly?"

She frowned. "Around midnight, I think. Maybe a few minutes before."

"I see." The pencil scribbled a note. "Did she cry out, then?"

"What?"

"I asked if she cried out, or called to you."

"No, she didn't call to me. I told you, she died in her sleep. Or so I thought, anyway."

Holliman looked up from his pad. "Then I'm a little confused, Mrs. Vanetti. If you weren't summoned, what were you doing there with her, at midnight?"

At that, her face seemed to sag even further. She looked as if she might be about to burst into tears. Holliman didn't know if it was because of her memory of what had happened or because of the fact that he had asked her about it.

She drew a shaky breath, then said, as if each word was painful to her, "My room's down the hall from hers, and I always listen to the radio until late. Before I went to bed myself, I always went back in to check on her."

"Why was that? Did she have trouble sleeping?"

"It was just my routine." She seemed a little irritated. "She couldn't see well enough to read much, so I read to her every night around nine-thirty. It usually took half an hour or so. I would leave her room around ten, she'd go to bed at eleven, and I'd come back to check on her at midnight." She stared dreamily down at the tablecloth for a moment. "I look in on her again at seven every morning. She's always asleep both times, but I check on her just the same."

Suddenly Ruth Vanetti's face changed again. She looked surprised, and embarrassed. Her right hand came up to cover her mouth. "Oh my," she whispered. "I said that as if… as if everything were still the same."

Holliman thought he saw tears shining in her eyes.

"I can't believe she's really gone," Ruth Vanetti said.

Neither of them spoke for a while. As he waited Holliman could hear sparrows playing in the trees behind the house. Somewhere nearby a dog yapped, and what sounded like a large truck rumbled past in the street.

"Could I see her room?" he asked.

<hr>

Clara Endicott's bedroom was bright and warm and spotless. Inspector Holliman stood in the center of the room with his hands in his pockets for a full five minutes or more, scanning everything, trying to picture the scene as it had been two nights before, when the old woman was alive and breathing and lying there in the bed after Ruth Vanetti had left and returned to her own room. The coroner had been emphatic about one point: that particular poison took perhaps an hour to do its work—an hour and a quarter at the most. If what the housekeeper had told him was true, Clara Endicott must have ingested the poison between ten and eleven o'clock. The question was, how had it happened?

The bedroom was simply, almost childishly, furnished: bed, dresser, wardrobe, nightstand. The bed was large but plain, covered with a thick flowered spread with ruffles around the hem. Pictures in wooden frames littered the top of the dresser; most were of small children holding pets or dolls or Christmas presents. The nightstand was a large bedside table stocked with a vase of dried flowers and a clock and a cupful of pencils. No radio on this table. Sunlight filtered into the room through thin pink curtains.

Holliman frowned. Something about the room bothered him, but he couldn't put his finger on it. Finally he nodded and followed the housekeeper out the door and down the stairs to the kitchen.

"Mrs. Vanetti," he said when they were seated again at the table, "was anyone else here that night? Did she have any visitors at all?" He had taken her up on the offer of tea this time, and sipped from his glass as he waited for her answer.

"No," she said. "Only me."

"What about during that day?"

She shook her head. "No one ever comes here anymore, Inspector. Certainly not to visit."

He pondered that for several seconds. "Let me make sure I have something right. You left her at ten, listened to the radio until twelve, then went back and found her dead. Correct?"

"Yes."

"Did she have a bedtime snack, possibly? Or anything to drink?"

"Not to my knowledge."

"What do you mean by that?"

"I mean I didn't bring her anything. There's always the chance, I guess, that she went and got a snack or glass of water on her own, but I doubt it. She doesn't—didn't—get around very well, and I don't think she'd have tried to tackle the stairs by herself."

Holliman ran a finger along the rim of his glass, thinking. "I suppose you ate together that night, the two of you?"

"Yes, we did. Right here at this table, matter of fact."

"Could she have carried something to her room with her afterward, that you didn't know about?"

The housekeeper sighed. "She could have, I suppose. Again, I doubt it. She just didn't do those things."

A silence passed. Ruth Vanetti was looking more weary with every passing minute. For the first time, Holliman realized he could hear the soft chiming of a clock somewhere in the house.

He took another drink of tea, then set his glass down and studied it a moment. Finally he asked, "You and Mrs. Endicott were the only two people in the household for many years, is that right?"

"That's correct."

"Who bought the groceries?"

"The groceries?"

"Did you go out and buy them yourself, or were they brought in?"

"I bought the food myself. With money she gave me for that purpose." For an instant the challenging look returned to her eyes. "I was very careful about the accounting."

"I don't doubt that, Mrs. Vanetti. Bear with me, here." His notepad was out again now, and open. "It has been established that she died of poison, taken orally. That means, to me, food or drink. Did you buy *all* the groceries?"

"Yes."

"Well then, did you buy anything that she ate and you didn't?"

That caught her by surprise. She seemed to give it some thought. "Not that I remember. I ate some things she didn't, but not the other way around."

"Even drinks? Soda, coffee, lemonade, juice—"

"Clara only drank water. Nothing but. Morning, noon, and night." Ruth Vanetti allowed herself a weak smile. "She said it was the secret to a long life."

"And you're sure someone else couldn't have given her something?"

"Everything went through me, Inspector Holliman. I think I wish now that it hadn't."

"And you're positive no one else came to the house that day?"

"No one but Freddie. He comes every day, but only to the front door. He gives everything to me."

Holliman narrowed his eyes. "Freddie?"

"Freddie Barton. He works now and then at the filling station around the corner. Before I started here full time, Clara used to pay him to run errands for her. Afterward, we just kept it up. He didn't have much else to do, and it was kind of handy."

Holliman took down the name. "What kind of errands?"

"All kinds. Bank, post office, general store, anything she needed. Even when she didn't, he brought the mail and the newspaper."

"And he gave it to you?"

"That's right."

"And you gave it to Mrs. Endicott?"

"Inspector, I told you—she saw no one but me. She wanted it that way."

"But he did come that day?"

"Freddie? He comes every day." Ruth Vanetti seemed to be tiring of this, and it showed on her face. "You want some more tea?"

"No, thanks." He paused for a beat. "Why didn't she want to see anybody?"

She heaved a sigh. "That's quite a story. She was a very wealthy woman, you see, before the medicine started taking all her money—"

"Wait a minute," he said. "The medicine?"

"Her heart medicine. Expensive stuff, that was."

"She was taking heart medication? How often?"

"Three times a day."

"Including late at night?"

She shook her head. "Only before meals. And we had supper at seven that night, like always."

"Could she have smuggled some to her room with her? Taken it without telling you, maybe, before turning in?"

Another sigh. "I guess it's possible, Inspector, but it would have been totally out of character for her to do that. I gave her all her medicine. I never found any in her room in all these years."

He thought that over. "What kind of medicine? Liquid, from a bottle?"

"No, they were pills."

"Capsules?"

"Some of them. Others were tablets."

"But if some were capsules..." Holliman pondered that for a moment, remembering the commercials he'd seen for "time-released" headache relief. That could be a possibility. "Where were the prescriptions filled? Here in this area?"

"That's right. Robinson's Drugs. Surely you don't think—"

"We'll check it out. Right now I'd like to go back to something else. You said Mrs. Endicott was wealthy before she got sick..."

"Right. But it's the *way* she got wealthy that caused the problems. You see, there used to be a cotton gin out on Highway Twelve, and a hosiery mill over in Redford, and a bank and a lamp factory downtown. They were all Clara's. Actually they were her husband's, but he left them to her when he died." A sad look crossed her face. "Those are gone now. Torn down, or sold and revamped. She got rid of them all. Before she was through she put half of this side of town out of work."

"So you're saying a lot of people around here never forgave her?"

"I'm saying a lot of people around here hated her guts."

"What about the druggist, Robinson? Was he an admirer?"

She chuckled without humor. "Even the ones who didn't hate her weren't admirers, Inspector. But to answer your question, Hiram Robinson had no special grudge against her. Not that I know of, anyway."

Holliman glanced at his notepad. "And… Freddie Barton?"

"That's a different story. Freddie's sister had a stroke and died the day she was laid off from the hosiery mill."

"Is that so. And he had had recent contact with the deceased."

"Well, indirectly. Through me."

Jim Holliman stayed quiet a moment. "The thing that really bothers me is the poison. After all, it wasn't strychnine, or arsenic, or anything common. It was rare and exotic, practically inaccessible." He chewed on his lower lip, then asked: "Could Freddie Barton have had any history or connections outside the country? Relatives in foreign service, vacations abroad, that kind of thing?"

"People around here don't take vacations abroad, Inspector. Freddie went somewhere way off with a church group a while back, but I don't know where."

"A church group? Like missionary work, you mean?"

"I think so."

"Where? Africa, maybe? Asia?"

"I really don't know, Inspector. You'd have to ask him."

"I will." Holliman mulled on that awhile, then rubbed a hand over his eyes. "Okay," he said. "Can you think of *anyone* else who might have come here to the house that day? Salesmen, a minister, a repairman…"

She looked pained. "No. Certainly none of those. Clara hated salesmen with a vengeance, all preachers were off-limits, and there hasn't been a repairman here since the day the pipes froze under the house last winter."

Holliman gave her a stare. "You thought I had come to fix the lawnmower," he reminded her.

"I thought you had come to *buy* the lawnmower. It's out back, in the shed, never has run right. A gas mower, of all things, as if a plain pushmower isn't good enough. Besides, you would have been the first to answer the ad Clara had me put up on the church bulletin board."

Holliman scratched his cheek with the eraser end of the pencil. "Hmm. So you're sure Clara Endicott never had a moment's contact with anyone the day of the… the day of her death."

The housekeeper shook her head. "Not face to face. She wrote to her children and grandchildren all the time, and a few old acquaintances from her hometown back East—"

"I thought she couldn't see well enough to read."

The irritated look returned. "I said she couldn't read, I didn't say she couldn't write. It was mostly chicken-scratching, but it did the job, or so she thought. Anyhow, it didn't matter much—nobody ever wrote back to her." Mrs. Vanetti drew a long breath and exhaled. "The truth is, she was a lonely, pitiful old woman, right up to the very end. She had no real family and no real friends." As she spoke these last words, Holliman could once more see tears in her eyes.

This was one complex woman, he told himself. Over the past half hour he had seen her demonstrate every emotion from fear to anger to surprise to sadness, with very little transition time from one to the other. But the strangest thing was that all these emotions seemed to be genuine. Holliman sighed. He was no psychologist, but in the course of his career he had become good at recognizing a killer when he saw one. This lady was no more guilty of murder than his Sunday School teacher.

Finally he closed his notebook and put it away. "Well, thank you for your time, Mrs. Vanetti. I'll be in touch."

They stood.

"Aren't you going to tell me not to leave town?"

He smiled. "Don't leave town."

She swallowed, looked around at the kitchen, then turned to face him again. "It's the house, isn't it? That's the reason."

"I beg your pardon?"

"The fact that she left it to me. It was a total surprise, you know. It never entered my head she would do something like that. I never even knew she had a will." A tear spilled onto her cheek, and she brushed it away with the back of her hand. "Then again, I guess we spent a lot of time here together, she and I."

A response really wasn't required, and he didn't make one. He just stood there and watched her, waiting.

Finally she straightened up a bit and stared him in the eye. She looked as thoroughly miserable as anyone he had ever seen.

"I told you I listen to the radio a lot, Inspector," she said. "*Dragnet, Nightbeat, Barrie Craig, Johnny Dollar*—from the police point of view, I'm the ideal suspect. Opportunity and motive. Am I right?"

He started to say something, changed his mind, then said it anyway.

"I think you'll come through this fine, Mrs. Vanetti. I shouldn't be telling you that, but I think you will. If I'm any judge at all, that is."

She gave him a sad smile. "Maybe so," she said.

They walked together down the gloomy hallway. As he was about to leave, he turned to face her. "One more thing. You told me you read a book to her that night, until around ten o'clock."

"That's right."

"And then you went to your room."

"Right."

"And you came back at midnight to find her dead. Two hours later."

"We've been over all this, Inspector—"

"Hear me out. Is what I've said correct?"

"Yes."

"And you also told me she went to sleep around eleven o'clock every night."

"That's right."

Holliman stayed quiet a moment, deep in thought. "When you took me to see her bedroom," he said, "there was no radio there. No radio, no record player, no books, no magazines."

"Right again."

"Well, that's what's bothering me."

She just looked at him, puzzled.

"What did she do in the meantime?" he asked, turning his palms up. "What did she do for that hour every night, between ten and eleven?"

"Oh." Ruth Vanetti smiled a little, as if at a fond memory. "She wrote her letters."

"Her letters?"

"They were always there on her nightstand every morning, sealed up and addressed and ready for me to carry down and give to Freddie to take to the P.O." A look of sad reality passed across her face. "Like I said to Freddie a while back, those were just about the only two things left that she could do all by herself."

Holliman frowned. "Two things… ?"

"Writing letters," she said, "and licking stamps."

We kick away the somber mood with our next story, a wicked take on what has become known as the Cabot Cove Syndrome. How is it that dead bodies keep popping up in cozy towns?

Nothing But the Sleuth
by Diane Arrelle

Gretchen glared at the headline with disbelief. *How'd that no-talent cow do it again*, she wondered for probably the fiftieth time.

"Will ya look at that!" she shrieked.

Bill looked up from a typewriter and glanced at the newspaper Gretchen was holding in a white knuckled grasp, wrinkling the text into illegible creases.

"I presume you are not ranting about the sports scores or last night's Borough meeting?" He asked with a sigh.

"I'm talking about April Later. She supposedly solved another murder for the police. I swear that woman has no writing ability and that our police force must be a bunch of morons who could be replaced by a bag of potato chips and still be as effective if not a tad more compassionate to a person going just a few miles over the speed limit while rushing to get to work on time."

Bill shot Gretchen a cruel smile and said, "Gosh, Dear, could that be sour grapes I'm hearing, and perhaps one of the worst sentences ever uttered by a writer?"

Gretchen glared at her husband. "Leave my writing out of this. I'm a damned good reporter and I know I'm a better author than April Later. I just need a good break."

"Like your neck," Bill muttered.

"I heard that! But I'm serious, I write damn good mysteries and I could solve crimes just like her, if you'd only give me a chance to do some investigative journalism."

Bill swiveled in his office chair, his white shirt sleeves rolled up above his elbows, his thin tie loose around his open collar and faced his wife. "Gretchen, I know we are married, but I am still the editor here and I'll have to say it again, you are a good correspondent, one of the best I have at covering town events, but you are not logical enough, nor talented enough to be an investigative reporter. April Later may be lucky with her mysteries, but as our village's only amateur sleuth she is a living, breathing wonder. Face it, she's damned good and we, in this burg, appreciate it."

Gretchen glared at Bill a moment and then turned and walked over to a battered filing cabinet. Yanking open a drawer, she pulled out a fat file and waved it at him. "Look at this. Later, April. Her file is so full it frightens me. Don't you think that it is strange that there are so many murders in such a small town. Don't you think it's strange that everywhere this woman visits somebody dies?"

Bill shook his head and went back to his typing, hammering at the keys. "Why don't you go home, dear, and work on your newest attempt at a mystery."

"That's just what I'm going to do," Gretchen muttered storming from the office. "I'm going to solve myself a little mystery. Yeah, I'm going to find out why April Later is always around to solve the crime."

Getting into her Edsel, Gretchen snapped on the radio hoping to hear something by Pat Boone or Frank Sinatra, something to calm her nerves, but all she got was that Elvis trash. She began to drive home when she passed a phone booth. She pulled over and, leaving the car running, got out without straightening her skirt. Once in the phone booth, which smelled awful, she put in a dime and got the operator to call April Later.

"April? Gretchen Harris here. Say, are you busy? I was wondering if you'd meet me for lunch. I'd love to do a feature on you."

Fifteen minutes later Gretchen was seated at a local restaurant. She sipped a whiskey sour, while waiting for April to arrive. "I need a way to trip her up," she mumbled and signaled for another drink. She had just finished that drink when April entered the dark restaurant twenty minutes late. She stood silhouetted in the doorway for a moment and then moved into the room and joined Gretchen. April fluffed her perfectly coifed silver hair, lightly touched her pearl necklace and smiled her million dollar greeting letting her deep wrinkles turn up into smile lines.

"Gretchen, Dear heart. So good of you to call. How nice you want to do a feature on me, your paper has always been so kind. And I have another novel coming out soon, so the publicity will be great."

Gretchen signaled for for the waiter to take April's order and refill hers then stared into April's deep-set blue eyes and got to the point. "April, I want to do an article on your superb deductive skills. There are so very, very many of us who want to know how you do it, solve violent crime after violent crime. Why, you've probably solve more real murders than fictional ones."

April smiled, and slowly sipped her Singapore Sling. "I guess I just have to say it is my writer's natural curiosity. Must have been a cat in a past life."

She laughed and Gretchen gulped down her drink and waved for another. *More like a dog,* she thought with a smirk. *A great big silver bitch, one that kills just for the fun of it, maybe even a wild dingo.*

"I just have a knack for finding clues and once I uncover one clue, I'm hooked until I can solve the case. I know I'm just an old busybody, but if I can help this community, if I can pay back my fans for their support by putting criminals where they belong, then I feel like my life has been worthwhile. After all, I feel that we are all put on this good, dear, earth for a reason and I know my reason has to be more important than writing silly, old books. I mean, Gretchen dear, you are a fine newspaper writer, don't you feel like you should have a bigger purpose?"

"Uh… sure," Gretchen said trying to concentrate on making the room stop spinning. She took another sip and tried to sit up straighter. "I want to right society's wrongs too, and I plan to start by proving that someone in this area is a ruthless killer!"

There, she nodded to herself, *I've put all the cards on the table, exposed my hand, let the cat out of the bag. Now the ball's in her court. Oh my God, I'm thinking in stale cliches, I need another drink.* Gretchen waved a limp hand to the waiter for another round.

April was smiling, her bright blue eyes sent the message that she seemed to be enjoying herself immensely. "A murderer? A mystery that needs to be solved and I've missed it. Well, good luck, dear. Now, if you will just excuse me for a moment I must go powder my nose."

Gretchen thought about getting up, but decided to wait for the restaurant to come to a complete stop.

April was back in no time at all, as far as Gretchen was concerned, but perhaps she'd just grabbed a little nap while the older woman was gone.

"So, Gretchen, how is your writing going? Still trying to sell a mystery?"

Gretchen groaned as she tried to hold onto the edge of the table before it threw her to the ground.

"I take that as no luck yet. Tell you what, Dear, why don't you send me one of your manuscripts and I'll ask my publisher to critique it for you."

Struggling to find the words, to force her tongue to respond, Gretchen spat out a slurred tirade. "Critique my ass, send it to him and he'd buy it. You're just scared that I'm onto you. So you want to buy my cooperation. Well, just you wait and see, I'll get the goods on you lady. I'll prove that you aren't solving murders, you're doing 'em. I just can't figure out how you've bamboozled everyone else in this dump of a—"

"*GRETCHEN!*"

She stopped yelling and turned to see Bill behind her, his baggy sports jacket misbuttoned like he'd rushed there.

"Gretchen, I could just kill you for this." He bent down and helped her rise to wobbly feet. He set her felt hat straight on her head and said, "April, thanks for calling me. I'm truly sorry for my wife. She didn't mean it, it's the jealously speaking."

April smiled at them. "No harm done, a little controversy never hurts book sales you know and I know she has a good heart. It was the alcohol mixed with the green-eyed monster speaking, not dear, sweet, Gretchen. I'm sure that someday she'll make it as a writer."

"If she lives that long," Bill said and half-walked half-carried Gretchen to his car.

That evening when Gretchen woke, the house was dark.

"Bill?" she called. "Bill, are you home?"

She got up on unsteady legs and staggered to the bathroom and threw up. After a shower, two cups of black coffee and a handful of aspirin, Gretchen called Bill at the office. No answer. "Must be out on business," she said knowing that he probably wasn't. This was one avenue she didn't want to investigate at all.

Investigate! That's right, she remembered. She wasn't finished yet, in fact now that she had blown her real intentions toward April, she really had to act fast. Throwing on her calf length wool coat, she walked the half mile to April's ivy-covered, gingerbread cottage. "Too damned cute for words," Gretchen said eyeing the dark domicile. "I bet she's got plenty of ugly evidence hidden inside."

She tried the knob and was surprised to find the door unlocked. "Some mystery writer. Trusts people just because small towns are supposed to be so safe." She went inside and took a flashlight from her pocketbook. She searched the entire house then noticed the basement door. She went down and turned on the light. The entire back wall was lined with filing cabinets. She opened the first five and found them filled with manuscripts, contracts and news clippings. But the last two were it. "Aha the evidence is down there!" she whispered with triumph. "I just need to swipe all of this and I'll have the news story of my life." She rifled through the folders, one for every person in town. Each was full of gossip and facts, each held the life story of a real person. Gretchen was so involved that she didn't hear the sound behind until it was too late.

She felt the cold steel against the back of her head.

"Yes, Gretchen Dear, it is a gun and if I shot you dead right now, it would be an open and shut case of breaking and entering and the unfortunate aftermath of assumed self defense against a robber. But I'd like to avoid that."

"So would I, April," Gretchen said with a shaky voice.

"Now Dear heart why don't you take out your folder and tell me if my facts are correct."

Gretchen read through tears of fear and tears of humiliated anger. *Yes, all the facts were there.* Single until she was 40 when she met and married Bill five years ago. A borderline alcoholic, a so-so reporter, a failed mystery writer, a bitter and burnt out human.

"Now dear, take out Bill's."

Gretchen read on with a sinking feeling as all her fears were realized. She'd trapped Bill with a false pregnancy and he'd stopped being faithful about three years ago. An unhappy man in an unhappy marriage.

"See, dear, you really are pathetic, not only ruining your own existence but poor Bill's as well. Such a shame, such a waste of a nice man."

Gretchen turned slowly and looked at April, "You going to kill me?

April shook her head no.

"Why all the files?" Gretchen asked. "You really are the killer aren't you? I just don't understand how you did it and got all those innocent people to confess?"

April laughed, her voice sounding like happy jingle bells. "Let's go upstairs and sit down, I'm too old to be standing around in damp basements."

She waved the gun, motioning for Gretchen to go first and followed a safe distance behind.

Once in the living room, Gretchen was shocked to see Bill slumped on the couch apparently asleep. "Is… is he… dead? Did you poison him? Are you planning to pin this on me? It won't work you know. I won't confess."

April motioned for her to sit in the armchair across from her husband. She giggled, sounding like a schoolgirl. "Dear me, he's quite all right, just in a deep hypnotic state. I'm a hypnotist you know. Worked vaudeville as a young woman. Quite successful actually. Did that for a living before I started writing. Wrote for the magazines for quite a while. Anyway dear, Bill is all right for now and I promise you that I won't hurt either one of you."

Gretchen stared at her nemesis and shuddered. *What was going on? What was this woman planning?* Gretchen knew she'd been right all along, that April Later was a cold blooded killer, so why was she lying to her?

"What now?" Gretchen asked. "Why have you done this to my husband?"

"To set up the scenario. Dear girl, you were almost on the money. I've caused every crime since I've moved here and decided to become a mystery writer. You see, I'm not very imaginative, a fatal flaw for a novelist. I needed the crimes to be carried out before I could write about them. I needed to see it, to write it. I was good enough to set the scene to provide the motivation. I was just not good enough at the description. So I had others do the crimes for me."

"But how?" Gretchen asked, interested in spite of her fear.

"You know that old saying that you can't hypnotize someone to do something that they are morally incapable of doing?"

Gretchen nodded, looking at Bill with a chill of fear.

"Well, I got around that by studying people and finding out what they would do. That is how I got them to commit the crimes. I hypnotized them to do what they secretly wanted to do. And then I pretended to solve the murders. It was easy and the police here really aren't very sophisticated. The murders helped me with my writing the books, and this amateur sleuth business helped sell them."

Gretchen looked at Bill slumped over and shuddered at all the grief she'd caused him. "And now?"

"Well, Gretchen, because you were so clever, I'm now afraid that I'll have to cause another crime. If you started asking too many questions others might follow suit. Right now, I'm just a beloved and sacred celebrity here. No one suspects me of any of the coincidences because fame makes the masses blind. Nobody wants a hero to be mortal."

Gretchen sat in silence, finally wordless.

"So here's the plot. I've hypnotized your husband and he's now going to take you home. Everyone heard him threaten you this afternoon and nobody will really blame him, actually they'll feel sorry for him. Poor, poor Bill, turning to other women for comfort and love. Poor Bill, humiliated at work as well, as all over town by that alcoholic shrew. I won't even have to solve this one. Even the police will be able to see Bill did it and with good cause.

Gretchen found her voice. "Bill won't do it."

April laughed. "This time you are dead wrong. Now I really must leave." April went out the back door and called into the room, "Bill, you will awaken now and respond when you hear the command. Gretchen you'll really like this. Bill, the word is *Sleuth*."

Gretchen shivered with horror as Bill snapped awake and stared at her with the most malevolence she had ever seen.

She started to call to April to stop him.

But he was already dragging her out the door and toward home, using a tight two handed grip to the throat.

A woman has lunch with the man she jilted five years before.
She was on a mission, a very personal one.

A Dish Best Served
by M.M. Elmendorf

Villains, as well as heroes, can live with manicured lawns in cheery looking houses right next door. They can have polite smiles to greet you with in the morning, inquiring after your health and chit-chatting about the weather. Sometimes they can walk with a limp from a childhood accident, and sometimes they can glide on an effervescent wave. Some might dress shabbily, hiding their nature behind a cocoon of unassuming garb, while others might dress in the latest fashions, their natures equally invisible behind the blinding glamour.

The greatest villains, in conjunction with heroes, are such because they take us by surprise; they challenge our assumptions that we can tell the difference between good and evil. They remind us that the gilding of morality can be put on and taken off by absolutely anyone, and at any time. After all, it is not only snakes who need shed their skins.

Elizabeth Miller's wrist-length, white gloves tightly gripped the steering wheel of her 1951 teal two-door sedan. The Kasier Henry J had been a "please come home" gift sent to her by her mother. At first she'd balked at the idea of keeping such a thing when she had no intention of returning, but she'd later thought better of it; having this sort of independence would suit her intentions just fine. The layers of tulle that made up her petticoats rustled as she switched her foot from brake to accelerator, following the speed of traffic in downtown Memphis. The scent of liquid sediment hung heavy in the mid-summer heat, an ever-present reminder that The Big Muddy slithered alongside the city's western border.

The heat: oppressive. It was only when the car moved that it became slightly more bearable. Even then, Lizzie felt sweat staining the back of her teal and white polka dotted shirtwaist dress. She'd earlier unbuttoned the top buttons of the bodice to allow more air to move around her restricting brassiere. Sitting on the plush benchseat beside her lay her matching teal purse, the waist belt she'd have to reattach before leaving the car, her wide-brimmed white hat, and her white ballet slip-ons. It was obvious that she'd given up on propriety in the name of surviving Tennessean humidity and it was no wonder that perfectly coiffed women dropped in exhaustion like old fruit flies.

If Mother could see Lizzie now, she'd probably draw her already thin lips into such a line as to give no indication that she'd ever had lips. Her button-sized eyes would narrow and pinch shut as she'd ready herself to use both silence and carefully measured words as weapons against Elizabeth.

"You must rise above your past, Elizabeth Marie." Mother always used Lizzie's first and middle name whenever she did something that could be deemed "unseemly" by the surrounding families. If Lizzie disappointed Mother, which was a near daily occurrence, she'd be reminded of her differences from the other "more cultured and refined" children. *"You aren't like the others, Elizabeth Marie. You have innate weaknesses that they will never have. You must fight harder than they ever will to overcome your inferiorities."*

Of course, Mother's chastisement was passive aggressive and in "good taste." Father's, on the other hand, was more to the point and, in retrospect, Lizzie much preferred the blatant disgust of

Father to the feigned care of Mother. *"For the price we paid for you, I could've gotten a yacht and a nice-looking broad to go with it."*

Lizzie pulled into a metered parking spot along the main thoroughfare. She was a block away from the joint and, glancing at her faux diamond Crestwood watch, she had twenty minutes to spare before they were set to meet. She began the process of setting herself to societal rights: putting her shoes and belt back on, securing her hat, checking that her lipstick was not smudged, and fluffing the bottom of her curly bob. Satisfied that she looked the part of demure woman of decent standing, Lizzie stepped out of her car and paused to allow the breeze to detach her dress from her clammy skin. Then she joined the ranks of passersby on the baking sidewalk. Lizzie placed the keys in her purse and gave a momentary press to the small waist pocket of her dress. It was still there. She smiled to herself and continued her way.

A brightly colored window display had Lizzie pausing. Somewhere nearby, crooning through the open doors of a shop, came the distinctive melody of Nat King Cole's "Pretend." As she continued to study the window display Lizzie mouthed along with the lyrics, *"Pretend you're happy when you're blue, it isn't very hard to do, and you'll find happiness without an end whenever you pretend."* Looking further down the street she spied a bookstore and, noting their additional signage of "air conditioned," Lizzie wove her way through the throng until she leaned into the door and crossed into the cool haven. Just inside was a rack of older magazines, advertised for cheap, and after double-checking her watch, Lizzie picked up the closest one.

It was a 1950 issue of *Woman's Home Companion*. She'd never much liked the magazine for its reminder of Mother and the expectations she'd long since shed, but Lizzie was always amused by the advertisements. The first one she came across was a Reed and Barton Sterling Silverware ad. Pictured was a romantically drawn bride and groom with the phrase, "It's your life from now on..." written across the top in bold letters. Lizzie's smile grew as she re-read the phrase. How true that was. A second ad she flipped to was a Sherwin-Williams Weatherated paint ad. Leaping off the page in bright letters was written, *"KNOW THE TRUTH"*, followed by a series of explanations and claims by the company. Lizzie, however, didn't move beyond the initial phrase and the shiver of nerves it brought upon her.

A rush of heat from the opening door had Lizzie looking again at her watch. She replaced the magazine and allowed herself to be belched back onto Madison Avenue. The same store that had earlier been playing Nat King Cole now played Frankie Laine's "Jezebel" and her ears recognized it just as he sang, *"Who's seen Jezebel? She was born to be the women we could blame…"* Lizzie crossed the street towards the entrance of *Britling's* before she could hear anymore.

She'd never eaten at this cafeteria-style restaurant before, but she'd eaten at plenty of similar establishments. Ever since she'd begun her quest to make impassable the canyon between herself and her fabricated past in New York, she'd preferred places like this. The rows of free-standing square tables set up in a grid, typically with walls lined with plush-seated booths, allowed for large numbers of people and a great commotion of conversation, and yet there was always a comfortable sense of anonymity. The entrance walls were always lined with compartments filled with daily specials. Moving like ants behind scenes, workers replenished these displays as quickly as they were depleted. Then, further on down the line, were more delicacies to fill your tray with if none of the earlier displays whetted your appetite. Everything was always so colorful and easy.

This chain restaurant was one of the originals of its kind and the outside boasted gleaming black glass and stainless steel. When Lizzie moved inside with a small crowd of fellow patrons, she noted the black and white octagon-shaped tile floor along with the notable teal theme of the booths. She smirked at the realization that she'd managed to match her outfit to both her car as well as this restaurant.

Quickly falling into line, Lizzie grabbed a compartmentalized tray and proceeded to fill it with *Britling* Chicken Salad, *Britling* Corn Beef and Cabbage, and risked her wasp-waist by adding a slice of *Britling* Red Cherry Pie. She didn't feel much hunger, due partially to heat and the other to nerves, but she had to at least fulfill the expectation of having a meal at a mealtime meeting. She read the motto of the store as it hung on the wall behind the cashier: *Good food is good Health.* Only a fool would ever classify traditional southern-style food as healthy.

She paused to see if he'd already arrived. Lizzie couldn't spot his telling red-hair among the masses of profiles and bobbing heads in the cafeteria. Choosing the furthermost booth from the door, she sat with her back facing the entrance. She wanted to give him a bit of a challenge to find her. It wouldn't do to let on that she'd looked forward to seeing him. It had been in another lifetime, the one she was purposing shedding, that they'd been an item. Though, for as distant as that life seemed to be, Lizzie could still remember his scent on her skin if she kept her eyes closed long enough on a lonely night.

The strange thing about specters, they often appear when pictured, and he wasn't any different. Almost as soon as her mind drifted down the memory lane marked "forbidden," he appeared at her side. She jerked at the sight of him despite her best efforts to remain cool. If he noticed her surprise he kept it to himself and dropped into the booth opposite her, not bothering to wait for an invitation. They both knew he'd been invited, and this meeting arranged. After placing his tray on the table, he extricated a patterned sport coat and a simple Tremont and placed both on the bench beside him. His white button-down was miraculously not sweat-stained and his hair was still perfectly combed. He looked as cool as if he'd never set foot on the hot streets of the city. The only indication that he felt the Memphis heat at all was that he'd loosened his narrow, regimental stripe tie and had unbuttoned the top two buttons of his shirt.

Lizzie drew her attention back as he began to study her. She resisted the urge to fluff her hair or double check her makeup. She'd already put her hat on the bench, along with her purse. Her gloves, she'd kept them on. She couldn't risk touching him.

A playful smirk spread his lips wide when he began quoting one of her least favorite movies, "Of all the gin joints in all the towns in all the world—"

"Really Ronny?" She interrupted him before he could carry on. "That's your opening line?"

He shrugged his shoulders and for a moment Lizzie remembered what it felt like to grip them, flesh against flesh, feeling the sinewy muscles move beneath her touch. His voice had her snapping off the "forbidden" lane almost as quickly as she'd tripped onto it.

"Would you rather, 'I haven't seen you in years and I don't know why you asked to meet me out of the blue but here I am because you've never left my mind even after you jilted me.'"

Lizzie recoiled, "Not holding your punches today are you?"

"I must be the biggest sucker in the history of suckers," Ronny spoke as if he'd not heard her, "for here I sit with the same dame who blew me off almost as soon as I came back from the war and disappeared into who knows where without so much as a line, zip, nada." Though the words he spoke carried heavy weight into her gut, Ronny was gentleman enough to not carry his voice above what was the norm for such a place. "You've got a lot of nerve, Lizzie. It's been five years."

"I know." She dropped her eyes away from the strength of his green gaze, finding solace in the congealed innards of her cherry pie as it bled out onto the plate, victim of gravity.

"Where have you been?"

It was her turn to shrug, "A few places." She finally looked up to find his hand coming back from the middle of the table to clutch at his tray. She chose to ignore his almost touch and hid behind a polite smile. "Most recently, Little Rock. I'm on my way to the eastern side of the state now. Got some business to attend to."

"Business?" Ronny raised his eyebrows. "What sort of business have YOU got out there?" Though he'd been working in the south in a district attorney's office for a few years now, Lizzie could still hear the northeast in his accent. It most likely mirrored her own.

Seeing this as the opening she needed, Lizzie reached into her pocket and withdrew the carefully folded document. She slid it towards him and withdrew her hand before there was risk of his fingers brushing hers. He snorted at her movements but took the paper nonetheless and studied it. His expression of curiosity grew into one of confusion and his questioning eyes met hers across the table.

"Where did you get this?"

Lizzie shifted on the seat, tulle petticoats itching at her skin, "Little Rock. Though that's just a copy. The original is somewhere here in Memphis. Doubtful it'll ever be found. I was assured that most such documents have already been disposed of or filed in such a way that they'll never be found."

Ronny studied the document again and read aloud, "Frances Clara May Robinson." Lizzie closed her eyes at the name. She'd said it many times over the miles from Little Rock. Every time she said it aloud, she'd wait a moment, to see if there was some part of her soul that would awaken and sing out, "*Yes!*" But it'd never happened. Instead she was left with a strange sounding name on a piece of paper that was testimony of what could have been while she legally bore a concocted name of what had actually happened.

"Are you going to explain what's going on here, Lizzie?"

She jerked alert and back into the present. At some point he'd set aside the re-folded paper and had reached across the table to finally lay a hand atop hers. At the look of pained alarm on her features, Ronny frowned and retreated.

"You remember what I told you about my life with Mother and Father?"

Ronny nodded and spoke dismissively, "None of us had a particularly spectacular childhood despite the luxuries our parents bestowed upon us."

"Father always said he could have bought a yacht for the price he paid for me."

"Births in upstate private hospitals can be expensive, Lizzie, that's nothing new. And private tutors and ivy league education are also pricy. You know even my father threw similar remarks at me over the years."

Lizzie shook her head and switched tactics, "Do you remember what was going on around the time I disappeared?"

Ronny grew quiet, his eyes trained on the ceiling, as he worked to recall time and place. After a spell he spoke again, "It was around the late summer of 1950. I was working with Taylor on a number of investigations but, if I recall correctly, Governor Browning pushed Taylor to home in on the case against the Tennessee Children's Home Society." Ronny adjusted in his seat and leaned his elbows on the table, his voice lowering to a conspiratorial tone. "At the end it was a shame too because the leader of that black-market ring if child trafficking died only a few days before we published our findings and could officially charge her. A Miss Georgie Tann. Cancer."

Lizzie nodded, her heartbeat quickening, "Do you remember anything else?"

Ronny stared at her for a few quiet moments. Lizzie felt his gaze as keenly as if he were touching her skin. She knew he could see her flush and she hoped he'd connect it to the mid-summer heat and not the memories that leapt into her imagination unwelcomed. Ronny took to twirling his fork on the table as he leaned back again. He seemed as uninterested in his meal and she'd been hers.

"There were many particulars about that case that left me feeling sick to my stomach and I remember I took a lot of showers. I know not everyone involved got their comeuppance either, but that was at the end of a long era of corruption that Governor Browning and Taylor's offices were trying to dismantle. We're still working on it in fact." Ronny glanced down at the paper again then back at Lizzie. "Are you going to tell me what that has to do with Frances Clara May Robinson, and you?"

Lizzie took a deep, steadying breath. This was to be the final blow to her old life. Even Ronny would want nothing to do with her after this. No amount of lingering affection on his part could change who she was and what she'd done. The skin must be shed.

"Its 1924, in a rural town of southeastern Tennessee. A young unwed woman gives birth to a little girl, whom she names after her own mother, Frances Clara May Robinson." Lizzie nodded towards the paper. "The particulars of time, place, and that sort can be found on the birth certificate." She paused, wondering if Ronny had guessed it already.

"Go on." He seemed unwilling or unable to jump to the natural conclusion of this story.

Lizzie sighed and shook her head, "This young woman, Mrs. Robinson, would later be described as unfit and incapable of proper parenting. Her only crime was that she took a chance and handed Frances Clara May over to a woman who came to her rural house, offering aid for her sickly child. Frances Clara May was never returned to her birth home. Instead, Mrs. Robinson was served a notice by the state stating that because of her dire circumstances and the status of the child, Frances Clara May would be placed in a more suitable environment. This child was then taken to the Tennessee Children's Home Society. She was renamed and adopted out to a young, childless yet affluent couple in upstate New York. Everything was hush-hush, the proprietor of the Society was a professional after all, and for a price of approximately seven-hundred and fifty dollars, Elizabeth Marie Miller made her debut in the world."

"You can't possibly think that you're one of the Society children!" Ronny reared back. "You have no proof."

"I have a drunken confession from Father, made a few nights after your findings were published, and stern silence from Mother when subsequently questioned. I have a clandestine and fortune-favored discussion with a distraught Miss Hollinsworth, Miss Tann's adopted daughter, also soon after the publication of your findings and Miss Tann's funeral. And I have my own investigation out in Little Rock, which led me to that birth certificate as well as to the narrative of my origins. It is little wonder that

Mother always told me to rise above 'my past' and other such strategically worded cuts."

Ronny leaned forward again, "What investigation in Little Rock? Is that where you've been all this time?"

"You said earlier that not everyone got their comeuppance, referring to those outliers who were connected to the case." Ronny nodded and Lizzie was surprised that for all his brilliance he hadn't yet connected the dots. "Do you remember the 'Little Irish Judge'?"

"Judge Camille McGee Kelley, yes. There were many rumors that she got a cut of the profits for her support of the trafficking from the court system, but we never found any paperwork or records to prove it. Soon after our findings were published, she retired from the bench."

"Do you know where she went?" Lizzie pressed.

"No. That case has been closed and so many others have come since then that I haven't much thought of it. I would really rather never think about it again, in fact." Lizzie sighed. It seemed he was determined to not see. She would have to spell it out for him.

"Mrs. Kelley did retire from the bench and she moved in with her son, Heiskell Kelley, an attorney for the Department of Agriculture in Little Rock, Arkansas." Ronny maintained a blank but expectant gaze. "After piecing together Father's confession, along with Miss Hollinsworth's, I decided to take care of things myself."

"'Take care of things'?" Ronny began to frown.

Lizzie nodded matter-of-factly, "Your investigation stated that well over five thousand children were taken by the Society during its years of operation, and the number of deaths could not be counted for certain but at least five hundred had been noted. This is not a mere case to dismiss and be done with after publishing the findings, Ronny. Justice must be served, for the living and the dead." Her voice had taken on a quality she'd never quite heard before and she spoke in such a cool tone that it surprised ever herself. She proceeded to explain the details to

Ronny in as clear a manner as possible, "Miss Tann died before she could face the full force of the law, so her part in this narrative was finished and nothing more could be done. Her adopted daughter, Miss Hollinsworth, I found, was as much a victim as any of the stolen children, allowing her to live with her guilt was punishment enough."

Ronny shook his head. "Do I want to know anything else that you're about to say?"

"You wanted to know where I've been and what I've been up to."

Ronny rubbed both hands over his face, "You're right. Go on."

"Miss Tann's personal attorney, Abe Waldauer, testified in your investigation to always acting in accordance to the law, following through with the legal papers issued by the court. So, though implicitly connected, it can be argued that he acted in true ignorance and, he is still so prominently connected to the local community, to get close to him would require much more effort and the likelihood of walking away from such an endeavor would be slim."

"What do you mean by 'walking away from such an endeavor'? Lizzie, you're not making any sense."

She smiled and this time she initiated the physical contact, reaching across the table and patting the back of his hand. "I am making perfect sense, Ronny, you just don't want to piece it all together." Ronny stared at her hand atop his own but before he could move to take hold of it Lizzie pulled away. She continued her sordid confession. "Mrs. Kelley never wore judicial robes in court. She liked to wear colorful dresses, jewels, and always had a flower pinned to her shoulder. She said robes scared the children and they responded better to a well-dressed lady on the bench. Did you know that?"

Ronny nodded.

"She wrote three books and was intricately involved with the application of confidentiality laws adopted by the General Assembly. She worked thirty years in Shelby County's Family court and spoke at length of how she made sure to punish the crime and not the child."

"Where is this all leading, Lizzie?" Ronny's voice had taken on a pleading note and Lizzie again felt her gut clench at the reality of the severing she was causing with her brutal honesty.

"Mrs. Kelley used her place in court to alter, destroy, or misfile birth records to the extent that it is now impossible to determine the true parentage of thousands of children. She received payment for services rendered from Miss Tann and was fully aware of the extent of Miss Tann's network at all times of the operation. Before you ask, 'how do you know this, Lizzie,' Mrs. Kelley told me herself. From her deathbed."

Ronny grew very still. "She's dead? But you just said she moved in with her son-"

"That was five years ago. She died January of this year. The official story is stroke."

"Official story." Ronny parroted back, his eyes wide and his mouth agape. "What is the unofficial story then?"

Lizzie smiled; it seemed Ronny was finally starting to follow along. "You remember I used to sneak into the kitchen because I always wanted to learn how to make those perfect desserts cook made. Mother said I would get fat from so many but I couldn't help myself, they were too delicious! You remember that don't you?" Ronny mutely nodded. "And I even flirted with attending culinary school, and not just to annoy Mother either. I genuinely wanted to become a culinary artist. She always said that though such a vocation suited my past, I had since grown beyond and I was much better suited for a well-matched marriage." Lizzie smiled. "I've been perfecting my culinary skills over the past five years. Worked in quite a few well-to-do family kitchens even, gathering up enough references to recommend me to just about anyone anywhere. I can bake a mean German chocolate cake now."

She paused but Ronny didn't seem to want to say anything now. "Do you know what a 'gift of the Borgias' is?"

Ronny shook his head.

"Apparently one of the quickest ways to acquire property during their time was to dispose of the owner of said property and by canon law this property would then revert to the church. Before you ask how I know this, let's just say I've made great use of many libraries in the past years."

Ronny snorted. "You always did like to dig into the scandals and taboos of the past."

Their table fell silent, though their hearts continued to speak to one another. It took herculean effort on Lizzie's part to drag herself off the beachhead of the forbidden shores that was their shared past and get back to her severing of the last of their connection. She shook herself and sighed.

" Right. The Borgias. In any case, if a victim's would-be executioners knew how to use an odorless, tasteless white powder known as arsenic diligently, well, these men could profit greatly from each and every dinner party they hosted. And did you know that this same white powder is still quite prevalent today? It can be purchased without much effort in a number of different places as it is used for all sorts of things, though now the intended purpose is typically less heinous. Typically."

"Lizzie," Ronny's voice sounded strained, "What have you done?"

She watched the color drain from his face, his features now devoid of anything except horror.

"'For the children of a forever grieving mother. I have no one to love me now.'"

"What?" Ronny raised his eyebrows.

"That was written inside the bible of one of the victims of Miss Tann's Children's Society. Your office published it in your investigation. You don't remember it?"

"Lizzie," Ronny tried to reach for her, but she placed her hands in her lap, "no one is above the law."

She snorted, "Yet you said so yourself, some got away with it. Why should that be allowed? Age and gender do not exempt you from reaping what you sow and time distance from the crime should also not determine whether or not justice should be served."

Ronny's body slumped and he dropped his head. They sat in silence and for the first time Lizzie became aware of the fact that the lunch hour had passed and Ronny would most assuredly be late getting back to work. She glanced around and saw that they were one of perhaps a half-dozen other customers. All of them were couples, speaking in similarly hushed tones, either being confessed to or doing the confessing.

"What business do you have in the eastern part of the state?"

Lizzie returned her wandering gaze to Ronny, "Hmm?" Ronny repeated his question and Lizzie gave a soft smile. "I'm going to try to find Mrs. Robinson."

She knew it was a long shot but now that her wounded soul was satisfied that everyone involved with this Society had been served their due she had no other purpose to set her compass to. She couldn't go back to New York. Not now. She also couldn't stay here; that'd ruin Ronny. Studying him across the table now, Lizzie noted that he looked older. Her confession had aged him. She grieved the loss of his innocence, at least as he'd reflected upon her, but it'd had to be done. This was the final nail in the coffin of her phony past. No, the only thing to do was to go east and to see what sort of ghosts she could stir up.

"Why did you tell me this, Lizzie?" Ronny reached across the table but let his hand fall open, and empty, in the middle.

"I guess," Lizzie squared her shoulder and lifted her head, "I guess I wanted you to know that everyone got what was coming to them, though it took five years." She dropped her eyes a moment to gain bravado before she tentatively placed her hand in his and met his gaze, "I guess I wanted to hear my name, my real name, come from your lips, even if it was spoken with confusion and now revulsion."

A waiter dropped a tray in the back of the restaurant and they both jerked as if that was the death knell itself. Ronny looked at his watch and swore under his breath. He reached for his hat and coat, not bothering with his tray of food. Lizzie mimicked his movements and they walked towards the entrance as any other normal couple: his hand on her lower back, steering her before him. Only, they both knew there was nothing, and now would be nothing, normal or couple-y about them.

Once outside they stood awkwardly in front of each other. Ronny: gripping and releasing the brim of his hat. Lizzie: tightening her hold on her purse.

"You," Ronny stopped, seemed to think better of whatever it was he'd been about to say, then started again, "I hope you find what you're looking for," he paused again then carefully added, "Frances Clara May."

She smiled and nodded in return, "Take care of yourself, Ronny." He started to turn away, but her voice stopped him and he looked over his shoulder, "'We'll always have Paris.'"

He smiled and nodded before turning away completely. Lizzie watched his back a moment before she too made her to her car. Sliding into its heated confines, she flipped on the radio and after scratching through static settled on a clear station. Leaning against the bench seat she again kicked off her shoes, removed her waist belt, unpinned her hat, unbuttoned her top bodice buttons, and this time she added to the pile, her pristine white gloves. As she finished shedding, the tune of "Mister and Mississippi" filled the Henry J.

"I can't recall my mother, I don't remember dad. Mister and Mississippi was all I ever had."

Francis Clara May turned the key in the ignition and let the car idle a moment while she checked traffic.

"My cradle was the river, my school a river boat. My teacher was a gambler, the slickest one a float."

Seeing an opening, Francis Clara May pulled back onto the thoroughfare but came to a stop when the traffic light switched. She turned up the radio and began to singalong as she waited.

"I'd love a tiny village, a quiet country town. A house, a little garden, with kiddies running 'round. You'd be a faithful husband, I'd be a trusting friend."

She glanced in her rearview mirror and spotted Ronny crossing the street coming in her direction. He pulled his Tremont tighter onto his head and tugged at his large patterned sport coat. His eyes seemed to be frantically searching as he moved among the crowd. Lizzie felt a tug in her gut and her hand moved of its own accord towards her turn signal.

A honk from the car behind her had Francis Clara May jumping and she waved an apology before accelerating away from Ronny and everything that could have been between them.

"Oh! I was born to wander, I was born to roam, and Mister and Mississippi made me feel at home."

Author's Note: Many of the characters referenced in this story, as well as the details of the Tennessee Children's Home Society, are true. The details connecting some of the outlying information, as well as the cause of the fate of some of the characters, have been fabricated.

A Desperate Act

by Herschel Cozine

It had been over half a lifetime since I last saw Rick Houston. He had been a major force in my life once, an unwelcome interlude that I have tried hard to forget. So I wasn't ready for the phone call. Nor was I prepared to deal with the memories that came with it. It was inevitable, I know. Rick's strange disappearance had never been explained, and the police kept the book open. Now it was over, and I guess in some ways I was relieved. But it will never "be over" for me.

A lot of water has passed under the bridge since Rick went away. I no longer lived in Oakville. But I suppose, like most people, I never really left the town. I loved it, and still do.

Oakville was not a town for the likes of Rick Houston. It was a small, secluded community, nestled in the foothills of Southern California. Life in Oakville was—how would one phrase it—idyllic. No drug problems. No gangs or other bad influences to disturb the peaceful existence of the two thousand inhabitants.

It was in the late fifties, a time before Viet Nam and the unrest of the turbulent sixties. I was entering my junior year in high school. I was looking forward to the school year, planning to try out for the baseball team and the junior play.

Then Rick appeared. A sulky, ill-tempered teen from Chicago, he moved with his divorced mother into the former Johnston house on the outskirts of town. Mrs. Houston, a small, mousy woman of indeterminate age, wore a look of perpetual sadness, as one would expect of a mother of an out of control teenager. She took a job as a maid at the local motel and kept to herself.

Rick was instantly a problem. Uncooperative with teachers at school, bullying with his classmates, and contemptuous of the law, Rick was constantly in trouble with the faculty as well as the local police. Most of his transgressions were minor: truancy, classroom infractions, and general behavior problems. But it disrupted the otherwise peaceful environment of the small school. No one was quite sure how to deal with him, and except for an occasional trip to the principal's office, Rick did pretty much what he wanted to do.

I met him on the first day of the new school year. For reasons I shall never understand, Rick was drawn to me. He bullied me, to be sure. But he was protective as well. I didn't welcome his bullying or his protection. I could do without the former, and I certainly did not need the latter. There were no threats or challenges from my schoolmates that I couldn't handle. And we had nothing in common. I was shy, introverted and studious. Rick was none of these.

Nonetheless, Rick sought me out, and in his own peculiar way treated me as his friend. In all of the time that I spent with him, I saw no one else whom he considered a friend. The girls were afraid of him. The boys kept their distance. He went out for the high school football team, and his natural physical ability along with his aggressive personality landed him a first string spot at fullback. But football, to him, was not a game. It was another form of legal violence in which he excelled and enjoyed in a sadistic sort of way. Often he would miss practice as well as games. The coach was patient, only because Rick's talent was needed to field a competitive team. But it was clear that the coach and the rest of the team were not happy with his lack of commitment.

It was toward the end of the school year when he collared me after school as I sat at the counter in the soda shop where I waited for the school bus to deliver me home. I lived on an orange ranch a few miles from the school, and, along with several others, patronized the soda shop while waiting for the bus to deliver students who lived on the west end of town. The school district was small, with limited funds, so one bus was all that was available. We didn't mind. It gave us a little free time before we had to get home to our chores and homework.

He slid on the stool next to mine, ordered a coke, and slammed a quarter on the Formica countertop. Sally, the soda girl, a pretty classmate, smiled nervously and twisted away from the grip he had on her wrist. He laughed and turned to me.

"Hey, pal. I don't know how you stand it here."

"What are you talking about?" I asked.

"This." he said, waving his arm around the room. "Boring!"

I followed the sweep of his hand. Having lived most of my life in Oakville, I saw nothing wrong with the way we lived our lives. I said nothing.

"Don't you ever want to break out and do something besides drink soda pop and wait for a goddam bus?"

"Yeah. I guess," I said, not certain how to answer his question.

"What do you do for excitement in this burg?"

I considered the question. Nothing exciting ever happened in Oakville. But we didn't care. Excitement was not high on our list of priorities.

"Dunno," I said.

Rick snorted. "What do you mean, you don't know, for Crissake? You must do *something* besides go to school and help your daddy pick oranges."

"Sure," I said. "We have a movie house. We ride horses. We go to the beach in Jackson in the summer. We have picnics." I paused to think of other events, but he cut me off with another snort, louder than the first.

"Jesus," he said. "You sound like The Beaver." He took the coke, removed the drinking straw from it and drank. Setting the glass back on the counter, he nudged me with his elbow.

"I want excitement, not a goddamn TV show. Where do you get your liquor?"

"Liquor?" I said. "I don't. I'm only sixteen."

"What the hell does that matter?" he said. "Does Jackson have a liquor store?"

I nodded. "I guess so."

"What about girls?"

"What about them?" I said.

Rick exploded. "My God, you're a piece of work. Back where I come from you could get anything you want if you knew where to go for it. Booze. Women". He winked. "I mean *real* women. Not the little tightasses you got here." He shook his head and sighed.

"You could get anything you wanted if you knew where to look."

"Marijuana?" I asked, intrigued.

Rick laughed out loud. "Kid stuff! Sure, you could get that anywhere. Hell, I could buy that from the school janitor." His eyes took on a reflective look and an enigmatic smile crossed his lips.

"Me and Joe had some great times," he said at last. Turning to me, still smiling, he said, "Have you ever hot wired a car?"

Before I could answer he waved a hand in disgust. "No. Of course not. I bet you don't even know how to drive."

"I do so!" I said.

Rick studied my face for a few seconds, then shrugged. "OK," he said. "Don't get sore. But I bet you never drove a real car. Your old man's Hupmobile ain't nothing more than a lawnmower."

I started to protest, thought better of it, and sipped my coke. In the short time I knew him I had learned that it was better not to argue with him. It could get physical fast, and I was no match for him.

"Hey!" he said, breaking the silence. "What do you say we drive over to Jackson?"

"Can't," I said.

"Why not?"

"I gotta get home and do my chores."

"It's Friday," he said, grabbing me by the arm. "Call your old lady and tell her you'll be late."

"But…" I started.

"C'mon," Rick said. "Live a little. God, man. You have the rest of your life to do what your mamma wants." He ushered me out of the soda shop and down the street to his car.

Rick's car was a flashy, if old, sports car, with a new coat of paint and chrome tailpipes. A decal of flame was on each side, giving it an appearance of power that both awed and scared me. With some reluctance I crawled into the passenger seat and locked the door. This was before the age of seat belts, so I gripped the armrest and dug my feet into the floorboard in anticipation of a fast, probably dangerous ride. Rick looked over at me as he started the engine and smiled maliciously.

"Ready?"

I nodded.

He pressed the starter button and the engine roared to life with a deafening noise that echoed along the otherwise placid street. The town's lone patrol car was nowhere in sight. I knew from previous conversations with Rick that he had been ticketed for various traffic offenses, primarily lack of a muffler. Instead of conforming, he treated the tickets like badges of honor.

With a squeal of tires, he pulled away from the curb and headed west, toward the coast.

"Where are we going?" I asked.

Rick didn't answer. Outside the city limits now, he accelerated, his eyes bright with excitement. I watched nervously as the speedometer pushed toward sixty. The road was narrow, with curves and hills that made driving over forty-five a dangerous undertaking. I dug in, wanting desperately to cry out for him to slow down. But my pride, or whatever it is teenagers have that keep them from acting sensibly in times like this, kept me from saying or doing anything "cowardly". Although I didn't like Rick, I felt the need for his approval. Swallowing my fears, I remained silent.

After what seemed an eternity, we were on the outskirts of Jackson. The town itself was not impressive. It was divided in two by the coast highway, with the beach on one side of the road and the main part of town on the other. Rick wheeled on to the Pacific Coast Highway, headed north, and passed a semi chugging up the small rise leading toward San Roberto. I held on, praying silently for the ride to end.

Rick slowed the car as we approached a service station. He pulled in, parked next to the gas pump and got out of the car.

"Wait here," he said.

I watched as he went inside. I could see him talking to the attendant behind the counter. Then, suddenly, before I realized what was happening, I saw a flash of light followed quickly by the sound of a shot. I watched in horror as the attendant slumped to the floor. I could see Rick fumbling with the keys of the cash register. A few seconds later he ran back to the car, got in and started the engine.

"You shot him!" I shouted as we sped away from the station.

Rick had a grim look on his face; not a look of fear as I expected. It was an evil, excited look.

"You shot him!" I said again.

Rick turned to me, the excitement flashing in his eyes. Taking the money from his shirt pocket he threw it in my lap. "Yeah," he said. "The stupid jerk wouldn't give me the dough."

"Is he dead?"

"I don't know," Rick said. "For Chrissake, do you think I was going to take the time to find out?"

"Rick!" I shouted over the roar of the engine. "We gotta go back and help him!"

Rick glared at me and sped up. "Are you crazy?" he said. "I just shot the guy. We gotta get out of here."

"But…" I started.

"Shut up!" he said, and for the first time since I met Rick I detected a note of fear in his voice.

I thought I was going to be sick. Rick must have realized it, because he left the main road and drove along a one lane unpaved road until we were out of sight from the highway. He stopped the car and sat back. I jumped out, ran over to a tree and threw up. Standing up slowly, I walked back to the car. I wanted to run. I wanted to get as far away from Rick as I could. But there was no place to go. Still feeling sick, I crawled back into the car and leaned back.

"Feelin' better?" Rick asked.

"Not really."

Rick laughed nervously. "Jeez, what a jerk!" He said.

"Me?" I asked.

Rick snorted. "No. The guy at the station. Sixty-five lousy dollars and he fights over it like it was a million bucks." He shook his head as he started the car. "It ain't worth risking your life for."

I didn't answer. Shaking and sick, I closed my eyes. Rick drove in silence, considerably slower than he had before.

"I want to go home," I said.

The drive back to Oakville was made without a word from either of us.

Rick dropped me off at the intersection near my home. I got out of the car and started to close the door. Rick reached over and grabbed my hand.

"Listen, pal. Not a word of this to anybody, understand?"

I wrenched my hand free, shut the door and started to walk.

Rick drove slowly along next to me. "We're in this together. You were with me. If anybody finds out about this we're both in trouble. Do you hear me?"

"I didn't shoot him," I said.

"You were there. That's all the cops care about. You're as guilty as I am."

Suddenly, without any warning, I started to cry. Rick stopped the car, climbed out and crossed over to me. Strangely, instead of getting angry, he put his arm around my shoulder.

"Hey, kid. It's goin' to be all right. Nobody saw us. Keep your mouth shut and we don't have nothin' to be afraid of." He reached into his shirt pocket and extracted the money. Peeling off a twenty, he handed it to me.

"Here," he said. "Your part of the take."

I pulled away. "I don't want it!" I shouted. "I don't want any of that money. It's dirty."

Rick shrugged and put it back in his pocket. "Suit yourself," he said, anger creeping back in his voice. "But remember, not a word to anybody. Understand?"

I pushed my hands deeper into my pockets.

"Understand?" he said in a threatening voice.

Finally, I nodded.

He visibly relaxed. Climbing back into the car, he started the engine. "OK, pal. Remember. Keep your mouth shut and nobody gets into trouble. That's the way it is. Welcome to the world." With that, he drove off.

My mother was waiting for me at the door. "Where have you been?" she said, a note of anger in her voice. "I was getting worried."

"Sorry," I muttered.

My answer only made her angrier. "Sorry? You were supposed to be home two hours ago. You didn't call. Then you come strolling through the door without a word of explanation. I..." She paused as she searched my face. Her mother's instinct took over.

"Bart, what's the matter? What happened?"

"I... I..." I started, fighting back tears.

"What? Tell me!"

"I can't," I said at last. "I can't talk right now." Before she could say anything, I ran to my room and closed the door. I skipped dinner,

By morning I had composed myself enough to face the world. My mother was in the kitchen. She eyed me with concern as I took a bowl from the cupboard and fixed a bowl of cornflakes. I avoided her eyes.

"Bart? What on earth is the matter?"

I had prepared for this. Having had all night to sort things out, I was ready with a story that sounded convincing.

"Nothing," I said. "I was upset last night because me and Judy had a big fight. She told me she never wanted to see me again."

Judy was my steady girlfriend. We had been going together for almost six months. My mother liked Judy very much.

"I'm sorry," she said. "Maybe you can work it out."

"I hope so," I said. I poured some milk over the corn flakes, spooned sugar on it, and ate. Putting the bowl in the sink, I headed for the door. "I'm going over there now," I said. "I'll do the chores when I get home, I promise."

My mother started to protest, but seeing the determination in my eyes she smiled and shrugged. "Don't be long. And good luck."

Of course I would have to tell Judy the truth. Having used her as an excuse for my state of mind, I had no choice but to tell her so that she would go along with my cover story.

Judy was horrified. "Rick killed a man?" she said. "How terrible. Why didn't you…"

"What could I do?" I shouted. "I didn't even know he had a gun. Hey, Judy, I didn't want to go with him in the first place. But you know Rick. Nobody says 'no' to him. Least of all, not me."

"You have to tell the police," she said.

"I can't. Rick says I'm as guilty as he is." I swallowed hard at the thought of going to prison. I didn't know if Rick was right or wrong about my being an accessory, but accepted his opinion. He was far more worldly than I, and had almost certainly been in trouble with the law before.

"Bart," Judy said, watching me with troubled eyes. "You have to go to the police. It's the right thing to do. It's the *only* thing." She reached out and patted my hand. "If you go now and tell them the truth, they'll understand. You weren't a part of it. You didn't even know it was going to happen until it was over."

She was right, I knew. Still, Rick's threat hung over me. Somehow he would see to it that I shared in the crime. People like Rick don't accept responsibility for their actions. They find ways to get others involved, and I certainly was the most obvious person to share the blame for the clerk's death.

"I know. I know," I said. "God, how I hate Rick Houston."

"I'll go to the police with you," Judy said.

"No," I said quickly. "You stay out of it. No sense both of us getting involved in this."

"You will go?" she said.

"I said I would," I snapped. Then, realizing what I had done, I took her hand and squeezed it. "I'll go. But I need a little time."

"No," she said. "You have to go today. Now. You can't wait."

I nodded absently, kissed her on the cheek, and left.

Rick was furious. "You told Judy?" he shouted. "What the hell's the matter with you, pal?"

"I had to," I said. "I had to tell *somebody*."

Rick was pacing up and down, cursing. "Jeez, I can't believe you could be so stupid." He stopped pacing and glared at me, his eyes bright with anger. "What the hell…"

"Hey, Rick," I said. "She won't tell anybody."

"The hell she won't," Rick said. "She wants you to go to the cops, don't she?"

I nodded.

"And if you don't, she will. You can bet on that."

"I… I don't know."

Rick snorted. "You don't know. Well, I do." He started pacing again. "We gotta do something about this."

"What?" I asked, concern edging my voice.

Rick stared at me with a look that sent chills down my spine. "What do *you* think?"

"I don't know."

He waved a hand in dismissal. "Forget it. Leave it to me. I'll handle this."

"What are you going to do? For God's sake, Rick what are you going to do?"

He didn't answer. Horror gripped my throat as the impact of what he had said hit me. He was going to kill her! I had witnessed the cold-blooded way in which he had shot the clerk at the liquor store. He was capable of doing the same with Judy.

"No!" I said. "You can't do this. You can't…"

Rick whirled and swung hard, landing a fist on my chin. I went down in a flash of pain and rolled over. Rick leaned down and held out his hand. "Sorry, pal. I didn't mean it. I'm just so pissed off about all this that I lost control." He patted my shoulder. "No hard feelings?"

I rubbed my chin gently. "Rick, you can't do this."

"Sure, pal," he said. "You're right."

The way he said it scared me. I didn't believe him. I didn't believe him at all.

"Let's talk about this, Rick."

Rick snorted. "There's nothing to talk about. What's done is done. We just have to deal with it."

"Well," I said, trying desperately to think of something that would change his mind. "Let's go somewhere away from here. I… I have to get away."

Rick studied my face with a look of disdain. He hated weakness, I knew. And I was weak. I could never measure up to his expectations even if I wanted to. Finally, he looked away. "OK."

While I sat sullenly silent in the car, Rick drove out of town to the hills overlooking the reservoir. It was dark, with a waning moon rising slowly over the mountain. A cool breeze swept through the trees. Under any other circumstances I would have enjoyed the ride and the view from the hilltop. But tonight all I could think of was a murdered man and an innocent girl who was in danger. I felt helpless, impotent in the face of a horror unfolding before me.

Rick was no longer a schoolmate, a companion. He was a killer, a dangerous young man who was as desperate as I, even though he didn't show it. I had never wanted to be his "companion" anyway. I never felt so desperately alone in my life. And now, alone with Rick miles from help, I should have felt fear for my life. Strangely, I didn't.

We walked to the edge of the cliff overlooking the reservoir. Rick picked up a stone and threw it over the edge. A few seconds later the plunk reached our ears. In the crisp night air it sounded loud and ominous.

"Rick," I said. "Don't do anything to hurt Judy," I said.

Silence. In the soft light of the moon I studied his face. It was a passive, cold look that sent chills down my spine.

"Rick? Do you hear me?"

Finally he nodded. "Sure, pal. I hear you."

"Well?"

"Things will work out," he said. "Let's get out of here. I hate this place."

"Go ahead," I said. "I'll walk."

Rick grabbed me by the arm. "It's five miles to town. Don't be a jerk."

"Leave me alone," I said.

Rick gripped my arm harder. "Get in the car."

"No."

I had never stood up to Rick before. His hard black eyes studied me for a minute.

"Listen, pal. You better not do anything stupid."

"I need to be alone. I'll walk home. I've done it before." I met his eyes. My heart was pounding so hard I could hear it. I knew what Rick was capable of doing, and up here where there was no one to see or hear us, I was sure he wouldn't hesitate to kill me. The way I felt at the moment, it didn't matter to me.

We stared at each other for several seconds. Then Rick released my arm.

"Suit yourself," he mumbled. He turned and walked away. I watched Rick's retreating form with a growing rage. At that moment I felt a hate I had never felt for anyone before or since.

<hr>

It was after midnight when I got home. The walk from the reservoir took close to two hours, and I was exhausted, physically and mentally. I closed the door softly and went to my room, careful not to wake my parents. I fell on the bed, fully clothed, and drifted into a troubled sleep.

As it turned out, there was a witness to the killing. A woman who lived nearby, out walking her dog, had seen Rick running from the station and getting into the car. She gave a good description of the car with its flaming decal and chrome pipes. Her description of Rick was less accurate. But the car was sufficient evidence to lead the police to Rick. Thankfully, she did not mention a passenger. I was never suspected.

Rick never returned home the night we went to the reservoir. His disappearance created a stir in Oakville. They had a murderer in town, a fugitive. In a strange sort of way, the residents enjoyed the notoriety. The local papers picked up the story and gave it prominent coverage. The Jackson Tribune printed an interview with Rick's mother, playing on the public's fascination with the case.

"He's run off before," she told reporters.

"Where would he go?"

"No place in particular. 'Specially if he's runnin' from the law."

"Are you surprised by this?"

"It don't surprise me that he did this thing. He's a bad one. Always has been. Just like his father. I brought him out here to the country hopin' it would change him. But a leopard don't change its spots, I guess."

Mrs. Houston didn't seem sorry that Rick was gone.

I never went to the police. Now that it was known who killed the clerk, I felt no need to go. Judy agreed. I loved her for that.

They never found Rick. Eventually, life returned to normal in Oakville. For me, however, life was never the same. Being a witness to murder and knowing things that no one else knew about Rick and his plan to kill Judy scarred me forever. Shortly after graduation I left Oakville, not because I wanted to, but because I could never live a normal life there in light of the situation.

I received the phone call about Rick from Judy. She had married a local boy, raised a family, and was still living in Oakville. Now a widow, she kept in touch by e-mail and an occasional phone call.

"They found Rick Houston," she said without preamble when I answered the phone.

I swallowed hard at the pronouncement. "They did? When? Where?"

"Yesterday," she said. Silence.

"Oh? How?"

"You know the reservoir?" she asked. It was not a question, but a statement. Everyone who ever lived in Oakville knew where the reservoir was. "The dam was cracked. They condemned it last month. They had to drain the reservoir."

I waited for her to go on. After a moment of uncomfortable silence, she said, "Bart?"

"What?"

"You knew about this, didn't you?"

"What do you mean?"

There was an edge to her voice. "You were with Rick the night he disappeared. You told me that, remember?"

"So?"

She sighed. "They found a car at the bottom of the lake. It was just off the south rim—the deepest part of the lake. Over eighty feet deep, I guess."

I thought back. The cliff overlooking the lake was primarily rock. No tire marks would be left. And it sloped downward, making it easy to push the car over the edge.

"It was rusted almost beyond recognition," Judy was saying. "But enough remained to identify it as Rick's car. They could tell the make and year. And there was even a trace of a decal on one of the doors."

"That's interesting," I said. "But what about Rick? You said they found him."

"They did. There were partial remains of a skeleton. They found a skull." Another pause. "They could tell from the condition of the skull that he had been hit with a blunt object, heavy enough to kill him."

Like a tree limb, I thought. There was no shortage of them at the reservoir.

"So he was murdered?" I said.

"Bart." Judy said, "I'm not telling you anything you don't already know. Ever since the night Rick disappeared you were a different person. I thought it was because of your being involved with the murder of the clerk. I never suspected you had anything to do with Rick's disappearance."

"And now you do?" I asked.

"Yes. I do. And I know why. You had no choice, at least in your mind. You were afraid he would try to kill me…"

"No," I interrupted. "I *knew* he was going to kill you. He almost said as much. I couldn't let that happen, Judy. Don't you understand?"

"I understand, Bart. Of course I understand. And I'm grateful. But…" Her voice trailed off.

"But what?"

"There had to be another way."

"Maybe," I said. "Maybe." I listened to the sound of her breathing and felt a surge of love for the girl I used to adore.

"God, this is so hard for me," she said. "I never dreamed you were capable of murder."

"Desperate people do desperate things," I said.

There was a long silence, broken by a muffled sob on the other end of the line.

"What are you going to do, Judy?" I said.

"Do?" she said. "There's nothing to be done. Not now. It all happened so long ago. What possible good could it do to resurrect it now?"

"Right," I said. "I'm just sorry it had to happen."

"Bart?"

"Yes?"

"Believe me when I tell you that I am not judging you. I can't begin to understand what you were going through. I just find this so difficult."

"I know," I said. "Forgive me."

"There's nothing to forgive. I called because I wanted you to hear it from me. Before you read about it in the paper. And I wanted you to know, too, that your secret is safe. I think I'm the only one who knows what really happened that night."

"I'm coming to Oakville in a few weeks," I said. "I'd like to see you. Will you be home?"

There was a long pause. "I don't think it would be a good idea. Let's remember things the way they were, Bart. I loved you once. I guess I still do. But things can never be the same. Not after all this."

I started to protest, then sighed. "OK. OK. Thanks for calling."

I hung up, a feeling of melancholy spreading over me. The police could close the book on Rick's disappearance. But now they had another murder on their hands. They would have to investigate, I was certain of that. But I wasn't certain how vigorously they would pursue it given the amount of time that had elapsed and the nature of the victim. It didn't really matter to me. Because of it I had lost a girl, a home and a way of life I had treasured. Let the police investigate. I suddenly realized that I wanted the truth to come out. It had consumed me for most of my life. Now I could have closure.

I reached for the phone. Obtaining the number from information, I dialed and waited.

"Oakville Police, Sergeant Madison," a voice growled over the wire.

"My name is Barton Howell," I said. "I killed Rick Houston."

The 1950s were big years in home ownership in the US as a wave of babies, later to be known as Baby Boomers were born, and multitudes of new parents moved to just-built suburbs. With her newly minted realtor's license, Sue Wright is about find out how easy it is to make a killing in real estate.

4BR/3.5BA Contemporary
by Margaret S. Hamilton

"At the end of Happy Valley, turn down the middle gravel driveway." Sue Wright, nee Streicher, looked up from her scrawled set of directions.

Her husband, Walt "Buy and Sell the Wright Way" Wright, scowled and down-shifted his Chevy. "Gonna be hell on the suspension."

Sue swore Walt loved his two-tone blue Impala more than his wife. She hummed to Frankie Avalon's "Venus" on the radio as they inched down the driveway.

"This is ridiculous. Who'd want to buy a house way out here?" Walt groused as he steered around a pothole. "You should've asked me to handle this."

Sue slid her steno pad into her handbag. "Mr. Gorman asked for me, not you."

Walt parked next to the carport across a gravel turnaround from the back of the house. "Honey, you don't have a real estate license. Feel free to wander around and get ideas for your pretty ads. I've got a potential listing contract to negotiate."

Sue freshened her scarlet lipstick and snapped the compact shut. "As a matter of fact, I'm now a realtor. My license arrived in the morning mail." She removed it from her handbag.

Walt threw his key case on the dashboard. "No way. Lemme see that." He pulled a small certificate out of the envelope. "Looks real." He yanked her hair, forcing her head against the seat back. "We don't have enough money for a six-pack of Schlitz, but you found a way to pay for real estate school?"

Sue wrestled herself from his grip and adjusted the headband on her shoulder-length flip. "Get your hands off me. I sit in the office all day waiting for the phone to ring. And while I sit there, day after day, I do freelance typing. You know that. I saved up enough to pay for real estate school and studied my eyes out for the exam." She opened the car door. "My father told Mr. Gorman I have my real estate license. He wants to list the house with me, not you." She slammed the door.

Walt started the car. "Find your own ride back to town. I've got rentals to show."

"The same moldy, roach infested places you showed last month and the month before? It's not healthy for people to live there but of course, that doesn't bother you." Sue tugged her navy linen shift over her hips.

"New dress? That come out of your typing money, too?"

"Mom made it. Now that I'm a realtor, I need more than a secretary's blouse and skirt."

"Fancy-shmancy." Gravel flew as Walt gunned the Impala, spun it around, and headed up the driveway.

Sue took a deep breath and walked toward the house, taking mental notes about the first contemporary she'd ever visited. It was built in a curved shape around the side of the hill, surrounded by woods. Bushes sculpted into bonsai shapes lined the back wall with a meditation garden and bubbling fountain placed next to the glass-walled dining room. Unusual for the Eisenhower era Cincinnati suburbs, but Sue was up to the challenge of marketing it.

Jim Gorman stepped outside. "Sue, thanks for coming. Why don't we take a few minutes to walk around the property?"

Sue sat on a wrought iron bench next to the kitchen sliding glass door. "Sure thing, Mr. Gorman. I'll change my shoes." She slipped off her new kitten heels and pulled a pair of immaculate white Keds from her bag.

He helped her up. "Please call me Jim. It's a pleasure doing business with you."

Sue looped her handbag over her arm and they walked side-by-side on a gravel path through the woods.

"I know it's a trek, but Dad put Adirondack chairs next to the creek at the bottom of the hill," Jim said.

Sue kept her eye peeled for poison ivy as she made her way down the slope. Blue jays shrieked, and cardinals sang in the trees overhead. She heard the distinctive rat-a-tat of a woodpecker nearby.

Jim stopped at the creek, where a slow trickle of water eddied around the tree roots. "This is where Dad swallowed a bullet."

Sue gasped and clutched a nearby sapling for support. "I thought he died of natural causes."

Jim gave her a grim smile. "That's what the police told the press. When your father filed the claim for Dad's life insurance, he got his hands on the medical examiner's report and told me what really happened."

Sue pulled a linen hankie out of her handbag and dabbed her face. "Oh, dear." She squinted as a shaft of sunlight hit her face. "Was your dad having troubles?"

"Dad was in excellent health. This house was the culmination of his dreams—he helped design it and selected the furniture. Sure, he missed Mom, but he enjoyed a busy retirement." Jim choked back tears and turned away.

Sue looked up at the house, which resembled an Oreo cookie with one bite taken out of it, set in the hillside.

"Did the police cover up what had happened so you could sell the house?"

Jim shook his head. "I don't know."

"Did he own other guns? Are they still in the house?"

"No guns. Somehow, he got his hands on a service pistol." Jim started up the path. "I'm with a Madison Avenue agency. Though I live in Manhattan, I still subscribe to the local paper. I noticed you have a real knack for ad copy. Ever thought about a career in advertising?"

"I've never considered it. Everything changed when I married Walt. He wanted to be a realtor. Dad lets us use the store-front building he owns and we live in the upstairs apartment."

"Does Walt have other listings?"

Sue sighed. "My father's friends gave him a few. I do all the detail work—the newspaper ads and some of the showings. I spend a lot of time reassuring the sellers, too."

"While Walt does what?"

Sue wrinkled her nose. "He drinks with his buddies and plays cards."

"I plan to give you the listing," Jim said. "But only if you promise Walt has nothing to do with our contract. I don't want him in the house or on the property. You handle the showings and coordinate with other realtors in town." He smiled. "I know your ads will entice customers, and the house will sell itself."

After Jim ushered Sue into the living room, she clicked her pen and started taking notes. Cathedral ceiling, floor-to-ceiling stone fireplace, a wall of glass overlooking a deck stretching the length of the house. "Chimney swept?" Sue pointed to the fireplace.

"Dad had it cleaned every spring."

Sue walked around the room, admiring the furnishings. A gold ball clock hung on the wall, the curved shapes of the soft green couch matched the early summer leaves outside. A floor lamp stood next to a tan leather steel chaise lounge near the window. Flanking the fireplace, low-slung cocoa brown swivel chairs accented the wooded view. Glass-topped tables in amorphous shapes completed the room. Sue noticed that the circular lines of the furniture matched the curved walls of the house, creating a harmonious whole.

Sue oohed and awed when she entered the kitchen. No one she knew owned a six-burner gas range plus wall ovens, with snazzy white stainless steel Eurostyle cabinets, and a double door restaurant-style refrigerator. The homemaker could stand at the sink and enjoy a view of the hillside garden planted with marigolds and petunias. She stroked the stylish Formica countertops, gray embellished with red and turquoise swirls, with a red and turquoise tile floor to match. A kitchen for a serious cook, with room for an herb garden on the small patio worthy of *Architectural Digest*.

As she toured the main floor, Sue noted spacious bedrooms with walls of windows opening to the deck, bathrooms with separate showers and tubs, plus sleek wooden cabinets with drawers under the sink—vanities. Just like the bathrooms in *House Beautiful*.

Jim ushered her into the main floor corner study lined with windows. "This is where Dad spent most of his time."

"It's a treehouse in the woods." Sue noticed two framed prints on the wall. "Charley Harper silkscreens?" One depicted chickadees and sparrows defending their bird feeder from a marauding squirrel, and the other, a single cardinal.

Jim smiled. "You know Harper's work? After they met, I ordered Dad two serigraphs of Harper's *Ford Times* covers. Charley lives in the woods a few miles from here, in Finneytown.

"I like Harper's prints. The birds are flat. No shading, but with appealing shapes, kind of like the design of this house." She glanced at Jim. "Are they valuable?"

"Not particularly. Each print was $4.50 plus shipping. The frames cost more than what's inside."

Jim guided her down a teak circular staircase, a small fountain burbling in a gravel garden at the bottom. A huge glass-walled family room overlooked the woods and lower deck. Two bedrooms and another bath completed the level.

Sue finished her notes. "Plenty of room for a large family, or even grandparents, down here."

Back upstairs, they sat at the dining room table.

Sue stroked the curved arms of a Thonet chair and hitched it closer to the table. A china cabinet filled with colorful glass vases and wall-mounted Breuer cabinet completed the room. "Are you the sole executor of your father's estate?"

"Yes." Jim drummed his fingers on the table.

Sue pulled out a folded listing contract clipped to her steno pad. "Let's fill this out before we discuss price." She had found the fourteen-digit parcel number for the house and the plat and lot map in the county records office. Flipping to the page where she had jotted square footage and selling price on comparable homes, Sue said, "The house sits on a two-and-a-half-acre lot. Do you know if the land can be subdivided?"

"No. Dad told me the county inspector wouldn't allow another house on this parcel, so the builder sold it as one large lot."

Sue showed him a list of recent sales. "This house has the same square footage as these properties, though none of them is a contemporary. Because of the high-end finishes and features, I suggest we price it at the top of the list." Sue circled a price on her pad. "With a top-drawer school system and easy access to the interstate, this location checks all the boxes." She looked up. "Does the furniture stay with the house?"

Jim rubbed his jaw. "I don't know. Dad paid a fair amount for some of the pieces. His lawyer hired an appraiser."

"And the decorative glass?" Sue had noticed pieces in every room.

"I'll have to make a decision about it."

Sue completed the contract and offered Jim the pen. "I'll check the house every day and, if necessary, tidy up."

Jim signed the contract and handed Sue a set of keys. "It's all up to you. Get me a fast sale at a decent price."

After they walked outside, he opened the door of his dad's red '58 Corvette. "No question, I'm keeping this baby. Want a lift?"

⁂

After he dropped her off, Sue raced upstairs to the apartment and hid Jim's set of keys at the bottom of the laundry basket, where Walt wouldn't find them. After changing into her usual workday clothes, a short-sleeved blouse and cotton skirt, she sighed as she entered the dusty office on the first floor. The fly-specked window was coated with a veneer of grime from the belching trucks clogging the downtown street. Sue dusted and swept, all the while composing ads in her head. She couldn't wait to pull the cover off her Royal typewriter and insert a yellow draft sheet.

First, the display ad:

EXECUTIVE CONTEMPORARY $99,900

Spacious 4/3.5 contemporary in private woodland setting, ideal for family living and gracious entertaining. Gourmet kitchen, sep DR with garden view, LR with cathedral ceiling &WBFP, sep FR, master suite. All rooms w/ floor-to-ceiling windows opening to expansive decks. Top school district, custom builder. Must see to appreciate. Wright Realty. AD2-6621

And the small ad to run in the local paper:

4/3.5 exec cont, Prv wd 2.5ac, gmt kitch, top SD. $99,900 Wright Realty. AD2-6621.

Sue called the city newspaper courier for copy pickup and walked her ad over to the local paper. No sign of Walt. Too lazy to hunt and peck a rental lease form, he always expected her to complete them. Where was Walt, anyway?

After the estate lawyer, Mr. Porter, called to confirm that the appraiser and cleaning service would be at the house the next day, Sue unlocked a storage closet and pulled out her camera and a roll of film. If she could get a few shots today, the camera shop could print up enlargements by morning. She grabbed the keys and made the two-mile bike ride to the house in under fifteen minutes. Another great selling point.

As she walked her balloon-tired Schwinn cruiser down the gravel drive, Sue heard men shouting. Curious, she leaned her bike against a tree and crept toward the house. Movers manhandled the dining room cabinet and table into the back of a panel truck parked in front of the carport. Sue gasped and retreated up the driveway, remembering that a woman from her parish church lived a few houses away. Sue raced down the street, sprinted up the front steps, and rang the bell. "Help me, please," she called. "I need to use your phone." She hammered on the brass door knocker.

A woman opened the door. "Sue Streicher? What is it, dear?"

"They're stealing furniture from Mr. Gorman's house. I need to call his lawyer." Sue pulled his business card out of her pocket and dialed Mr. Porter's office from the kitchen wall phone.

"Mrs. Wright, nothing leaves the house until the appraiser gives me his report. Call the police."

Sue dialed the operator, who connected her with the local police station. "Quick, they're stealing furniture from Mr. Gorman's house, 498 Happy Valley Lane."

"Wait for the squad car in the street."

Sue thanked the woman and walked to the top of the driveway. She could still hear the men loading furniture. After five minutes of anxious pacing, Sue looped the camera strap around her neck and slipped through the trees. Might as well get a photo of the front façade from the woods.

Still avoiding the poison ivy, Sue took shots of the house from different angles, a peaceful and serene setting despite Mr. Gorman's recent death. She shuddered, trying not to look at the chair where he had died.

She heard a police officer call her name, and scrambled back up the path. "Thanks for coming. Did you catch the thieves?"

"You're the Streicher girl, aren't you?" the officer asked.

"Yes, Sue Wright. I have the listing on the house. When I saw the men carrying out the furniture, I borrowed a neighbor's phone to call the lawyer. I suspect the furniture is valuable."

"Got the lawyer's phone number? The guys said Gorman's son hired them to move the furniture to a warehouse in town."

Sue pulled out Mr. Porter's business card and dictated his number.

The officer asked her not to leave, and went to the squad car to radio the dispatcher. Sue eyed the movers. They looked like day labor, not professional movers wearing coveralls embroidered with a company name.

After fifteen minutes, the officer received a radio response with instructions to return the furniture to the house and send the movers away.

"Ma'am, do you know where all this stuff goes?" the officer asked.

Sue gave him a faint smile. "Yes, I'll do my best. I toured the home earlier today."

When the furniture was back in the house, the officer stayed with Sue while she checked the door and window locks. She walked into the study and stopped. The framed Harper prints were gone, only two small nail holes left in the wall. The officer wrote down the information.

"Anything else missing?" he asked.

"Yes, the art glass from the dining room cabinet." Sue had an inspiration. She raced down the circular stairs to the lower level and pulled open a storage closet door. "Look, someone moved the Harper prints down here. And about ten glass vases."

"Think it was the guy's son?"

"I don't know who else would have been in the house."

"The lawyer told us the deceased owner had two children—a son and a daughter."

"What? If Jim Gorman isn't the sole executor, his sister should have signed the listing contract." Sue leaned against the wall. "I'll have to call Mr. Porter as soon as I get home."

Walt's Impala bounced down the gravel driveway. He climbed out and ambled across the gravel turnaround. "Honey, whatcha up to? Got a problem with the house?"

The officer nodded to Walt. "A misunderstanding. Mrs. Wright will call the estate lawyer from her office."

Walt looked at Sue. "Taking pictures?"

"Yes, a few black-and-white exterior shots for the office window display."

"How'd you get up here?"

Sue glared at Walt. "I rode my bike. Didn't it occur to you that I might need the car? Where have you been all day?"

Walt whistled and looked at the sky. "Around town, taking care of business."

"I need a lift, so I can drop this roll of film at the camera shop before it closes."

"Why don't you ride your bike? It's all downhill."

"Sounds like Mrs. Wright would appreciate a ride." The officer approached Walt, one hand on his holstered weapon.

"I don't have room for her bike in the trunk," Walt said.

"Why not?" The officer asked.

Walt turned on his heel, jumped in the Impala, and headed up the driveway.

"What that was all about?" the officer asked.

Sue frowned. "I have no idea."

"What does Mr. Wright usually carry in the trunk?"

"The usual—a toolkit, spare tire, and jack."

"I'll tell Sarge I offered you a lift because your bike had a flat." He heaved her Schwinn into the backseat of his squad car.

Sue thanked the officer when he dropped her in front of Wright Realty. "Excuse me for saying this, Mrs. Wright, but your husband doesn't treat you very well. In case you need help, do you have family in the area?"

She flushed. "Yes. Thanks for the lift, Officer. I appreciate it." Sue padlocked her bike to the fire escape at the rear of the building, and dashed to the camera shop. "I need an enlargement of the house exterior by tomorrow. Would you select the best one and print it?"

"Sure thing, Sue," the shop owner said. "Walt land a new listing?"

She smiled. "My first listing—it's a real beauty. I'm now a licensed realtor."

"Hey, congrats. You already do the heavy lifting for the business."

Sue inwardly sighed. Did everyone in town consider Walt a loser? She trudged home to call the estate lawyer.

shaking, she inserted the magazines back in the file box and returned it to the shelf.

Where was the ambulance? The firehouse was only a mile away. Sue patted Mr. Porter's jacket pockets until she found his car keys. She could lock the documents in the glovebox of his LeSabre. She slipped out of the study and pulled the housekeys from her skirt pocket. Unlocking the deadbolt, still holding the boning knife, she eased open the front door and tip-toed around the deck corner toward the turnaround at the back of the house.

"Rats!" Sue swore to herself.

Walt leaned the framed Harper prints against the rear bumper of the Corvette and tried to open the trunk. He turned and called out. "Jim, need the trunk key."

Jim Gorman appeared carrying a cardboard box filled with newspaper-wrapped bundles. "I've got the best pieces from Dad's collection. The rest are in the trunk of your car." He flipped Walt a key ring. "Let's get out of here before Porter wakes up."

"You ever find the will?" Walt asked, lifting the trunk lid.

"Nope. Maybe Dad had second thoughts about giving Jane all his money." Jim patted the framed Harper prints. "I've got more than enough right here."

"Those bird pictures valuable?" Walt asked.

"Let's say they were re-framed with care." Jim smirked.

Sue frowned. What had Jim hidden behind the Harper prints?"

Jim jumped behind the wheel. "Time to roll. I'll give you a lift."

Walt climbed in the passenger seat. "When's my payday? I did what you asked—stole a pistol and ammo off a vet."

"You'll get what's coming and maybe even a bonus. Sorry I couldn't give you the listing for the house. It would've looked suspicious."

"Better make it soon. Fancy pants Sue thinks she's in charge these days. I'll straighten her out tonight."

Sue's heart thudded. Walt had given Jim the gun his dad had used to kill himself. Or had Jim made it look like suicide? She had to tell the police. Would they believe her? The whole town considered Walt a loser, but the police always trusted a man's word over anything his little wife said.

"We'll leave the lights on for the rescue squad," Jim said. "Call them when you get home."

Sue watched them start up the driveway, the radio blaring Bobbie Darin's "Dream Lover". Walt was no dream lover—he'd almost ruined her life.

A Cadillac ambulance screamed down the driveway, followed by a squad car. Jim backed the Corvette down to the turnaround and sat behind the wheel. Walt jumped out of the car and bolted into the woods. Sue suspected he'd find his way back to the Impala and head for the apartment. Mr. Innocent, his wife out with another man, with a trunk-load of stolen art glass. He'd claim she'd stolen it.

Sue dashed into the turnaround and screamed. "Injured man in the study. Go through the kitchen to the front of the house." The rescue squad crew members grabbed their medical bags and went inside.

She approached Jim Gorman, holding the knife in front of her. "Stay put, Mr. Gorman. I overheard everything. Walt supplied the gun you used to fake your dad's suicide."

Jim looked at her. "You're wrong. I hired Walt to kill him."

A police officer approached. "Ma'am, put the knife down, nice and easy."

Sue put the knife on a large flat stone and held up her hands. "Sue Streicher. I'm the realtor. The estate lawyer, Mr. Porter, is injured. Jim Gorman knocked him out and tried to steal two framed prints and a box of valuable objects. My husband, Walter Wright, was with him, but ran away. Radio the dispatcher. Walt's cutting through the woods to his car parked down the street."

Her head spinning, her eyes unable to focus, Sue stumbled to a nearby bench.

"She's crazy," Jim Gorman said. "She went after me with a knife."

"No, she's not," a female voice said.

Sue looked up. A woman who could have been Jim's twin approached, holding a small suitcase. "I'm Jane Gorman. May I join you?"

Sue nodded. "I found the new will," she said in a whisper. "And Jim hid something important in the framed Harper serigraphs. They're in the Corvette trunk."

"Well, let's find out." Jane beckoned to a police officer. "I'm the sole beneficiary of my father's estate. I understand my brother stole valuables from the house. Please open the Corvette trunk."

After handing an officer the keys, Jim slumped behind the wheel.

Jane unlocked the trunk and pulled out the Harper prints. "Got a knife?" she asked Sue.

Sue collected the knife from where she'd left it. Jane put one of the prints on the bench, took the knife, and slit the brown paper backing. She pulled out a stack of certificates. "Well, what have we here? New York State Thruway bearer bonds." She counted the stack. "Good, they're all here."

Jane heaved the second framed print on the bench and slit the back. "U.S. Treasury bearer bonds. I'd forgotten Dad owned these."

Sue turned her back, yanked up her blouse, and pulled out the original will and other documents. "I found these in the *Ford Times* magazines." She handed them to Jane.

"Thanks, Sue. I suspected he'd hidden them in the magazines. I gave Dad the original prints and had them framed."

Sue frowned. "Jim told me he bought them."

Jane shook her head. "My goodness, you can't believe anything Jim says. I'll bet he told you Walt killed our father. Jim's bankrupt and unemployed. Dad wouldn't give him any more money, so Jim took matters into his own hands."

Sue heard an officer on the car radio. "Walter Wright. Yeah, the realtor. Blue two-tone Impala. Multiple counts of theft and suspected involvement in Gorman's murder. Check his car trunk for stolen goods. We'll arrest Jim Gorman and see you at the station."

The rescue squad personnel brought Mr. Porter out on a stretcher. "He's asking for both of you," one of the men said. "We're taking him to the ER for treatment."

Sue squeezed Mr. Porter's hand. "I found the will. Jane is here, and the police have Walt and Jim in custody."

He winced. "They really clobbered me. Good work, Susie Q. What a way to start your real estate career."

"Thanks, Mr. Porter. Now that I'm running my own real estate company, I look forward to working with you again."

Michele Bazan Reed brings our next story, a tale sparked by learning that Adolph Hitler's limousine was "lost" in a warehouse in Syracuse in the late 1940s.

Our author's work has been appearing in numerous publications in recent years, with a mini-mystery in Woman's World magazine, stories in several Chicken Soup for the Soul books, and stories in anthologies, including Wrong Turn (2018) and Detective Mysteries Short Stories (Nov. 2019).

The Hitler Heist
by Michele Bazan Reed

Adolph Hitler had been dead for three years when he robbed Syracuse Savings Bank on October 8, 1948.

Why the deceased leader of a vanquished regime would target a small city in Upstate New York was a question no one could answer. All anyone knew for sure was that every eyewitness agreed the ringleader of the robbers was the Fuhrer himself.

It was 1:42 p.m. on a Friday, payday for several local industries, so the tellers' drawers were full of cash.

According to the six tellers and fourteen customers present, Hitler and his loyal chauffeur threw open the ornate oak and brass doors of the 1876 gothic-style building. As they marched across the lobby, the chauffer shouted, "Everybody down, NOW." Then, almost as an afterthought, *"Ach du lieber!"*

Hitler, dressed in the grey wool overcoat and field cap so familiar from the newsreels, went right up to the head teller. He pulled open a grey duffel and silently motioned with his pistol, an iconic Luger, for her to fill it.

His chauffeur went down the line, ordering the other tellers in a gruff voice, "All the money right here, make it snappy. *Sau-*

erbraten!" Questioned later, the tellers expressed surprise that the chauffeur spoke English so well, but three insisted he did have a heavy German accent.

The customers lying on the marble floor held their breath as heavy boots stomped within inches of their noses. The robbers, the loot secured in their duffels, marched back across the lobby. At the door, the chauffeur turned and yelled, *"Auf Wienerschnitzel!"* and out they went.

A custom-made 1943 armored Mercedes limo sat waiting at the curb. The robbers hopped in and sped away down South Salina Street. Mr. Ralph Dennison, the assistant-assistant bank manager, stared out a mullioned arched window on the mezzanine. "Goering's in the passenger seat," he shouted to no one in particular. "Holy cow! We've just been robbed by a gang of top Nazis!"

Mrs. Peterson, the head teller, pressed the button under her window, alerting police to the robbery.

Within minutes, bubble-topped black and whites screeched to a stop in front of the bank, lights flashing and sirens wailing.

Sergeant Mack McKinnagh entered the bank and strode across the lobby, followed by three uniformed officers. "What seems to be the problem here? Who's in charge?" Mr. Dennison rushed down the stairs from the mezzanine, waving his arms and shouting, "We've been robbed by a gang of Nazis."

"Whoa, whoa, whoa. Settle down and let's start at the beginning. And what's this nonsense about the Nazis? The war ended in '45, man, and we beat those bastards," said McKinnagh.

He gestured to one of the officers, who pulled out a pad and started taking notes as McKinnagh continued questioning the assistant-assistant manager.

"Ha! Did you see the looks on their faces when I shouted *'Auf Wienerschnitzel'?* Betcha didn't know I knew so much German, did ya?" Sam slapped the steering wheel and let out a loud guffaw.

"You had to go and ham it up, didn't you? And besides, the word for goodbye is *'Auf Wiedersehen,'* you jamoke. *Wienerschnitzel* is some kinda sausage or something. Ow!" Pete grimaced as the glue from the fake mustache he was removing pulled at his upper lip. "Still, I guess it was kind of funny."

"I can't believe we pulled it off." Sam was practically crowing with delight. "You're a genius, that's what you are, Pete."

"Don't count yer chickens, as they say. We ain't safe yet. Now, pay attention to your driving. Last thing we need is you running a stoplight, and getting us arrested before we can stash this car back at the warehouse."

Pete opened one of the many secret compartments that Hitler had had built into the Mercedes so he'd have a gun ready at hand, no matter where he sat. He slid the fake Luger into the cubby and secured the cover.

"Yeah, yeah, but just admit it was a brilliant plan. I still remember that day last summer. You wuz doing yer favorite pastime, window shopping for cars..." Sam squinted through the bulletproof windshield, trying to read the street signs, looking for the turn to the warehouse.

"True, there I was, just moseying along Automobile Row on West Genesee Street, looking at all the new 1948 models. And there in Turner's showroom was this baby." Pete patted the armored dash with something akin to affection.

It was a hot July day when Pete first came upon the display of the Hitler car. Standing outside the Turner Brothers' dealership, drinking a Hires root beer, he saw a banner inviting one and all to see Hitler's custom-made limousine.

It cost two bits to see the Mercedes, but Pete was happy to pay it. He'd always loved cars, ever since his dad let him hand him wrenches as the old man worked on his Model A. Pete loved that old Ford. And his love for cars only grew when Pete got to serve in the motor pool for an Army regiment over in Europe, before he got wounded. Those were the days – driving officers around, ogling the *mam'selles* and working on jeeps.

He lifted the soda bottle to his lips and winced. That Kraut shrapnel ruined his shoulder and along with it, his chances for a good mechanic's job stateside.

Still, a guy could dream. So when the war was over, Pete cruised the strip of car dealerships on Syracuse's West Side every chance he got, eyeing the new models and getting odd jobs washing cars and parking vehicles.

But from the moment he saw it, Pete knew the Hitler car was going to change his luck.

"Can you believe those Frenchies brought that car to little old Syracuse?" He shook his head as he related the story to Sam later that July day.

French forces had captured the car at Berchtesgaden right after V-E Day and used to it to raise money for kids orphaned by the war. Crowds all over France paid to see the vehicle that had carried the evil dictator of the Third Reich all over Germany.

The Victoire war relief group next sent the vehicle on a circuit of North America to continue the fundraising. Syracuse was only the fourth stop on the tour, after Montreal, Toronto and Detroit.

Pete nodded his approval. Hosting the Hitler-mobile was a smart move on the dealership's part. Not only was it a patriotic thing to do, helping the war relief, but it brought hundreds of potential customers onto the showroom floor. With the war over, everybody was in a giddy mood. Guys were marrying their sweethearts, having families, and wanting to take those little tykes on vacations. Some would come to gawk at the Fuhrer-wagon and leave with new 1948 Oldsmobiles.

The car was on display for three days and Pete spent every minute of them studying that Mercedes, from the hand-painted license plate to the huge trunk.

"Did you know that thing has two carburetors and eight cylinders? I mean, it's actually got 800 horsepower!" he said to Sam one night over a Schlitz down at Sully's.

"Ya don't say." Sam was getting tired of his friend's obsession with the Benz. He took another swig of beer and listened to Peggy Lee sing *Mañana* on the jukebox. "And why do you drink that 'beer that made Milwaukee famous' anyway, when we got good old Congress made right here in Syracuse? My uncle works at that brewery. Give a guy a break. Sheesh."

"Yeah, yeah," Pete waved him off. "What I was saying is all them ponies under the hood makes it the perfect getaway car. The French guy that gave a talk about it said it could go 138 miles per hour. No cops would ever catch us in that thing." He pulled out his military-issue Zippo and lit another Chesterfield.

"Look at this," Pete said. He'd scribbled down some facts about the Mercedes on a brochure for the new Oldsmobile Futuramic 98 that he'd grabbed from a rack on the showroom floor.

Sam listened with a bored expression as Pete recited the Merc's attributes. "Three-quarter inch armor plating! No bullets are ever gonna get through that. And the bulletproof glass? One and a half inches thick!"

"Heh, heh, to protect your pretty mug." Sam had slapped him on the his bum shoulder.

"Ow! You can laugh if you want. That bastard Hitler ruined my life, and now, his car's going to fix it," Pete told Sam. "I was checking out the tires when I heard one of the Frenchies tell Mr. Turner that they're going to store the car down at Ryan's warehouse so no vandals can get at it. I'll get a job there and borrow that car for a little job of my own. Are you in?"

<hr>

"Hey, Pete! Pete!" Sam was slapping him on the shoulder. "You daydreamin' or what? I said, 'there's the warehouse.' Get out and open the door so I can get this baby in. Just like your plan."

With the Mercedes maneuvered back into its spot behind boxes of refrigerators at the back of the warehouse, Sam climbed out. "I still don't understand why we had to bring it back here. You said it had an extra 70-gallon gas tank. We coulda made it to Canada on that."

"Yeah, yeah, that was there so Hitler could escape to Switzerland if things got too hot in Berlin. But we Allies made sure he didn't get the chance!" Pete said as he pulled his duffel bag out of the footwell. "Don't be a dummy, if we tried to make it to the Canadian border we'd be caught before we were five miles north of town. This hardly looks like your uncle's DeSoto, now, does it?"

"Haha, dummy, get it?" Sam pointed to where Pete, who kept working as he talked, was pulling off his coat and hat, and replacing them on the near-perfect wax figure of Hitler that they had pulled out of the car's back seat before running the heist.

"It was pretty thoughtful of them Frenchies to provide us with the perfect disguises, eh, Pete?" Sam was dressing the chauffer dummy in his own costume.

"Well, we wouldn't have needed them if someone didn't get drunk the night before the job and forget to arrange disguises." Pete eyed Sam with a stern look. "But it did work out all right. You know, I heard the French organizer telling Mr. Ryan who owns the warehouse that these three dummies were worth 12 thousand bucks."

"You're pulling my leg. Maybe we should steal them." Sam turned the chauffer figure this way and that, appraising it.

"Now you're really being a dummy. Where the heck would you fence something like that? Big market out there for fake Germans. Right."

They finished replacing the dummies in the Mercedes and Pete stashed the duffel bags in the trunk of the car.

"What are you doing?" Sam looked aghast. "That's my money, too. Where's my share?"

"Have you listened to nothing I've been saying these last three months?" Pete shot Sam a pitying look. "The heat is on now. In a couple of days when things quiet down, I'll pull the loot and we'll get together and divvy it up."

Sam's face fell and he sputtered. "But... but..."

Pete reached in the duffel and pulled out a ten-dollar bill, tossing it to him. "Trust me. It's safer this way. And I'll be working all week, so I'll keep an eye on it. In the months I've been working here nobody, but nobody, has even touched this car. Now get out of here, Mr. Ryan's due back any minute now." And he picked up a broom and went to work sweeping the warehouse.

<hr>

Back at the bank, Sgt. McKinnagh held his head as he sat at Mr. Dennison's desk, which he had commandeered for the occasion.

"Seriously, Mrs. Harris, for the hundredth time, there are no Nazis in Syracuse," he said, his voice betraying the approaching end of his patience. He'd been questioning witnesses for two and a half hours and was no further ahead than when he began. To a man—and woman—they insisted on a scenario that he knew was impossible.

"Well, I only know what I saw. And heard," said the well-dressed customer. "When they left, that polite little chauffer wished us all *'Auf Weinerschnitzel.'*"

"*THAT'S* what he said?" McKinnagh's voice raised an octave and he tapped his notebook with his new Reynolds ballpoint pen. The matron nodded.

"Ma'am, I don't think that word means what you think it means. It's not goodbye, it's some kind of German sausage or something."

"Well, I never." Mrs. Harris fiddled with the veil on her fascinator, and looked at the sergeant with narrowed eyes.

"The point is a real German would never say that. Which proves we're dealing with a couple of imposters. A couple of very dumb imposters at that," McKinnagh concluded.

"Oh yeah? Well, if they're not really Germans, where did they get that grand Mercedes, and why was Goering waiting for them back in the car?" piped up Mr. Dennison, who was rather annoyed at being relegated to the corner of his own office. He was pretending to be working on a big green linen-covered ledger with brown leather binding, all the while eavesdropping on the interviews.

A big fan of "Suspense" and other radio mystery shows, Dennison was secretly thrilled to have been on hand for a real, honest-to-goodness bank robbery. No one got hurt, and customers' money was safe thanks to Mr. Roosevelt's FDIC, so why shouldn't he enjoy it? Now at least he had a story to tell at Mrs. Dennison's cocktail parties. He should be able to play that one out for months of barbecue cocktail franks and gin rickeys.

"That's enough from the peanut gallery!" McKinnagh's annoyance showed in his voice. Truth was, he had no answers for those questions. He was stymied. "Just get me those figures on the robbers' take. Send a messenger. I'll be at the stationhouse." With that the sergeant gathered up his notes and his officers, and stormed out of the bank.

Later that night, down at Sully's, Sam was still exultant over their success. "We're rich, buddy!" he hissed to Pete. Louder, he shouted, "Beers on me, all around!"

"Pipe down, you idiot," Pete said under his breath. "One of these lugs gets wind of it and we're done for." He took a drag on his coffin nail.

"Why are you so generous all of a sudden? Six years you been coming here, never stood a round." Jack O'Sullivan, aka Sully, eyed Sam suspiciously while he pulled drafts for the guys at the bar.

"Oh, Sam found a sawbuck on the sidewalk down by Edward's Department Store this afternoon," Pete said, before Sam could open his mouth and mess things up further. "Now he thinks he's Rockefeller."

"Haha, yeah, you'd think he robbed a bank or something," chimed in somebody at the end of the bar. Sam got a coughing fit and sprayed beer out his nose.

"No seriously, did you see today's *Post-Standard?*" Jack threw the paper down on the bar. "They say a bunch of crooks dressed up like Nazis robbed Syracuse Savings."

Pete and Sam stared at the front-page headline.

"Best part of it is, the cops are stymied," Jack continued. "They haven't got a clue."

Pete nodded to Sam, who drank up and they headed for the door.

"Where are you guys going? Aren't you gonna buy us another round, Mr. Rockefeller?" called out the wise guy who spoke before.

Pete and Sam just waved and walked out.

"How could they vanish into thin air?" McKinnagh slammed his fist down on his desk. He'd tried everything. He put out an APB for Hitler's 1943 Mercedes, and all he got were crank phone calls from jurisdictions from the Pennsylvania border to Montreal, offering him everything from John Wilkes Booth's horse to Al Capone's 1928 Cadillac.

He had a police artist draw sketches of the suspects from eyewitness accounts. That yielded more mocking and still no leads.

The robbers wore big leather gloves, so no fingerprints. And prints of the soles of their boots showed them to be authentic German Army issue.

Worse yet, the stolen bills were unmarked and in small denominations, the way the factory workers cashing their paychecks—or rather the wives they brought the money home to—liked them.

The only physical evidence somewhere out there was a simple canvas money bag, with Syracuse Savings Bank imprinted on it, that one of the tellers had shoved, full of cash, into the chauffer's duffel bag. Needless to say, it hadn't shown up either.

October, November, December, January. Autumn in Syracuse gave way to winter. Fierce lake effect snow storms and the car accidents that went with them kept the cops busy.

McKinnagh was counting the days to retirement. He just didn't want to have to turn in his badge with that robbery unsolved.

On February 4, a man with a French accent walked into the police station and reported a missing car. A representative of the French Victoire war relief effort, he told the oddest tale.

Back in July, he told the desk sergeant, his group had brought a very special car over from France for a display at the Turner Brothers' showroom on West Genesee Street. It was a 1943 Mercedes once owned by Adolph Hitler.

He explained that the group had used it to raise money for French war orphans, and the campaign was a great success. They raised $800 in Syracuse alone. However, they didn't have another show lined up and so put the car and three wax dummies representing Hitler, his chauffer and Hermann Goering into storage at a local warehouse. And promptly forgot where the warehouse was.

"*Alors,* it is ze mystery, *ne c'est pas?*" he asked with a typical Gallic shrug. "We have a new city to go to now, but no car. Can you help us find it?"

As soon as he heard the words Hitler's Mercedes, the desk sergeant called McKinnagh and asked him to come right down.

McKinnagh listened while the Frenchman recounted his tale once again. "It is very valuable, *Monsieur,*" he lamented to McKinnagh. "Zat car is worth thirty-eight thousand of your dollars and the figures, also many thousands. That model of Hitler was perfect, from the peak of his cap down to his authentic German boots."

"Where did you say you stored it?" McKinnagh asked the Frenchman.

"*Merde,* I cannot remember, your words are so odd. Someplace with a name like a river. Danube? Rhine?"

McKinnagh slapped his forehead. "Ryan's, that got to be it! I can't believe no one's come looking for that car before now." He commandeered a patrol car, and he and the Frenchman headed to Ryan's Warehouse.

***

Mr. Ryan couldn't believe it either, and he pulled out an invoice, demanding payment of $200 in storage fees and proof that the Frenchman was the rightful owner before he'd let the valuable car go.

Meantime, McKinnagh and his men prepared to search the vehicle for clues. They didn't have to look far.

Neatly folded on the passenger seat was a plain canvas bag with Syracuse Savings Bank printed in black ink. Pinned to it was a note that read, "Changed the oil and gave her a tune-up. Polished her all up nice. Thanks for the loan of the car. *Auf Wienerschnitzel!*"

***

The next day, the *Post-Standard,* carrying a banner headline that read, "Hitler Car Tied to Bank Robbery Found in Local Warehouse. Cops Say It Was Perfect Crime," sailed through the open garage door of Pete's Motors on the West Side of town. The owner rubbed his shoulder as he put down his wrench, picked up the paper, and grinned.

Agent Provocateur
by Michael Allan Mallory

Elliot Crandall had one of those faces. Nobody ever noticed him. Even old friends sometimes walked by him on the street without a second glance.

Until today.

Elliott sat on a park bench along the Tidal Basin Loop Trail opposite the Jefferson Memorial, enjoying the summer sun and an egg salad sandwich. A long stream of tourists walked nearby. Lifting his eyes from the Alistair MacLean paperback, he saw her. A beautiful woman was looking at him from the sidewalk. More than looking. Staring. She was young and sleek, with long lustrous hair the color of mahogany and a face that could have graced the cover of *Cosmopolitan*. From her body posture she'd been walking along the sidewalk and had stopped dead in her tracks. Sightseers out for a stroll had to walk around her. Exquisite dark eyes regarded him as if he were a marvel of nature. Reflexively, Elliott glanced behind him, certain her attention was directed at someone else. There was no one else. It was him! He checked his shirt, wondering if he'd spilled egg salad on it. That wasn't it. Did he know her? Not that he recalled. Confused, he returned a timid smile for a few seconds before returning to his thriller. Seconds later, he couldn't resist. He had to look. She was gone.

He sighed with disappointment. From nearby, a tinny pocket transistor radio played "Johnny Angel." The corner of his mouth pulled back dreamily. Maybe one day he'd be someone's angel. He glanced at his Timex, saw he had half an hour left and returned to his book.

A minute later he was interrupted by a honeyed voice.

"Hello."

Elliot looked up.

Oh, my god! It was her.

"Sorry to bother you. Is this seat taken?"

For an awkward instant he forgot how to work his vocal chords. "Please," he managed to croak out, dearly hoping he wasn't embarrassing himself in front of her. Elliot drew in a deep breath as he cleared away his lunch bag and wrappers.

With an easy grace the young woman lowered herself onto the bench. The ends of her dark hair flipped up at her shoulders like Jackie Kennedy's. "Lovely day, isn't it?"

It was! And getting better every second. She was even lovelier up close, with soft, regular features, an impudent nose and vibrant dark eyes he felt in danger of falling into. "A beautiful day," he grinned. "The sun's warm and there's no humidity. Pretty good for August."

She nodded at the Jefferson Memorial across the gleaming water. "I love how the sun shines off the stone. So peaceful and picturesque don't you think?" Then back to him. "Do you come here often?"

"Almost every day in summer. Either here or the National Mall. For lunch."

Shapely eyebrows quirked beneath dark bangs. "You must work nearby."

"Good guess. At the Museum of Natural History over there."

"Oh, what d'you do?"

"I'm a scientific assistant in the invertebrate zoology department. I work with the specimens. Packing and unpacking, getting them ready for exhibit. Stuff like that. And you?"

Nice work, Elliot. Keep her talking.

Making small talk with strangers was never easy for him. Oddly, with her it almost came naturally. This woman put him at ease, had a way of listening to him like it really mattered.

"I have a government job," she said. "Another transplant who came to work in DC. Are you a native?"

His narrow shoulders gave a slight shrug. "I'm from Duluth originally. Moved to DC two years ago"—Elliot smirked with a note of pride—"about the same time JFK took office. We started around the same time."

They sat in silence for half a minute when she turned to him. "What's your name?"

A flush of warmth. *How nice she asked.* "Elliot Crandall."

"Susan Miller. May I call you Elliot?"

"Please do."

She moistened her lips and took a preparatory breath. Something was on her mind. "You saw me looking at you earlier. I apologize for staring. The thing is you look like someone I know. In fact, I thought for sure you were him—and that was impossible. That's why I had to come over."

"A friend of yours?" he asked, deflated as the real reason for her visit became apparent. Silly of him to think she might have any other objective.

Susan elaborated. "I work for the State Department. I'm Agent Susan Miller." From her handbag she produced a laminated ID badge. She took a great photograph. No surprise. "What I'm going to ask you is highly irregular. The State Department does not usually involve private citizens in active missions but we're under a deadline and, to be honest, we've run out of options."

His scalp pricked at the phrase 'does not usually involve private citizens.' It was plain now her interest in him had to do with her job. Why else would a woman like her be drawn to him?

Agent Miller moved closer and he became aware of the scent of lilacs. Before continuing, she glanced warily around her. "Dr. Manfred Auerbach is a visiting diplomat from West Germany. He's worked closely with NATO on a new arms treaty with the Soviet Union. You could say he's the main architect of the treaty. A very important player. In fact, he was at the White House two days ago."

Elliot sat up with interest.

She inched closer. Elliot was keenly aware of her proximity. "Dr. Auerbach was kidnapped by KGB operatives yesterday. The Soviets are trying to scuttle the talks."

"Sounds serious. Why are you telling me this?"

Her eyes locked onto his. "Elliot, you look like Auerbach."

"Excuse me?"

"You're almost a dead ringer. I swear, when I first saw you I couldn't believe it. The FBI and Secret Service are frantically scouring the eastern seaboard for him, thinking him a prisoner in a dark cellar and I see him leisurely sunning himself in a park eating a sandwich!" Agent Miller tilted her head to side and smiled at him beguilingly. Long strands of her hair fell across her eyes in peek-a-boo fashion.

Elliot was at a loss.

Seeing his discomfort, she rushed to explain. "The longer I looked at you the more differences I saw, in your face and hair. That was under bright daylight. In evening light the differences wouldn't be as noticeable."

Evening light? What did that mean? A pang of dread wriggled in his gut. He didn't like the direction the conversation was headed. His face must have betrayed his feelings. Susan Miller reached out and took his hand.

"Please hear me out," she pleaded with a sense of urgency. "We've narrowed Auerbach's location to six possibilities. The Soviets tend to use the same safe houses. We hope a special assault team can rescue him before the talks. However, that can only be done if we can pinpoint where he's being held."

"Sounds like a challenge. Good luck."

"I was hoping you could help us with that."

"Me? How?"

Susan Miller spoke her next words with care. "There's an informal diplomatic function before the talks. Call it a low key cocktail party, a kind of get-to-know-you event. The West German ambassador will be there, so will the Soviets. Dr. Auerbach is supposed to attend with the rest of the West Germans—except he can't because the Soviets have him. Imagine their shock if Auerbach actually made it. They'll have to verify he's still their prisoner. Someone will be sent to find out. We'll have phone taps and licensing devices in place. That's when we hope to learn where Auerbach's being held."

The realization hit Elliot like a sledge hammer. "You want me to impersonate this guy, don't you?"

"Yes."

"I-I can't do that!"

"It's asking a lot, I know."

"This is crazy. You want me to attend a diplomatic party and pretend to be a man I've never met. I'll never pull it off."

Her lovely face radiated confidence. "Yes, you can, Elliot. You can do it for ten minutes. That's all I'm asking. Ten minutes."

"Just ten minutes?"

"And you don't have to say a word to anyone. Ten minutes and we'll leave, just long enough for the KGB to see you. Oh, and I'll be with you the whole time."

Elliot blinked.

She'd be with him the whole time? Appealing as that was, his misgivings reared up like a cornered rat. "I don't know. What if something goes wrong?"

"We won't be alone," Agent Miller emphasized. "We'll have agents from multiple agencies present. Armed agents. They'll always be close by." Still holding his hand, she pressed firmer. "I won't let anything happen to you, Elliot. I'm very good at what I do."

He didn't know what to say. The warmth of her skin was exhilarating. Gave him confidence.

"And," she stressed, "the reception will be in a public place. No one would dare do anything. Ten minutes, remember. By the time the KGB sees you and wonders what's going on, we'll be gone."

In spite of her assurances, one thing still bothered him. "You figured out I wasn't Auerbach. Won't they?"

Agent Miller released his hand and studied him like an artist appraising a blank canvas. "A little work with your hair, a touch of makeup, a new suit, a few lessons in protocol and you'll fool anyone for a few minutes."

"I suppose…"

"And there's only one man we need to fool: Anatoly Krenko. That's the KGB officer I was telling you about. His men are holding Auerbach. Krenko will be at the reception."

It was a lot to take in. Elliott leaned back against the bench. His eyes drifted to the tourists enjoying the sights. His attention was drawn to a pair of teenaged girls. One dressed in a white pullover and capri pants spoke animatedly to her blonde friend in cotton pedal pushers. They laughed together at some private joke. Elliot envied how carefree the girls were. Well within their comfort zone. He was miles outside of his. What Agent Miller was asking him to do was potentially dangerous. The thought of helping her, of spending more time with her, was the only reason he was even considering it.

"Suppose I agree to this," he ventured. "When would it be?"

"Tonight."

"*Tonight!*" Elliot glared back in horror. "That's too soon."

"It has to be tonight. The treaty talks start tomorrow. After tonight Auerbach's life may be forfeit—or he'll be flown away to some Soviet gulag."

He exhaled a ragged breath and looked at her with woeful eyes.

Her voice filled with emotion. "I know it's asking a lot. I wouldn't ask if I thought you'd be in any danger. You can do this. *Please?*"

On the verge of hyper-ventilating, he calmed himself. "Is there enough time? I have to get back to work in a few minutes. We have to prepare—"

"There's time," she insisted. "You won't go back to work. We'll spend the afternoon getting you ready. My supervisor will call your manager and will explain that you're helping the State Department on a special assignment for one day. He's got the weight of the United States government behind him. Don't worry, you won't get into any trouble."

Elliot shook his head in awe. "You've thought of everything."

Hope glimmered in Susan Miller's face. "Does that mean you'll do it?

The words, when they came out, surprised even him. "Yes, I'll do it."

The grandeur of the Windsor Marriot Grand Ballroom turned Elliot's legs into rubber. A lavish oriental carpet, intricate hand-woven wall hangings, embossed gold-leaf cove moldings, and banks of sparkling chandeliers spoke of riches and prominence. Even after special grooming and a new tailored suit, he was painfully aware how out of place he was. The same couldn't be said of Susan Miller, who most definitely blended in with the sumptuous surroundings. She looked like a million dollars in a simple black dress. Stepping into the ballroom with her was a surreal experience, like walking on stage with a cast of famous players he'd seen on television or in newspapers: senators, congressmen, diplomats, military leaders, even heads of major corporations. Movers and shakers schmoozing with easy familiarity. All of it intimidating. Elliot's confidence wilted like fresh spinach in a frying pan.

Agent Miller, whose hand rested on the sleeve of his new pin-striped jacket, felt the reluctance. "Elliot?"

"I'm all right." He mustered a wan smile.

"Hang in there."

"I'll mess this up, I know it."

"You won't. I have faith in you." Her voiced soothed, her fingers on his sleeve assured. "After your makeover and that new suit you look so much like Dr. Auerbach even I'd have to get really close to see the difference."

She made it sound so easy. He needed that. "Thanks."

"Remember," she added, "ten minutes."

He nodded. Though ten minutes couldn't pass quickly enough.

As they stepped further into the ballroom, Agent Miller surreptitiously pointed out two men among a group of people whom she indicated were Secret Service agents there to watch over him. In the confusion of meandering party guests, he didn't catch which two men they were. All men in the room were dressed in dark suits with crisp white shirts. No matter. Just knowing they were there eased frayed nerves.

This way," she said above the chatter of partiers, guiding him to the appetizer table. Afterward, with plates and beverages in hand, they migrated to a clearing well away from the others. "The point of these things is to mingle and meet people, but we're keeping our distance." A grateful Elliot was happy to focus on nothing other than crab cakes and salmon canapés.

The respite was not to last. From the direction of the bar ambled a portly man with horned-rimmed eyeglasses and a jovial face. Round and bursting with purpose, he sailed toward them like a tug boat at full steam. Elliot's initial alarm faded as he recognized the West German ambassador from the photograph in Agent Miller's briefing earlier.

"Good evening!" Gerhard Schaumberg spoke with a mild accent and too much enthusiasm. After a quick inspection of Elliot, he took a long sip of his cocktail. Then to Agent Miller, "You were right, he looks remarkably like Manfred. I'd swear it was him. I'll see what I can do. *Auf Wiedersehen.*" Schaumberg raised his glass in salute and moved to intercept a group of men and women showing interest in joining them.

"United Nations delegates," Susan Miller said out of the corner of her mouth. "Schaumberg's telling them you have a sore throat and are saving your voice for the talks."

Elliot was grateful for Schaumberg's intervention, happy for anything that kept strangers away. He was barely holding it together. On a nearby table, he set aside his empty *hors d'oeuvres* saucer and glass, looked up to determine where it was safest to stand and froze.

He was being watched by a pair of the most openly hostile eyes he had ever seen.

Seventy feet away a well-built, silver blond man eyed him with the disapproving scowl of a Kremlin politburo minister. Seconds later he called over an associate who was visibly shaken to see Elliot.

The mother of all heartburns seized Elliot but he found his sea legs and willed them forward to rejoin Agent Miller. He leaned in confidentially. "Two men are staring at me."

"Where? Don't look. Tell me."

"Behind you, towards the wall near the flower arrangement."

Pretending amusement at some witticism he'd made, Susan Miller knelt to the floor and adjusted the strap of her shoe. She stole a glance to the side before straightening up. "The blond is Krenko, the KGB man I told you about." She smoothed back her hair. "The man we want to see you."

"Mission accomplished, I'd say." Elliot didn't like Krenko's looks. He had heard stories of the KGB's oppressive methods and Krenko had the look of man capable of that: the judgmental stare, the commanding posture. Elliot felt naked before him, as if the word FRAUD was tattooed across his forehead. He tried not to stare back but the compulsion to look was too difficult to ignore. Krenko and the man next to him, a brutish thug with a crooked nose, were clearly discussing Elliot.

"Agent Miller, I think it's safe to say Krenko knows I'm here. Don't you think it's time we left?"

No one answered.

Concerned, Elliot shifted. No Agent Miller. She was no longer standing next to him.

He wheeled about.

She was nowhere to be seen. Gone! He anxiously searched the attendees in hopes of finding her at a serving table. No luck. Then he was struck by a terrible thought: had the Soviet's taken her? Was he next? Damned if he'd stand around to find out. Elliot looked for the nearest exit and made fast tracks toward it.

As he got near the portal his way was blocked by a big man with dark brown hair slicked back with a little more than a dab of Brylcreem.

Then a hand clamped down on his shoulder.

Krenko!

"Don't make a scene." The KGB man spoke in a low, threatening tone. "No one needs to get hurt."

Elliot, heart in throat, nodded once. To his dismay no one seemed to care when he was escorted out of the ballroom. Anxious eyes scanned for the Secret Service men who were supposed to be looking out for him. Before he could protest, Elliot was ushered into the back seat of a Ford Fairlane and whisked off across town to an imposing building and deposited unceremoniously into a small conference room. Two men, the same two associates he'd seen with Krenko earlier, took positions by the door with their arms crossed. Elliot sat meekly in an uncomfortable wooden chair. The blond-haired Krenko sat opposite. He leaned forward, resting imposing forearms on the desk. "The game's up. Why don't you make it easy on all of us and tell me the name of your target?"

"Target? What target?"

"Answer the question. Who's your target?" Krenko glared back daggers.

Elliot swallowed. "I don't know what you're talking about. Listen, you're making a big mistake. I'm not who you think I am. My name is Elliot Crandall. I'm an American citizen." This last was added for whatever it was worth, although it occurred to him that Soviet agents ruthless enough to abduct a West German diplomat in the heart of the U.S. capital might not care much about his constitutional rights.

A hint of uncertainty appeared in Krenko's face. The moment passed. "Mister Crandall is it?"

"That's right. I know I look like Dr. Auerbach but I'm not him. You've got the wrong guy."

"Auerbach?"

"Yes, Manfred Auerbach."

Krenko drew a blank and turned to his confederates who both shook their heads. "Who's Dr. Auerbach?"

"What's with you guys? Don't you know the name of the people you kidnap?"

Krenko eyed him as if he were speaking gibberish.

"You've make a mistake," Elliot persisted. "You've got me mixed up with someone else. I'm a nobody. I only came to the reception as a favor."

Krenko's gaze narrowed on him sharply. "You just happened to come to a diplomatic reception on the arm of a Soviet agent?"

Elliot blinked.

Soviet agent? What was he talking about? And come to think of it, why was Krenko speaking perfect English without a trace of a Russian accent?

Elliot couldn't take it anymore. "Who are you guys?"

Doubt, real doubt, appeared on Krenko's face for the first time. He scrutinized the man across the desk. After a moment, he slumped back. "This isn't Vasilev."

At the door, the man with the crooked nose seemed confused. "Whaddaya mean? He's gotta be Vasilev."

Krenko shook his head. "I tell you it's not him. Looks like him but it's not him."

Elliot couldn't take it anymore. "Vasilev? Who's Vasilev? And what does he have to do with anything?"

"Vasilev's the reason we're interested in you," answered the blond-haired man on the other side of the desk. "Yure Vasilev is a hired assassin."

"Assassin? You think I'm an assassin? Jesus!"

A mirthless laugh was his answer. "Listen to him, Talbot, does he sound Ukranian? This isn't our guy. I'm Special Agent Gary Nash, FBI. Behind me are agents Talbot and Severson." Nash showed him his identification.

"FBI? The American FBI?" Elliot stared back.

"Yes, Mr. Crandall, the American FBI."

Emotions flooded him. Elliot was relieved he wasn't going to be hustled off to a Soviet gulag. Or murdered. Glad he was safe. *He was safe, wasn't he?* "Wait, how do I know what you're telling me is true? Agent Miller told me you were KGB."

"Agent Miller? Who's Agent Miller?"

"Susan Miller of the U.S. State Department. The woman I was with."

"That's what she told you her name was?" Nash smiled in admiration. "Her real name is Elena Petrova. She's a high level operative of the SVR, the Russian foreign intelligence service."

"Russian foreign intelligence? And you're FBI? Maybe you are, maybe you aren't. Why should I believe you?" Elliot threw up his hands. "I don't know what to believe anymore!" Words alone were meaningless, so were ID badges; he needed proof. Concrete proof.

"I understand," agreed the other.

It didn't take much effort to convince Elliot that Special Agent Nash was who he claimed to be: a brief tour of the FBI building, seeing politicians he recognized walking the halls, a well placed phone call. His resistance caved under the preponderance of evidence. After they returned to Nash's office, a visibly shaken Elliot slumped into a chair.

A far less confrontational Nash regarded him now. "Mr. Crandall, I believe you're who you say you are. You check out."

"You already had me checked out?"

"We *are* the FBI." He slid a thick manila folder toward him. "Open it."

Elliot peeled back the cover and let out a faint gasp. The face of his father looked back at him from a black and white photograph. Not his father, he realized after a second, though an uncanny likeness of how his father had looked as a young man, a face eerily similar to his.

"That's Yure Vasilev," Nash explained.

Unsettling as this was, Elliot's eye was drawn to an image on the other page, a candid photo of the woman he'd known as Susan Miller walking along a busy sidewalk. Real name Elena Petrova, Russian spy. The realization was a punch to the chest. She'd used him. He felt mortified. Elliot sank deeper into his chair and lifted his eyes to Nash. "You must think I'm pretty gullible."

"Don't beat yourself up too much, Mr. Crandall. You weren't the only one fooled. How did you meet Miss Petrova?"

Holding back nothing, Elliot told the story of how he'd been recruited by Agent Susan Miller, his makeover and the plan afterward.

Impressed, Nash leaned back with a shake of his head. "And she said you were impersonating a West German diplomat named Auerbach and that I was a KDB officer named Krenko?"

"Right."

"Wow, she *is* good." Nash cleared his throat. "By the way, the West German ambassador who came up to you at the reception, Schaumberg, is in reality a senior communist party bureaucrat from the *East* German delegation."

Elliot hung his head. Things just kept getting worse and worse. He looked up. "I'd never've guessed she was Russian. Her English was flawless."

"That's because she grew up and was educated in the West," Nash explained. "We became aware of her a few months ago. She keeps a low profile. It was only last week we intercepted a Telex about her. The message linked her with Vasilev, who we knew was in the country to take out an unknown high level target." Nash drummed his fingers on the desk. "In time we learned Vasilev was in the DC area. We managed to obtain a photograph of him taken a few years back in Yugoslavia. I was at the reception to keep my eye on Schaumberg, whom we suspected was a contact for Vasilev."

"Then I showed up," Elliot said with bitter frankness.

Nash gave a fatalistic wave of his hand. "Yes you did. Seeing Vasilev—or who I thought was Vasilev—at the reception pulled the rug out from under us. While we scrambled to figure out what was going on the real Vasilev managed to slip away."

There was no accusation in the way Special Agent Nash addressed him, no rancor or implication of any wrong doing, yet Elliot couldn't help feel culpable for his part in the deception. He held out hope for one thing "You'll find Vasilev, right?"

Nash shrugged. "Hard to say. We aren't giving up. But he also has a network of people helping him. You were lucky, Mr. Crandall," Nash inflected grimly. "You got mixed up with some dangerous characters. Things could have turned out differently for you. And not in a good way."

<hr>

After his release from the FBI, Elliot went home, returned to work the next day and tried to get on with his life. It took a while for him to adjust. For the first few weeks he paid attention to news events. No assassinations were reported, nor any other high-profile deaths.

Time moved on. Summer was fading, so he went back to his bench by the Tidal Basin walk to enjoy a few last days of lunch in the sun. On a Tuesday in late August, while reading the latest issue of Scientific American, approaching footsteps caught his ear. Elliot looked up. A young boy was walking toward him. Ten or thereabouts, with curly hair and chubby cheeks. Striped T-shirt, dungarees, and red Keds High-Top sneakers.

"I'm supposed to give you this." A small hand held out a folded paper.

Elliot took it. "What is this?" he asked.

"I dunno. A lady paid me five dollars to give it to you."

Having done his task, the boy turned about and trotted back to his friends on the walkway. Elliot unfolded the paper. In a flowing feminine hand were the words:

I'm glad to see you still come to the bench. I was hoping you would. Sorry if I got you in trouble.

Below the script was faint impression made with pink lip-stick.

His eyes flicked up and searched the mall greenspace. Too many sightseers walking in every direction, a jumble of shapes and movement. Elena Petrova had disappeared among them. Awash in emotions—chagrin, anger, sadness—he looked again at the note that rubbed the whole embarrassing situation in his face. Better to rip the thing up—

He hesitated.

He couldn't do it. Couldn't destroy her note. Eyeing the graceful handwriting, he read the words one more time. Was it meant as an apology? Perhaps he'd been more to the Russian spy than simply a disposable object; he liked to think he'd made a connection with her, however fleeting. She could have done nothing. Instead, she went out of her way to leave him this message. Didn't that mean something? Or was he reading too much into the gesture?

With a wistful sigh, Elliot folded the note and carefully tucked it into his pocket. He took a bite of his sandwich and gazed out beyond the tourists into the distance clouds.

Back we head into the dusty gloom of a PI's office, where a rare blooming of an odiferous plant plays a part in murder.

The Corpse Flower
by Adam Beau McFarlane

It was the late morning of Wednesday, July 18. A cool breeze through the blue sky cut the sunny summer heat. I sat in my office, wondering if it was too early to get zozzled on bottled corn mash. From the sidewalk below, smells of the roasted cinnamon almonds cart wafted through my open window. A yachtsman painted on the side of a brick building across the street was enjoying his cigarette, and I almost believed him.

The knock at the door was light: three gentle raps. An amorphous blob appeared at the pebbled glass.

"It's open," I hollered.

For a full-grown woman, she was short. Her skin was so pale that traces of blue vein were visible. Her pixie haircut was white-blonde, her indigo skirt was pleated, and she wore a teal cardigan over a polka-dotted blouse. Spectacles magnified her periwinkle eyes.

"C'mon in. Take a seat." I didn't have a secretary. Answering my own phone and poking the typewriter keys myself, I charged more by the hour than if I had a secretary do it. Plus, no overhead. The fact that every secretary I'd ever hired had slapped me and quit was beside the point.

She sat and looked down at a small stack of notecards. "I'm a circulation librarian, second class, for the Southeast Branch Library." Her voice was high and tiny.

I should spend more time at the library. Most of what I learned came from the evening newspaper or the television in the display window at Gilbert's Department Store.

"Joe Smith. But you knew that already." I offered a smile.

Her hands trembled. She flipped the top card to the back and read the next one. "My responsibilities include new patrons, overdue books, and fines."

Before she started another card, I said, "What's your name, miss?"

Breaking her concentration caused her to fumble with the cards, nearly spilling them onto the floor. "Uh, sorry. It's Margaret. I mean, Miss Martin. You can call me Margaret, though."

She needed a jigger of juniper juice to calm down. "Can I get you some water?" I asked.

She shook her head.

"Just relax and don't worry about your notes. Let's begin with the man, the woman, or the money; my work usually starts there."

She looked down, folded her hands, and took a deep breath. "There is a man—Richard Lee—who has three books overdue for one month. All checked out on the same day."

Overdue books? I got mystified.

Digging in her purse, she pulled out three library checkout cards. She dealt them on my desk. Each had a loopy signature and May 29 stamped as its most recent entry.

"When we send overdue notices, I wouldn't normally notice this. But all three cards were together in the day's stack, coincidentally. And I couldn't help it if I read the patron and title on each one." She shrugged. "Professional curiosity, I suppose."

The titles at the top of the cards were: *Encyclopedia of Poisons*; *True Crime*, volume 5: *Unsolved Cases*; and *Ending it All, the Suicide Option*.

"At our last staff meeting, I presented this. Intervening in a patron's use of materials? That violates our ethics code. But, based on the privileged information we have, we can hire a third party to check on his health and safety."

"Those books taught him how to make an 'end of life decision'?"

Using her forefinger and thumb, she tweezed a twenty-dollar bill and a phone number from her purse, then laid them on the desk.

I asked, "Twenty bucks, just to call him up?"

"Twenty dollars to verify that our materials didn't cause harm," she said. "Please."

I don't like taking money from little young ladies, but I figured it wasn't her money. It was taxes. I screwed everybody. Spread out over each taxpayer in the city though, it was just a little.

I picked up the phone. "Operator? I'd like to place a call to ROscommon six, one nine six one."

It rang.

It rang again.

I watched her watching me.

It rang a third time.

I hung up and said, "Okay, Margaret. Maybe I should see if he's home."

She pinched another twenty out from her purse, and she discarded it atop the first one. "Will this cover enough to continue? You can send an invoice for the rest."

The way she handed over money, I should've been a librarian. "You know where this guy lives?"

She extracted a notecard from her deck and trumped the two twenties. "This is the address I mailed his overdue notices to. It's also in the phone book. I cross-referenced; we keep phone books next to the foreign language section."

Since it was in Roscommon, I could stop on my way to the Fast Foto for a roll from last week's creep-n-peep case.

"My standard contract," I said, pulling open the file cabinet and taking out a blank copy. "You'll probably want your library kin to look it over before you sign it."

"Thank you."

"How do I reach you?" I was casting, hoping for a nibble. Maybe I could add some color to those cheeks.

Without so much as a blink, she said, "You can leave a message with the front desk. I work the day shift, Tuesdays to Saturdays."

"And when your shift gets done...?" I trolled my line through the water.

She paused for a moment. "On Saturdays, I take the K train home. Otherwise, it's the five o'clock express."

"Then you should expect a message at the front desk tomorrow."

I was a lousy fisherman, anyway.

Roscommon was an Irish neighborhood in The City That Never Snores, and it had the church and pubs to prove it. Lee's address was a two-story apartment building. With no parking lot available, I stopped along the sidewalk and strolled leisurely toward the lobby. It was a beautiful day to get paid by the hour.

Little Teddy Tucker chased his blues away at full volume from a unit inside. The lobby was so dusty, I could nearly taste it. The building superintendent stood on a stepladder, and he balanced a toolbox at its apex. He monkeyed with the light fixture. His eyes and brows were dark. He looked ethnic—not Italian, Mex, or Eastern European, necessarily. Just ethnic.

"I'm here for the delivery?" I asked.

"Yeah?" he said.

"Yeah."

He looked at me.

I waited.

"What delivery?"

"The one I'm supposed to pick up."

"From who?"

I pulled a random receipt from the bottom of my pocket, uncrinkled it, and pretended to read. "Richard Lee?"

"He didn't leave nothing with me. You have to talk to him. Second floor, first door on the left."

I went up the stairs and knocked on the door. Down the hall, Teddy Tucker sang the chorus and another verse. I twisted the doorknob: locked. If this was night time, if the case was going to trial, and if the client wasn't so gosh-darn innocent-looking, I'd have picked the lock. Instead, I went back to the super.

"No answer," I said.

"Why do I care?"

"Look, you're the one who told me where his apartment is."

"So?"

"So, I did. And he wasn't there."

"You want I should let you in?"

"Nope."

"Okay." He started rummaging through his toolbox.

I stood there, waiting.

He tossed a screwdriver down. "I'm gonna unlock the door for you. Then you get your package and get outta here, right?"

"Not my package," I said. "I'm just here to pick it up."

Grunting, he clambered down to the carpet and led me back up to Lee's door. He unlocked it.

"Mister Lee?" I said as I stepped through.

It was a studio, and no wall was bare, thanks to the door, a television, a refrigerator, and a bed. The Northware icebox—streamlined and trimmed in chrome for the Jet Age—and a plywood-clad television were costly luxuries, I guessed, between the electricity bill and his installment payments.

The corners of his emperor-sized bed were trimmed and tucked in. Even the white grout between the pink tiles in the kitchenette looked scrubbed. It was smaller than a submarine. But it was as clean as a detergent commercial.

"I don't see no package," the super said.

"Say, what's the big idea? You trying to pull a fast one on me, mister?" I feigned suspicion.

"What do you mean?"

"There is no package—you said so yourself."

No noose hung from the ceiling, no acids filled the sink, and not even a suicide note was smeared in blood on the wallpaper. Richard Lee might not make *True Crime*, volume six.

"It's gotta be around here somewhere," he said. "Start looking."

I should have been a burglar.

Beside a bunch of bananas, an empty white wine bottle rested on the counter. The bananas were yellow and speckled: soft but not overripe. A Monday newspaper from July 16—two days ago—was folded into the trashcan.

"What if it's something that's got to be kept cold?" I asked.

He scratched the fuzzy laurel of hair. "You mean the refrigerator? I don't know…"

But he opened it anyway. Inside was a bottle of milk, a can of Bavarian hopwater, and a cut of meat wrapped in a butcher's white paper.

I grabbed the milk and side of meat, took a sniff of each, then put them back. Neither smelled funky.

The superintendent stared at me.

"Um, I'll go check his bathroom."

The bathroom smelled like hairspray and perfume. Only shaving cream and a razor rested at the sink. I returned to the main room.

The wasp in the ointment was the closet; its door was open and contents spilled out.

"Did he leave it in here?" I said, pushing aside empty hangers and remaining pieces of denim and leather. Lined up at the back were shoeboxes, some open, some closed. Inside the first shoebox was letters. Lots of letters. Arranged chronologically, they started as simple subscription forms to the Monthly Gardener Club. The stack developed into small cards, big cards, little notes, then folded stationery. Each contained notes of breathless love. The name written on the box's lid was Shirley Brown.

The next shoebox looked virtually identical—right down to heart doodles and lipstick kisses. The love letters matched, too.

I blew out a low whistle.

On that lid, the name was Betty Murphy. Mrs. Betty Murphy.

Richard Lee was a dastardly Don Juan.

Maybe it was easier to seduce other men's wives than get your own—you never needed to take them out for dinner or a movie or anywhere in public, and you didn't have to put up with them the day after, either.

Maybe I should have been a professional womanizer. I wonder if there's money in that.

An evening here, a lunch hour there opened up his schedule to autograph several dance cards. Fooling around was serious business. If Richard Lee was an opportunist, he made the most of every opportunity.

The other shoeboxes remained lidded. Counting them equaled five married lonelyhearts.

"Maybe he changed his mind about the package?" the superintendent said, pointing.

The row had an empty space like a missing tooth in a smile. Poking out from the coat dump, a shoebox looked like it had been crushed underfoot until it was flatter than a flapjack.

With only a hunch to go on, I drove to the address on the Monthly Gardener Club forms. I skipped the new four-laner and took the long way along Highway Nine—Sunrise Drive, as the locals called it. Eminent domain had cut shoreline away from the moneyed estates of Lake Isabella to create a picturesque thoroughfare. On one side, drivers saw the morning sun over misty waters. They ogled historic mansions across long lawns on the other. The rich still claimed it as lakefront property, and they enjoyed watching worker ants motor into the city while they sipped mimosas.

I followed a wagon train of pastel convertibles until they veered off toward real boats at the Enchanted Bay Marina. Nearby, the Griffin Botanical Gardens stood inside Grandmont Park. Hidden within, the only clue of its existence was a full parking lot at the edge of a manmade forest.

The conservatory was an enormous grid of steel beams and glass panes. A three-story solarium dominated side rooms decorated as classrooms and offices. Fountains, flower beds, and docents filled the main area. I'd never visited before, but I was surprised to see a crowd waiting to enter. They let people in every fifteen minutes. Once in, I followed the herd to a central stage featuring one plant and its botanist.

It was a beast of a plant: six feet tall with a flower larger than a basketball. The ugly bloom was pale green with a sickly yellow spike like a calla lily that stuck out like a phallic corn cob.

"Thank you for coming to see our corpse flower," the botanist said. "*Amorphophallus titanum*. We've had it for eight years, and this is its first blossom. Does it smell like rotten eggs in here? Does it?" He faked a frown and nodded to children in the audience. "That's the corpse flower, emitting a scent to attract insects. They're attracted to the smell of rotting corpses that it gives off—hence the name, corpse flower—then they carry its pollen and help it reproduce."

Maybe I should have been a botanist. Since I wasn't, I wandered to the atrium's edge where volunteers pointed toward bathrooms and watched for rough-housing kids. One stood beside a small tree—Siamese magnolia, according to a little sign. Its branches pushed out a cloud of pink petals over rows of iridescently blue Diana tulips.

"Looking for Richard Lee's office?" I asked.

"Technically, he doesn't have an office with us; he rents space. Let me show you." I followed her along the room's perimeter. With her khaki uniform and short, blonde bob, she was tomboyishly cute.

"Attendance to the botanical garden has really gone up since he started."

"Oh yeah?" Not knowing what to say, I just feigned interest.

"He also uses some of our other spaces." She nodded to a room as we walked by it. "Cooking classes for adults, scavenger hunts with little ones."

"Oh yeah?" I repeated.

"Who knew playing with dirt could be such good, clean fun?" She grinned.

I pretended to laugh but oversold it.

Her smile flipped, and she pointed to a door. "I'm sure you can manage the rest of the way."

Once I'd reached that door and opened it, I caught a fresh whiff of sulfur, more concentrated here, as if a juvenile delinquent had thrown a stink bomb.

Self-contained and enclosed in glass, his office was isolated. Yet, it looked integrated with the atrium and other offices. In addition to standard office tools—typewriter, Rolodex, flask, etc.—his desk kept packets of seeds. They filled the left drawer, and they were organized by seasons and months. The right drawer held blank order forms for Seventh Street Print & Letterpress. Each form had a template grid for page layout, plus blanks and boxes for total copies, color selection, font, etc.

Atop the desk's blotter, a ledger book was tattooed with income and expenses across various accounts. Richard Lee was sole proprietor of the Monthly Gardener Club. Annual membership got you seeds, a newsletter, and passes to horticulture events. He was clever with marketing and product diversification: group discounts for schools and garden societies, additional perks for a heftier membership fee, and cross-promotional advertising with the conservatory and its arboretum.

He did everything but celebrity endorsements and secret decoder rings.

I spun the Rolodex, then flipped through names randomly. Shirley Brown, Joyce Clark, Patricia Harris, Betty Murphy, Carol Taylor—

"Sweet John the Baptist," I whispered profanely.

In the corner with his legs spread wide, Richard Lee sat with his eyes closed. The room's rotten smell didn't come from the *amorphophallus titnum;* that plant only misled anyone who would have found him earlier.

If seeing a corpse flower was a once-in-a-life-time chance, then folks would have to wait for reincarnation. When the police came, they closed the conservatory and questioned every employee. The plant's blossom closed, wilted, and dropped before the solarium re-opened.

On Friday, July 20, I arrived at the Southeast Branch Library. Shops were closed for the lunch hour, and people lounged in an adjacent park. From the brickworks outside of town, cadet grey blocks of argile bleu clay were stacked into a squat rectangle striped by a row of windows.

If I were robbed, stabbed, or bamboozled, I wasn't likely to call the cops. But if I thought a killer should be in jail, I called Lieutenant William Davis. He was an ex-GI who had traded in his bayonet for a badge and a nightstick. The rubber soles of his suede deerskin shoes were silent. He kept his panama hat on inside, as if he were too important to stick around much longer.

I led him through a door marked "PRIVATE" into a dense honeycomb of desks. We trespassed into the librarians' inner sanctum. At various stages of innocence and spinsterhood, women sat at desks with ashtrays and stacks of books.

When I pointed at Margaret, she stood up and touched a heart-shaped pendant on her necklace. A burst of glitter was suspended inside it.

Davis glanced around the room; everyone stopped and stared at us. "Miss Martin, if you'll come with us; you're under arrest."

The boss librarian marched over to us. A long section of ash bent the tip of her cigarette. Her tightly-bunned hair was nearly as white as the string of pearls that laid over her fire hydrant-shaped physique. She stink-eyed us. It was as if the thought-police had come to burn her books. Whispering *sotto voce*, she said, "Who are you?"

Margaret Martin sat back down.

Davis pulled at his coat, showing a badge pinned to his vest. "Who are you?"

"Anderson, Barbara. Circulation librarian, first class."

"Margaret killed Richard Lee," I said.

"That's impossible," she said, breaking her stage whisper. "In fact, we hired a private eye to make sure he was alive and well."

"I'm the eye," I said. "And Richard Lee was, up until two nights ago. I found him dead at the Griffin Conservatory."

Eyes widening to half dollars, she sucked wind in horror.

Davis added, "Funny thing, poisons. They don't work like in the movies and kill you right away. Usually takes hours or even a day or two."

I said, "My guess is Margaret spent the night and brewed a mean—really mean—cup of coffee before he went off to work the next day."

"I don't understand," she said.

I turned to Margaret Martin. "You were his lover. His beautiful little rosebush, and he cultivated you like a blue-ribbon winner. Much to your surprise though, you weren't his only rose. He had a whole garden of other women, members of his subscription flower club. And when you found out, you busted up inside."

Start with flower gardeners. They were women, mostly. A lot of them weren't affair material. But they all mailed in birthdates and addresses on subscription forms. So recruiting promising candidates was easy. The Monthly Gardener Club wasn't just his job; it was his pastime, too. The six shoeboxes meant he'd had a harem of part-time mistresses.

I should have been a florist.

First-class circulation librarian Barbara Anderson shook her head as if that could clear her mind. "What about the overdue books? She came to us, asking to find him."

"It was a ruse," I said, looking at Margaret again. "You took the books yourself, forged his name on each of the three books' checkout cards, and backdated them with your stamp. That way, you killed him Monday morning, but it looks like he could have disappeared up to two months ago. Your checkout cards are stamped May 29. But May 29 was the last Monday in May. That's Memorial Day, a national holiday. The library was closed. He couldn't have checked out any books then; the date was faked."

Letting an awkward pause fill the air, Margaret's face was blank. "Am I supposed to say something? It didn't sound like a question."

"Not if you don't want to," Anderson said. "You have rights."

This case got me thinking about plants for months. You start with a seed. By its looks, you can't tell what it will grow into.

But somewhere in that little thing is all the information coded into microscopic instructions. Once you plant it—if it's in the right dirt and a certain amount of light—then a fruit or a flower will develop over time. Margaret Martin was a wildflower seed at first, and Richard Lee never realized she would grow into a full-bloomed maneater.

Handcuffed, Margaret Martin bowed her head and clasped her hands together as if in prayer.

"Richard Lee? *Dead?*" another librarian said, pulling her shawl tightly around her. She was as fresh-faced as a new graduate of librarian school, but she wore a wickedly experienced shade of lipstick. Like a monocle, a tear in her eye caught the light.

"Afraid so, Shirley Brown," Lieutenant Davis said, turning to read her desk nameplate.

Shoebox number one.

As we led her away, Margaret said to Barbara Anderson, "Will you water my plants while I'm gone? This month is carnations."

Back now to the gritty world of a struggling auto-repair shop on the north-side of Chicago in the late 1940s, and two brothers of color whose presence in a lily-white neighborhood is not welcome.

Ashes to Ashes, Dust to Dust

An Aaron Guerevich– Ann Berendt Mystery
by Mel Goldberg

The explosion at Nick and Sonny's gas station rattled windows for an entire block in the Scottsdale neighborhood. Fortunately, no one was at either of the regular or unleaded gasoline pumps when the blood-red billowing fireball erupted fifty feet into the afternoon sky. An eerie silence followed the eruption, as if the world had become momentarily mute.

Simultaneously, shopkeepers and homeowners scurried into the street from their buildings in a choreographed move. Then a few of the braver ran toward the little Sinclair Oil service station at the end of the block. Others moved tentatively, like dogs approaching a plastic bag flapping in the wind. In the distance, sirens wailed, and within minutes a police car skidded to a stop in the street.

Officer Wayne Williams exited his black and white Plymouth Concord and looked around. "This place is history, Dan." He crunched bits of broken glass underfoot and looked at what once was an aluminum overhang, now twisted, one end touching the driveway. As he took a few steps toward the burning building, he kicked aside bits of splintered wood.

Dan Siebens stood next to the car, radio in hand, the curly pigtail cord stretched from to the dash. "Dispatch. This is five-two-zero. Call Guerevich. Suspicious explosion at a service station. Mariposa and 85th. Possibly gasoline. Fire inside building. You copy?"

A female voice responded. "Affirmative five-two-zero. Will do. Ten-four."

Dan walked around the car and stood next to his partner. They could see fire through the doorway of the partially demolished building.

"Part of the roof's gone, Wayne."

A Maxim Pumper fire truck and a Rescue Response vehicle arrived. Four firemen, wearing hard helmets and dressed in blue uniforms, leaped from the truck and sprinted into the building. Two rescuers followed and waited outside the building. After a few minutes one of the firemen looked outside the doorway. He shouted that they had the fire was out, and signaled it was safe to enter.

"Careful," he cautioned as the officers and the rescuers approached. "These walls could come down."

They slowly ventured through the bent and twisted doorway into what was left of the building, kicking aside pieces of brick, wood, and glass. They shouted, more to discover survivors than to warn potential perpetrators.

Looking around the typical auto repair facility, they saw a large open room with two lift racks. In the back, a doorway in the cinderblock wall led to another room. Its door hung by one hinge. Shattered glass shards surrounded the window in the center of the rear wall. Along the bottom of the wall, thrown by the force of the explosion, rested a jumbled pile of bricks, fan belts, cables, and an assortment of tools, tires and rims. The metal garage door bowed out, like a sail in a strong wind, and both lift racks were down. Fragments of the metal roof covered part of the first rack. The wall next to the further lift rack bore streaks of black, like huge fingers pointing to the missing section of the roof.

The body of a man lay pinned under the rack, his badly charred head exposed. Above him on the rack was the smoldering wreck of a car, water dripping to the floor.

One firefighter walked toward them and pointed to the body under the rack. "No one's in this room except that poor guy."

As he spoke, a second fireman pushed the hanging door aside and peered in the back room. "Someone's back here in a wheelchair," he shouted as he entered the room.

The rescue men ran into the room, reappearing moments later, one pulling and the other pushing the wheelchair with an unconscious Negro man in it, blood oozing from the top of his head. The name *NICK* was sewn over the left breast pocket of his work coveralls. As they rushed him outside the building and started to examine him, he opened his eyes and flailed his arms.

"Who are you?" he shouted. "Leave me alone. Where's Sonny?"

A medic tried to calm him. "You took a bad hit to your head. You may have a concussion. We need to get you to the hospital."

"Ain't goin' to no hospital." He looked toward the sky and wailed. "Sonny." He emitted the name a second time, the sound softer, between a wail and a groan. " *Sonny.*"

After cutting a section of Nick's pants and squeezing his thigh to hold the muscle firmly, the other medic took out a syringe and injected Parafon Forte. Nick pushed the hand away. When they started to wheel Nick toward the ambulance, Siebens and Williams stopped them. "Who else was in the building?"

"Just me and my brother. Sonny. Working under a Pontiac on the rack."

Siebens looked at Nick and shook his head. "I'm sorry."

A moment after Siebens spoke, Nick closed his eyes. Tears streaked down the plaster dust on his cheeks and he wiped them away with his hands, giving his face a clown-like appearance.

"Lucky you were in the back from the looks of things," said Williams. "That cinder block wall probably saved your life."

The medics began pushing the wheelchair toward the ambulance again.

Nick started shouting and flailing his arms. Then he reached down and pushed the brakes. "No hospital, no hospital."

After arguing with Nick for a few minutes, the medics told the police officers that Nick refused treatment and transportation to the hospital. "You need to watch him." Then they drove away.

Officer Dan Siebens looked at the man in the wheelchair, folded his arms across his chest, and shook his head as he surveyed the wreckage of Nick and Sonny Johnson's two-pump gas station.

He turned to his partner. "Wayne, go see if you can get any statements from the crowd standing around gawking."

As he spoke, the two firemen returned to the truck and grabbed large prying tools to extricate the burned body from under the rack. A few minutes later, tires crunched to a stop on the asphalt outside and Detective Aaron Guerevich stepped out of his Ford Club Coupe, his suit jacket wrinkled and his tie loose.

Siebens turned around. "Hey, Aaron, what the hell took you so long?"

"Like I sit around waiting for you to call. Get any statements from the concerned citizenry?"

"Williams is doing that now."

"Who's that?" He pointed to a bagged body being wheeled out on a collapsible gurney.

"Not sure yet. Probably Sonny, the brother of Nick, the guy in the wheelchair."

Williams returned, notebook in hand. "Near as anyone can tell, there was an explosion that literally blew the roof off. Then the fireball. The station is owned by two brothers. Negroes. Nick and Sonny."

Guerevich looked toward Nick in the wheelchair, sitting alone crying. "Negroes?"

"Yeah. Only one guy really talked to me." He consulted his notebook. "Name's Edward Castle. Seemed kind of nervous. Said maybe they thought people wouldn't notice they were trying to pass because they had light skin. Said he knew there was going to be trouble and he stayed away from the station. Didn't want any "of them" working on his car. Then he said he didn't want to answer any more questions and walked away."

"Staying away is one thing," said Siebens. "Blowing up a place is another."

"What happened to the other brother?"

"The explosion likely blew out the hydraulics and the car came down on top of him. The fire roasted him pretty bad, but the medics said he was probably dead before the fire got him."

"Wasn't the safety bar set?" asked Guerevich.

"Don't know yet."

Guerevich really hated situations like this one. But more, he hated that he was sent because he was Jewish. "The department has a whole section for homicide crimes," he muttered to Siebens, "but you had to send for me."

"Awww," Siebens teased. "That's because you're such a nice guy."

Nick was staring emptily back at the ruined building when Guerevich walked toward him.

He was a big-chested man in a tight one-piece blue work uniform. The sleeves barely came to his wrists. His uniform was peppered in small fragments of splintered wood and white plaster dust, as if he had been baking bread. It clung to his kinky hair, flecks covered his cheeks behind his glasses, and lay in patches on his shoulders and on his lap. As Guerevich approached, Nick brushed his clothes, white dust falling in small clouds and collecting in the creases in his large work shoes. It fell to the ground around his wheelchair and swirled into abstract patterns in the oily surface.

Guerevich estimated that Nick would have been well over six feet tall standing and reached to help him. "I'm Detective Aaron Guerevich."

"I don't need no help to dust myself off." He spoke with a strong southern accent and shook his head. "I saw them take my brother away on a stretcher. To die like that ain't right." He pounded the arms of his wheelchair repeatedly as he spoke. "After all he been through. The war and the hatred. "

"The war? And what about the hatred?" asked Guerevich.

"World War II. Hatred in the army and hatred here. People in this community are hypocrites. My brother fought in Italy. Got a Purple Heart after he was wounded. I knowed it wa'n't a German bullet."

"Did you report it?"

"Yeah. But nothin' ever came of it. I thought people here'd be happy our gas and our labor was cheaper than ever'one else's. But they stayed away. We got hate mail and crosses spray painted on our windows. I hoped things would get better. And now this." He put his head down and covered his face with his hands, his elbows on the armrest of the wheelchair.

"I'm sorry that your brother died in such a horrible manner. It must anger you."

"It ain't anger. I'm past that. I'm sad now I'm gonna be alone. But he's with Jesus now."

"Any idea how this could have happened?"

""He had just completed a conversion from gasoline to propane. There must have been a leak. Maybe he dropped a tool and it sparked on the concrete. Or maybe something else."

"Wasn't he using brass tools?"

"All our brass tools was stolen a few weeks ago. We turned in a report, but we didn't expect the police to do anything. We ordered new ones."

"Well, the coroner will have do an autopsy, but the cause of death seems pretty clear.

"I want to go home. I got to make some phone calls to people and tell them what's happened. Got to make arrangements for Sonny's cremation."

"You really ought to go to the hospital. Just for evaluation, to make sure there's no serious problem."

"I ain't going to no hospital. I've had enough of hospitals in my life, and I don't need to go for a little bump on the head. After growin' up in Alabama, death don't mean too much. I've been in a chair since I was twelve, after I got hit by a car. Driven by a White woman. Nothin' ever came of that neither. We believed we was living on borrowed time anyway. God just gave him a shorter plan."

Nick took leather gloves from a pouch hanging behind the wheelchair and wheeled himself away from the building. One wheel struck a piece of wood that turned his chair slightly. Guerevich walked over, kicked away the stick, and Nick rolled toward his car, giving Guerevich a look of surprise.

"Thank you, but I really don't need no help. I managed by myself before you guys came along, and I gonna manage long after you is gone."

He removed one arm of his wheelchair and set in the carry bag on the back of his chair. The chair rolled backward a few inches until he reached down to set the hand brakes. He braced himself with one hand on the second arm of the wheelchair and his other hand on the seat of his car. Using only his arms, he pushed himself into his car. Then he reached out of the car door, removed the other chair arm, folded up the wheelchair, and slid it behind his seat. After the chair was in place, he picked up his legs and slid them into the car. Then he adjusted the seat and drove away.

Guerevich watched, a smile of admiration brushing his lips.

"Not as upset as you might think for someone whose brother was killed and his business destroyed," said Siebens.

Guerevich nodded. "Yeah. Strange that he didn't even ask to see the body."

"You think he was squeamish, especially since his brother was burned so badly?"

"I don't think it was squeamishness," said Williams. "I don't think he realizes it really happened.

Guerevich started walking toward the building. "I'm going to have Ann follow up on who wanted the conversion to propane. That seems odd. Williams, go to the house of that 'I-told-you-so' guy. See if you can get any more information from him, and ask him to come down to the station as a person of interest ."

Looking at the car lift, Guerevich observed that the safety bar was missing. He wrote down the license of the burned hulk. In the back office, behind the wall that saved Nick, Guerevich went through a small metal file cabinet and found the paperwork for the tank replacement. The invoice bore the name George Abbott.

That afternoon, Guerevich visited Ann at the forensics lab and told her about the explosion and Sonny, being crushed and burned under the car rack.

"Sounds pretty gruesome, and I'm used to gruesome," she said.

"Yeah. Do some research for me. Find out whatever you can about the Johnson brothers. When they bought the station, how they were doing financially. They had to have enemies, being Negroes owning a business in a White area."

"Sounds like you don't think it was just an accident."

"I don't think it was, and I intend to find out. There are too many odd coincidences. Like why'd Sonny decided to change a gas tank for a propane tank without brass tools? And why propane?"

"Not so strange. Chicago just outfitted a lot of busses to run on propane. Burns a lot cleaner than diesel."

"Maybe so. But why was the safety bar on the lift removed? Doesn't seem logical. By the way, here's the invoice on the conversion. See what you can find out about George Abbott."

He left the lab before Ann could protest. That evening, Guerevich went to his apartment and spent time reviewing his notes about the case. Although he and Ann had been together for four years, they kept their own places. It gave each a sense of independence, and sometimes he enjoyed being alone. He called her before he went to bed that night to ask her to meet him for breakfast. Then he stripped to his shorts, washed up, and stepped on the scale. He weighed himself twice a day, once in the evening and once in the morning, knowing his morning weight would be a few pounds lighted than his evening weight. He tried to keep his weight under two hundred twenty pounds.

Ann walked into the restaurant the next morning and dropped a folder on the table as he sat drinking coffee.

"This is it? One thin folder?"

"You think I work for you? There'll be more as soon as the coroner completes the autopsy report."

"I think I'll go down to the morgue. Maybe I can speed things up a bit."

"More likely it'll slow things down. You have a tendency to impede progress when you don't know what you're doing. But I know you'll do whatever you want. Let me know how you make out. I've got three other cases I'm working on, so I certainly won't stand in your way."

After checking in at his office and attending a mandatory meeting with local community leaders that he viewed as a waste of his valuable time, Guerevich went to the basement to the coroner's office. As soon as he walked in, his nose was assaulted by the overpowering smell of formaldehyde. Tears formed in his eyes.

"Aaron," greated Al Witz, the coroner. "Let me see if I can guess why you're here. The Johnson autopsy, right? I was planning to complete it after I finish lunch."

Guerevich wiped his eyes and nose with a tissue. "Any way you could finish it now? I'd like to watch."

"Always in a hurry. The answer is no. But I'll let you watch after lunch, as long as you don't get in my way. I've got an extra sandwich, and I was planning to eat in the lab."

"In the lab? I don't think so. You really eat in here?"

Al laughed. "Just kidding, but you get used to the smell after a while. Really, I was going out to lunch. If you're still kosher, there's a restaurant not far from here. I can tell you what I found so far."

As soon as they were seated, a tall dark-haired waitress appeared.

"Hi, Doc. What'll it be today?"

"I'll have the steak sandwich today. You want one, Aaron? They're good."

Guerevich nodded his assent.

Al turned back to the waitress. "Make that two, and bring a full pot of coffee."

As soon as she left, the coroner looked at Guerevich and smiled. "I don't usually discuss autopsy results over lunch, but you want information about Johnson fast, right?"

"Right."

"Well, it was hard to do a typical autopsy. We usually start the "Y" cut just at the shoulders and proceed to the groin, but he was burned so badly that…"

"Hold it," said Guerevich. "I'm interested in the results, not the process."

"So you don't want to know how we opened his head?"

"Not really. Maybe I should just read your report."

"You're such a sissy when it comes to autopsies. You surprise me, being a cop. You came to get information, and I intend to tell you what I found. But since I'm such a nice guy, I'll let you finish eating first."

As soon as Guerevich put the last bite in his mouth and took the first sip of his second cup of coffee, the coroner put down his cup and said, "Ready to hear about the autopsy as far as I've gone?"

Guerevich looked at the ceiling and took a breath. He folded his arms with his elbows on the table. "Go ahead."

"It was what we expected. He died as a result of massive trauma to the chest. The fall of the auto rack with a car on it crushed him pretty badly. The fire came after he was dead."

"So it was an accident?" Guerevich pushed his cup away.

Al sipped his coffee and held his cup in his hand. He spoke unemotionally. "Looks that way to me. There were two odd things, though. We discovered a brain tumor the size of a small lime in the parietal lobe. That's near the back and top of the head."

Guerevich sat up. "You telling me he had brain cancer?"

"Probably. I sent the specimen tissues to a lab to find out the grade."

"Cancer is graded?"

The waitress came by with a pot of coffee. Guerevich shook his head.

"Indicative of the degree of malignancy," the coroner continued. "If the tumor was high grade, and he hadn't died in the accident, he would have been dead in a year or less. Unless it was treatable, which I doubt. He had to know. The skull is bone, so it can't expand to make room for even a small growing mass, which presses on some part of the brain. The pressure may damage or in some cases even destroy brain tissue. He must have had symptoms caused by the pressure."

"What kind of symptoms?"

"In plain terms? He might have had trouble naming things, or distinguishing left from right. Problems focusing his eyes, or hand and eye coordination, things like that."

"You said there were two things."

"Yeah. Blood analysis showed enough pain pills to knock him out, but not kill him." The coroner looked at his watch, drained his coffee cup and put it down. "Sorry to cut this short, but I need to get back to the lab. Still want to watch?"

"No, that's all the information I need."

"I'll send you a copy of the complete report in a few days." He pushed back his chair and stood, smiling. "Since you insisted on this meeting, the lunch is on you.

After paying, Guerevich returned to his office. A sergeant stopped him as he walked toward his office. "We brought Edward Castle in for questioning in the Johnson case. He's the one Williams identified in his report. The captain wants you to talk to him."

Guerevich walked into the small interrogation room, which housed a six-foot table and four hard metal folding chairs. A single frosted glass window, covered with wire screening, let in hazy light, and a fluorescent ceiling fixture allowed the only other light in the dim room.

Guerevich walked around the table, took a seat, folded his hands and looked at the man who faced the window.

"You want some coffee, Mr. Castle?" Guerevich tapped on the door and a uniformed black woman opened it. "Can you bring us some coffee, Emily?"

Castle looked at the woman and said to Guerevich, "I don't want anything that she touched."

A few minutes later Emily brought a mug of coffee into the room.

"Thanks, Emily." Guerevich smiled and thought he could bait Castle into betraying his bias. "So you have a problem with her because she's black?"

"Them niggers? They need to go back where they came from. Why'd they come up here is what I'd like to know. And how the hell did they get the money to buy a gas station?"

Guerevich ignored the comments. "I heard people were boycotting their station.""

"I go to the Mobil station over on 85th. I got a right to go to whatever station I want. Costs a few cents more. I felt a little sorry for the guy in the wheelchair. I fought in the Pacific. What could he do?"

"What kind of work do you do?"

"Right now, I don't have a permanent job."

"How long have you been unemployed?"

Castle folded his arms, his mouth downturned in a sneer. "I'm not. I been working at a temp agency for the last year until I can find something permanent. Before the war, I worked in a munitions plant in New Jersey."

"Were you at the Hercules High Explosives Plant?"

"Yeah."

Guerevich leaned back and sipped his coffee. ""Isn't that the one that blew up?"

"Yeah. So I heard. Fifty people died. I worked there for a few months after the accident. Then I enlisted."

"A couple of weeks ago, Johnson's station was broken into and their brass tools were stolen. You know anything about that?"

"Look, I don't know nothing about their tools or that explosion." He paused and leaned toward Guerevich. "I'm not under arrest, am I?

The detective flashed his best sincere smile. "Of course not."

"Then I gotta go. I got work tonight. Taking inventory at an auto parts store."

"We just hoped you might have some insight on the hatred the neighborhood feels for them."

"They're out of place. We want to take our business to, uh, other stations."

"Where were you when the explosion occurred?"

"I was home, reading the want ads, and having breakfast."

"Alone?"

"Yeah. Alone." He stood up, walked to the door, and put his hand on the doorknob. Then he turned to face Guerevich, who had remained seated. "Y'know, these people come here and then expect everyone to welcome them. Well, it don't work that way."

After he left, Guerevich called the district attorney. "I need a search warrant for Edward Castle's apartment. I think he's more involved than he wants to admit."

The next morning, three plainclothes policemen appeared with Guerevich at Edward Castle's apartment. Over his protests, they began to go through everything. In his small desk, they found pro-White propaganda bulletins from a racist organization The local president of the group was listed as Edward Castle. Under his bed they retrieved a poster-sized sign nailed to a stick with a cross inside a circle and the words *WHITE PRIDE WORLD WIDE* around the circle. In the trunk of his 1940 Plymouth Road King they discovered a large canvas bag with Sinclair Oil stenciled on the side. The bag was filled with tools, among which were two brass hammers and an assortment of brass wrenches. Edward Castle was arrested and charged with theft.

Back at the station, Guerevich reviewed his notes to prepare a follow-up statement for the District Attorney. He spread the photos that had been taken by the police photographer across his desk and stood, poring over them. As he examined the photographs with a large magnifying glass, he studied Nick in his wheelchair. Something clicked in his brain. "Well, shit. No wonder he didn't want to go to the hospital," he said aloud. "Look at that."

He sat heavily in his chair and shook his head. Then he reached for the phone and dialed Ann.

"Forensics," came the voice with which he had become familiar over the years.

"Hi, Ann. It's me."

"And who's 'me'? Ralph? David? I know, it's Armando."

"Very funny."

"Oh. Aaron. It's you."

He could imagine the big smile on her face.

"Just keeping things from getting too complacent," she said. "What do you need?"

"I think Nick and Sonny traded places. I think it's Sonny in the wheelchair."

"But why would they do that? It doesn't make sense."

"We need to know more about the Johnson brothers. Especially hospitals and doctors. The autopsy showed that the dead brother had a brain tumor."

"A brain tumor? I'll get on it first thing in the morning. We just finished the Devereaux research. There's a mixed-up set of details for you."

"Well, I think you might find the Johnson case just as confusing."

The following night, Guerevich called Ann at her apartment. "Want a little company?"

"What makes you assume I've been alone for the past few days."

"Ouch. I've given up assuming when it comes to you."

"Well, then. Come on over. I've got some casserole left, and I'd hate to see it go to waste."

He made the short drive to Ann's. Before they ate, they sat on the sofa and watched the news. Then he put his arm around her.

"I know that move," she said. "You want to know what I found out about the Johnson brothers.

"That and other things."

"Let's get this out of the way. Work first, fun later." She went into her bedroom and returned with a folder. "This one's thicker than the last one. Do you want it all?"

"It's late. Give me the short version."

"The Johnsons bought the gas station about three years ago. They paid cash because they couldn't get a loan. They struggled financially and Sonny was the mechanic."

"What about George Abbott?"

"There are five George Abbotts in the directory, but none of them had a propane conversion done. I ran the license plate. The car was owned by Sonny Johnson."

"So he was working on his own car. But why invoice it in another name? That would show income they didn't have." Guerevich shrugged his shoulders and looked puzzled. "This gets more confusing by the minute. What about the medical?"

"About six months ago, Sonny took Nick went to the emergency room at County Hospital. The record shows Nick had complained of severe headaches and problems with reading and speaking. The doctor scheduled him for a cerebral arteriogram but he never went. That's a new technique for scanning the brain. But since there aren't too many places that do cerebral arteriograms, I checked around. Nick did have the scan. He went to Verde Valley Medical facility. The doctor who did the arteriogram said he'd only speak to you in person."

The next day, Guerevich and Ann drove to the Verde Valley Medical facility and met with the doctor.

"All I can tell you, Detective, is that the tumor looked suspicious. But without a microscopic examination, I couldn't give an exact diagnosis."

"What was your opinion?"

"It could have been anything from a grade one benign adenoma to a high-grade malignant sarcoma. But from his complaints of headaches and periodic inability to focus, my guess was a malignancy. We wanted to do a follow-up, but he never came back, nor did he ever return my calls."

"And you're sure this was Nick Johnson. Nick Johnson, the paraplegic in the wheelchair."

"Absolutely. I told him and his brother that if the tumor was malignant, Nick would probably be dead in less than a year."

They thanked the doctor and returned to Scottsdale. The next morning, Guerevich received the autopsy report, opened the plain brown envelope, and pulled the text and photos out. As he set the pictures aside, he glanced through the first page of information about the external examination. Sonny Johnson. Age 42. Height five feet three inches.

"That fits what I thought," said Guerevich aloud. "But it's Nick who is five feet three inches. Sonny Johnson is over six feet tall. Except the names should be reversed." Guerevich read the medical examiner's report. The victim's legs were deformed and the muscles badly atrophied. "Sonny must have assumed he'd be able to have his brother's body cremated before anyone examined it."

That afternoon, a warrant was issued for Sonny Johnson. He was brought to the station and wheeled into an interrogation room.

"You've got the wrong person," he insisted. I'm Nick, not Sonny."

"Really?" Guerevich bent down and put his face inches from the face of the man in the wheelchair. "It's a simple thing to find out. We compare your fingerprints with those on file with military. Why not just save us the trouble and tell us what happened."

Sonny slumped in the chair and hung his head, a man defeated.

"We know your brother was dying."

"Yes," he said. "He was." He looked up. Tears ran slowly down his cheeks and stained his shirt. Guerevich handed him a tissue to wipe his face. "After all he went through. When he was twelve, he pushed me out of the way and was hit by a car driven by a white woman. No charges were ever filed. That's how he ended up as a cripple."

"Why'd you want to change places with him? Why'd you want to become Nick in a wheelchair instead of being Sonny?"

Sonny took a deep breath and then sighed.

"You know, Detective, for a man in a wheelchair, my brother was full of life. He was happy. He always said his chair give him freedom. Me, I was the one who was bitter and angry. What an irony that he gets the cancer."

"I agree, but why did you pretend you were him?"

"For the insurance. He couldn't get no life insurance because of his condition. But I had fifty thousand in insurance. I was able to increase it through the military And double for an accident. That's a hundred thousand dollars. If I were to die, he would have gotten it all."

"So you killed him to collect the insurance?"

"Kill my brother? No. This was his plan. He said it was now my turn to help him. He didn't want to wait to become totally dependent on me."

"How'd you do it from the other room?"

"I didn't. He told me my part in his plan was to get out of the way and let him take care of it. He wired it so when the engine fired, the spark caused the explosion. I didn't think the explosion would be so big, or that rack would come down. He said the fire would obliterate the traces of who was who. And the cremation would finish it.

"So was this a mercy killing or a suicide?"

"Neither. It was an accident."

"But he was unconscious from the Vicodin."

"No he wasn't. He had built up a tolerance."

"And you agreed to all this? And did nothing?"

"I tried to talk him out of it. But he was my older brother. How could I refuse him? This is something I'll live with for the rest of my life. Do you think I did the wrong thing? Would it have been better to watch my brother slowly become a vegetable, unable to speak, to read, to have no dignity at all in the end?"

"I can't answer that. But I can tell you that you did wrong to pretend you were Sonny to collect the insurance."

"Yes. I am guilty of planning to cheat the insurance company. But I haven't made the claim. I couldn't."

Guerevich knew there were times when being a good cop meant not following the letter of the law. He gathered up the various pieces of paper and stuck them back into the folder. "I don't there's any reason for us to pursue this further, Mister Johnson." He headed for the door and was opening it when Sonny stopped him with a question.

"What made you suspect I was Sonny and not Nick?"

"In the photograph, I saw plaster dust in the creases of your shoes. A cripple in a wheelchair wouldn't have creases in his shoes."

We continue our exploration of the underside of mid-century America in our next story in which PI Malloy's good deed late one night gets him caught up in a twisting tale of both death and recover

Year of the Pig

by Karen Keeley

The duo beams from Malloy's headlights lit up the lettering on a cardboard box, General Petroleum Products, Mobilgas and Mobiloil, the box smack dab in the middle of the road. It was darker than pitch and Malloy was driving Balaclava south of Broadway in Kitsilano, a September rain pouring down. Even in the dark, he knew the leaves on the trees had turned colour, many now lying soaked and trampled in the street, more leaves littering the lawns and the sidewalks. The box, about the size of a small dog-house should not have been there.

Malloy took his foot off the gas pedal, shifted from third down to second and swerved around the box. His '47 Chevy coupe grumbled a throaty growl. He glanced in the driver's side-view mirror and a kid was climbing out of the box. He pulled a U-turn at the intersection of Balaclava and West 10th and headed back to the box, the kid standing there frozen in the headlights, a little lad stiff as a corpse—a corpse in rubber boots, a knitted sweater vest and flannel pyjamas. Malloy shoved the gearshift into neutral and put on the parking brake. He then got out and hollered at the kid, "Whaddya think you're doing? You trying to get killed?"

That was incentive enough for the kid to skedaddle, a little guy no more than three or four years old. Why he was outside in the rain at ten o'clock at night was anyone's guess. Malloy turned up the collar on his trench coat, pulled the brim of his fedora low on his brow and followed the kid to a nearby semi-detached, everything dark. The kid had raced up the wooden steps, across the veranda and in through the front door, neglecting to close the door.

Malloy stood on the porch under the eve and banged heavily on the wooden doorjamb three times. The sound echoed throughout the lower half of the darkened interior. It took awhile but eventually a lady came, she too, childlike in her appearance, maybe twenty-one, auburn hair dishevelled, sleep in her eyes. She flicked on a hall light. "Your kid," said Malloy. "I just spotted him on the road, hiding in a cardboard box. Damn near ran him over."

The blood drained from the lady's face. "Petey! You come now—where are you?"

The kid sheepishly appeared from the kitchen, thumb stuck in his mouth, wet curls stuck to his pink scalp. His face betrayed him, guilt at having been caught, fearful of a reprimand. The lady grabbed him, gave him a good hard shaking. The little tyke burst into tears. "Jesus, mister—I thought he was upstairs in bed. Thank you for bringing him home."

The lady plunked the kid on the cold linoleum and yanked off his rubber boots.

Malloy hadn't actually been invited inside but he took the initiative anyway, stepping across the threshold and out of the rain. "I just followed him home. Name is Syd Malloy, private investigator."

The lady quickly stood and regained her feet. "Are you investigating me?"

Malloy shook his head. "I was on my way home, downtown, took a shortcut through your neighbourhood. Thankfully there was only me on the road, a night like this. Someone else might have thought it a lark to slam into the cardboard box. I didn't. I hope he's learned his lesson."

"Petey—have you learned your lesson?" asked the lady.

The little lad gave a tentative nod, eyes downcast, nose snuffling. He looked up at his mother and then at Malloy. "No more playing in the street," shouted Malloy as the kid took off up the wooden staircase, presumably to his bedroom. "I'm a kind of police officer. You play in the street again and I'll come back and arrest you!"

The lady had stepped back during Malloy's outburst. She tightened the grip on the collar of her housecoat. "That was unexpected," she said. "But hopefully it does the trick. Petey hates being stuck in the house. I had no idea he'd graduated to cardboard boxes and playing chicken on the road well past his bedtime. Me and my Aunty Flo, she lives with me, we try to watch him but he is a handful."

"Well—good luck, Mrs—?"

"Hughes," said the lady. "Blanche Hughes. Widow, husband killed in the war. I work as a clerk in the toy department, Woodward's, downtown."

"Sorry for your loss," said Malloy.

"We all paid a price," said the lady, and with that, she gave Malloy something of a tentative smile which he took for gratitude as she slowly shut the door.

A week later, the rain having stopped, the sun having made a brief return, Malloy unlocked the frosted glass door to his second floor office on Broadway near Alma when a hand grabbed his arm. He turned, not having heard anyone come up the linoleum staircase behind him, and there—Blanche Hughes.

"I need your help," she said, her eyes full of concern, her hair just as dishevelled as the night Malloy had almost run over her kid, little Petey playing chicken on the road.

He led Blanche through the waiting room and into his office, to the single chair by his filing cabinet. The shared receptionist usually arrived around nine o'clock, her looking after Malloy and a publicist hawking magazines—Life, Look, and Cosmopolitan. A third guy—a fuller brush salesman kept an office but was seldom seen. Malloy closed his door, tossed his hat onto his desk, sat down and swivelled his banker's chair. He gave Blanche Hughes his full undivided attention.

Blanche set her cloth handbag on her lap and burst into tears. Malloy, never comfortable with a woman crying, got up, handed her his handkerchief. "Take it slow, start at the beginning."

Blanche told him her brother had been killed and Petey was missing.

"When?" asked Malloy.

"Yesterday," said Blanche. "I got the news about my brother in the morning, a hit and run on Robson Street downtown. Jerry lives with us, too—he's a deckhand on the Sarah-Lee. Right after the police came, I went looking for Petey, thinking he'd heard the terrible news, he loves his Uncle Jerry. I looked in all of Petey's favourite hiding spots but couldn't find him. And now, here we are twenty-four hours later and I still can't find him."

She twisted Malloy's handkerchief. Her little pillbox hat sat cockeyed on her head, she'd obviously been in a hurry that morning when she'd dressed. She wore a lightweight woolen suit, charcoal grey, calf length skirt and bolero style jacket, no doubt purchased at Woodward's. "I've been all over the neighbourhood myself, and I've told the police. They're combing the backyards, the parks, even as far as MacBride and Connaught but I can't imagine Petey having wandered that far. I'm frantic. I need your help—you said you're a private investigator. I remembered what you'd said."

"It sounds like the police are doing their job. There's not much more I could do," said Malloy. He'd loosened his checkered tie while Blanche spoke, fiddled with a paperclip, twisted it like a pretzel before tossing it in an ashtray, a memento from the Peter Pan café, the best bangers and mash in town.

"But Petey knows you—he'll remember what you said. He's afraid of strangers. He always plays alone, like when he invented that stupid chicken game with the cardboard box. With the police, he'll stay hidden. He'll think they've come to arrest him, what you said."

Malloy kicked himself for having scared the kid—he was just a little tyke after all. "I was only trying to help." Now who felt guilty?

"If you come and look," said Blanche, "call his name, maybe he'll come out from his hidey-hole, for you. Please, Mr. Malloy— you must come!"

Malloy straightened his tie, asking, "How did you get here this morning?" He was thinking about the movie he and his current squeeze, a leggy blond named Candy were supposed to see that evening—Dark Passage, a Bogie and Bacall film that was getting good reviews.

Blanche had taken a compact out of her purse, dabbed her nose and was now fiddling with a lipstick, fire engine red. "I took the crosstown trolley, found your name and address in the yellow pages."

Malloy took up his hat and placed it on his head. "We'll take my car. It's parked across the street."

While walking, Blanche told Malloy it was virtually impossible for a woman to get a mortgage—it had only been with Jerry's help that they had a home. With Jerry now gone, Blanche wasn't sure what would become of her, little Petey and her Aunty Flo. According to Blanche, Jerry had enlisted right at the tail end of the war, into the medical corp. He didn't see any fighting over-seas—just when he would've been deployed, the war was over.

After retrieving Malloy's Chevy from the Chevron station across Broadway and filling up, him thinking fifteen cents a gallon was highway robbery, it took him twenty minute to drive to Blanche's semi-detached in Kitsilano. The house didn't look as dismal or forlorn as it had the night of the rainstorm. He set the handbrake, rolled up his window. While Blanche was getting out of the car, Malloy lit a cigarette, his preferred brand Camels de-spite their nickname as coffin nails—he'd been smoking since the age of twelve. He tossed the spent wooden match in the ashtray.

Blanche waited on the sidewalk, and there, coming up the street was Detective Al Simms, fifteen years Malloy's senior and Malloy's former partner when he'd been a proud member of the Vancouver police force. Simms grunted when he saw Malloy, shoved his brown fedora back from his wrinkled brow, stared down his long nose at Malloy while his tongue waggled a toothpick side to side, making Malloy think the old bear hadn't changed much since he'd last seen him a year or so ago.

"Whaddya doin' here, Malloy?"

"Same as you, Detective. Looking for a lost kid."

Simms nodded to Blanche Hughes, "Ma'am," he said.

"Still missing?" asked Malloy.

Simms grunted in the affirmative. "We've been up and down the back alleys, poked into every hedge, discarded icebox, dustbin, incinerator and cardboard box we could find. We've checked out the parks and the schools, and scoured the neighbourhood including a half dozen paper shacks, them what house the Province and the Sun, in a six block radius. If the kid is here, he's hiding good and doesn't want to be found."

Blanche interrupted. "I've asked Mr. Malloy to help."

"And you two know each other how?" asked Simms.

"Long story," said Malloy. "I'll tell you later, right now let's keep looking."

"So you say," said Simms.

"I do," said Malloy, and with that he led Blanche Hughes up the wooden steps, past two flower boxes, home to mulch, dirt, dandelions and thistle, and across the veranda. "You go inside now, make yourself a pot of tea or a cup of Nescafé, whatever it is you drink. Keep your Aunty Flo company. I'll check back when I've had a looksee of my own."

Blanche tried to offer an appreciative smile but failed. During the drive, she'd told Malloy that Petey had a fondness for dark cramped spaces. Sometimes she or her Aunty Flo would come into the kitchen and Petey would've taken the pots and pans out of one cupboard, him hiding inside, the door closed, in the dark, pretending he was conducting an orchestra, the radio playing big band music or the blues or jazz.

Given that Petey had been playing his game of chicken smack dab in front of his own house, Malloy surmised the little fellow wouldn't have strayed too far, intending no disrespect or insult to Vancouver's finest who'd organized the massive search, even going as far as Jericho and Kitsilano beaches. But Malloy felt certain Petey was within a few blocks from home. And there were those who played their radios throughout the day. If Petey had discovered an open window and the homeowner was tuned to CBC or CJOR he might have heard the mournful wail from a sax or a clarinet, a tune he recognized, a way to console himself after hearing of his uncle's death.

While walking and smoking, Malloy could hear no music, only the sound of a police siren far in the distance and a couple of dogs barking. He saw squirrels, a racoon and cats sunning themselves on porch railings. He thought of little Petey, small for his age and about as bowlegged as a cowboy, according to his mother, now missing a full twenty-four hours which led Malloy to think that hunger too, might have pushed Petey to go looking for food. He was, after all, a resourceful little lad, and knowing his neighbourhood, he'd know where to go.

Malloy tried to put himself into the headspace of a four year old kid, thinking cramped dark spaces. His walk took him to a green grocer's located on the southwest corner of Blenheim and West 12th run by a Polish couple who'd lived in the neighbourhood for years. Yes—they certainly knew Petey. Often he accompanied his mother or his Aunty Flo when the ladies came to purchase vegetables and canned goods—baked beans and spam. The shop with its colourful striped awning in red, white and blue, and sandwich board advertising apples at thirteen cents a pound, ditto for a loaf of bread, also had fruits and vegetables in display bins on the sidewalk. The Kolinskis had not seen the boy.

Malloy flicked his cigarette butt into a puddle and wandered a few blocks over, many of the homes with a maple tree or a northern mountain ash in their front yard, the bright orange berries from the ash trees having fallen, the sidewalks stained with berry juice and pulp. Malloy didn't think the berries were poisonous but he hoped Petey hadn't eaten any, just in case. It was a school day, not many people about but those he did see, he asked if they'd seen a little boy—so high, blond, wearing a striped t-shirt and brown corduroy overalls but Petey had not been seen.

He then walked the alleys—mostly mud given the amount of rain the city had weathered the past month. He covered three long blocks, the alleys home to forty-foot telephone poles, part of BC Tel's growing infrastructure, a network of wires and cables overhead. He kicked at rusted tin cans—corn, peas and peaches, and discarded soda pop bottles—Nu-Grape and Orange Crush. Many of the yards had patches of rhubarb, now at the end of its season, the leaves having turned yellow and any remaining stalks worm infested. Malloy hoped Petey, like most kids, had ignored the rhubarb.

He returned to Blanche's house, found her in the kitchen. He followed his nose to a dish of Dutch apple platz sitting on the counter, something Blanche's Aunty Flo must have baked earlier that morning. The old woman was busy knitting, her arthritic fingers working on another sweater vest for Petey, this one navy blue with white stripes. She smiled an endearing smile and offered Malloy a cup of tea.

Malloy declined the tea and asked Blanche, "Does Petey have a favourite animal? If he had a pet, what would it be?"

"A black lab," said Blanche. "There's a family who lives on West 12th, six kids if you can believe. They have a beautiful black lab called Sadie, the gentlest dog in the world. Every time Petey sees her, he asks me, could we get a doggie like Sadie?"

Malloy had turned, was making for the front door.

"I'm coming, too," shouted Blanche, tossing a wet dishrag into the sink before hurriedly shoving her stockinged feet into her Cuban heeled shoes and running after Malloy.

Simms saw them, hollered for Malloy to hold up. "You got an idea? You onto something?"

The two men followed Blanche Hughes as she raced down the street, an Olympic sprinter in the making. Three blocks later, on West 12th she stopped in front of a single family home, white-washed veranda, faded hopscotch chalked on the sidewalk, a bo-lo-bat tossed into a hedge. Blanche, out of breath, leaned over and held her side as though she had a stitch. "Stay here," said Simms, him too, struggling to breathe. He knocked on the screen door, no answer.

"I'm going 'round back," hollered Malloy, his tie and suit jacket flapping. His long legged strides took him to the end of the block and into the alley. More mud, more puddles. He heard Simms huffing and puffing in an effort to keep up, Blanche too, hurrying in her high heeled shoes. Malloy hoped Simms wasn't going to inhale the goddamn toothpick and choke. They skirted the puddles and the dustbins, bicycles and rusted red-wagons and then, a backyard with a medium sized doghouse painted red, a black tarpapered roof.

Malloy opened the gate, strolled across the yard, mostly crabgrass and dandelions, a length of hose lying in the weeds. A damson plum tree grew near the doghouse, many of the blue tinged plums having fallen, some bruised and rotten, others still looked edible. He peered into the dark recess of the doghouse. Petey, fast sleep, lying on a dog blanket covered in dog hair. Malloy gently woke the lad who obviously remembered him, the kid pushing himself farther back into the shadows, seeking safety, fear in his big blue eyes. "It's okay, Petey—I'm not here to arrest you. You're not in trouble. Your mother is extremely worried," and as he spoke those words, Blanche Hughes knelt down, gazed into the dark recess of the doghouse. "Come to Mama, slugger— it's time to go home."

Petey came, eyes downcast, thumb stuck in his mouth. His dimpled cheeks were dirty, streaked with tears, his long-sleeved t-shirt and corduroy overalls blanketed in dog hair but no sign of the dog. Malloy spotted an empty milk bottle near Sadie's dog dish. The dish held three small plums, each half eaten. He picked up the bottle, Associated Dairies, their product delivered by horse and wagon in most neighbourhoods—families receiving homogenized milk, butter, eggs and cheese, the cost of a quart of milk fourteen cents. Petey must have heard the delivery, milk bottles clinking and stolen quietly from the dog house, taking one of the bottles.

Detective Al Simms approached the back door and gave it a good hard thump. Presently, a woman came, mousy brown hair, tall and thin wearing a house dress and wiping her hands on a frilly apron—what Malloy would have called froufrou. Suspicion clouded her dark eyes. Behind her, in the kitchen, a wringer washer hooked up to the sink, nozzle attached to the faucet, was busy churning away. A chubby little two year old sat on the floor playing with a Chinese checkers game, the marbles lined up in a row. The woman looked confused—who in blazes were these people in her backyard?

Simms explained about the missing boy and asked about the dog.

"Sadie died," said the woman. "A week ago today, hit by a car. There was nothing we could do."

Upon hearing that news, little Petey burst into tears, clung to his mother's neck, his legs wrapped around her as Blanche carried him home.

Simms grumbled, "You got a sawbuck in your wallet?"

"What for?" asked Malloy.

"Lunch, you're buyin'. Oh—and two-bits for a shoeshine."

The following Tuesday, another rainy day in the dreary month of September, the good detective stopped by to have a talk with Malloy. It had been a week since the death of Jerry White, and Simms knew Malloy had a connection with the sister. The police had no leads, no witnesses and no suspects.

"We've been to the house," said Simms. "Been through his room, not much to see, some clothes, sport pennants thumb-tacked to the wall, the Cardinals and the Cubs, baseball bat and glove, record albums—seems he was a fan of big band music, the blues and jazz." Malloy nodded, he knew that from Blanche. "The sister says Jerry was a deckhand on the Sarah-Lee, a tug working out of the Coal Harbor Marina off Hastings. I spoke with the tug's owner, a fellow named Walter Lynch. He said Jerry was a good worker, always on time, never any problem. Why he was on Robson at midnight, in the rain, is a complete mystery to him, and to the sister. Have you spoken with her? Gotten anything helpful?"

"Nothing," said Malloy. "My only dealing with Blanche Hughes was finding her lost kid last week. We haven't spoken since."

"Well—if you do, keep me informed." Simms stood, straightened his fedora, popped a toothpick in his mouth. "I'm batting zero with this one, Malloy. Anything you could give me would make my day."

An hour after Simms left, Blanche Hughes arrived, wide-eyed and dishevelled, little pillbox hat once again sitting cockeyed on her head. Malloy stood, thinking little Petey had again disappeared but no—Petey was fine. His Aunty Flo had taken him to see the woman who owned Sadie. "Remember her?" asked Blanche.

"Of course," said Malloy.

"She's gotten a new puppy, another black lab, only eight weeks old."

"That'll put a smile on Petey's face," said Malloy, and then as an afterthought he told her, he'd just had Detective Simms stop by.

"If he came to talk about Jerry, that's why I'm here," said Blanche.

She told Malloy they'd held Jerry's funeral on Sunday and then last evening Petey brought her a Duke Ellington album, *I'm Beginning to See the Light*, one of Jerry's favourites. The little fellow wanted to listen to the music, and when she removed the vinyl from the album jacket, a piece of paper dropped out. "Here it is." She handed the paper to Malloy.

He took it and realized he was looking at some kind of invoice: bok choy, leeks, water chestnuts, bean sprouts, white rice and mushrooms to be delivered to the Green Lantern restaurant in Chinatown located on East Pender. Malloy told Blanche he'd take a drive, see if anyone would talk to him, did they know Jerry? But first, he'd drop her at Woodward's downtown—she was, after all, late for her job.

The Green Lantern was closed, didn't open for another hour. Malloy used that hour to wander the area—he usually enjoyed the ambiance of Chinatown, the artistic script lettering advertising brick and mortar businesses, some with Pagoda style arches, and the patches of green space home to park benches and pigeons. But today the area was dark and grimy and grey.

He strolled the sidewalks in the rain, along with the pigeons. He couldn't remember when he'd last seen the Northshore, thick cloud cover right down to the ground. He adjusted the collar on his trench coat, pulled his hat low over his eyes. There weren't many on the streets, just a few locals scurrying past and muddy dogs rooting through tipped over dustbins. When the restaurant opened, Malloy entered and asked to speak with the owner. There were some discreet sideway glances which he ignored and presently a compact and somewhat feisty gentleman, wiping his hands on a butcher's apron came from the back kitchen. "You have question?" he asked. His name was Li Wei.

Malloy told him who he was, showed him his credentials and the invoice. "This was found in the possession of a fellow named Jerry White. Do you know him?"

Li Wie nodded with enthusiasm. "He come often, enjoy noodles and green tea. He friends with my son, Li Wang."

"Is he here, could I talk to him?"

Li Wei nodded, bowed with reverent grace and scooted back to the kitchen. Malloy's nose sniffed at the delectable aromas—ginger, garlic and green onions sautéing, the sound of something sizzling in a fryer. The owner returned with a young man, late teens, early twenties, very much resembling his father. Malloy showed him the invoice. "You knew Jerry White—you were friends. Did you know he was killed in a hit and run?"

The young man nodded, glanced back and forth between Malloy and his father.

Malloy asked, "Why would Jerry have this invoice?"

"Last time I see him, we sit over there, table by window," said Li Wang. "We have delivery, I go to help. Delivery is made in back alley through kitchen. Jerry come too, he my friend. He help unload, driver stay in truck, then driver give Jerry invoice. Jerry forget and not give to me."

Malloy pushed his hat back on his forehead. "Did you see the driver? Was he someone you knew?"

The young man shook his head. "New driver, never see before."

Malloy pondered that, did the driver get his knickers in a knot because Jerry was helping his friend? Two young men, acting as though they didn't have a care in the world, full of energy, probably kibitzing with each other the way young men do. Malloy knew there were those in the city who thought one race should not mix with another. Had the driver decided to teach Jerry a lesson—scare him on a dark rainy night? The invoice was from a wholesale delivery outfit called Federated headquartered in New Westminster. He asked Li Wang, "How did you know Jerry?"

Li Wang smiled, teeth bright in his boyish bronzed face. "He work on tugboat, I work on tugboat, belong to my uncle. We become friends."

Malloy thanked father and son and left the invoice with Li Wei, a man filled with gratitude, he did not know the invoice had gone missing. He then offered Malloy a table—did he want to stay to lunch? Malloy took in the Chinese silk artwork on the walls, fierce tigers and dragons, soothing cherry blossoms. He was tempted but he thanked Li Wei and said no, he had business back at the office. That business included looking up Federated in the yellow pages. The warehouse was near BC Distilleries not far from the Fraser River, a small wholesale outfit delivering locally grown product or items imported from the US.

Malloy found the owner, a harried man in his fifties, scurrying from railway boxcar to boxcar, carrying a clipboard, checking numbers against a stack of waybills. It was a losing battle, protecting his paperwork from the rain.

"Sure, I remember who made the delivery," he said, a soggy cigar clamped between his teeth. "I only got three drivers, it was Hank Winslow. He's been with me a couple of months. A rough and tumble character with an attitude, but he does the job."

"He here now?" asked Malloy.

The owner spit the stogie into the dirt, crushed it under the heel of his boot, and pointed to a small tarpapered shack nestled against a stack of wooden pallets in the northwest corner of the yard. "He'd be there, drinking coffee, waiting on his next delivery."

Malloy entered the shack, a few tables and chairs, Arborite and Naugahyde, cigarette smoke hanging thick in the air. A calendar featuring Betty Grable and her million dollar legs insured by Lloyd's of London was the only bright spot in the place. Hank Winslow sat at one of the tables looking through a stack of newspapers, Vancouver Sun and the Province, many of them yellowed and outdated. A lunch box and coffee thermos were on the table, the metal lid cup half full.

Malloy introduced himself, showed him his credentials.

"Whaddya want me for?" asked Winslow.

"You made a delivery to the Green Lantern in Chinatown a few weeks back."

"What if I did?"

"You gave an invoice to a young fellow name of Jerry White."

"What if I did?"

"Ever see White again?" asked Malloy.

"No, why would I?"

Malloy pulled out a chair, turned it back to front. "Maybe a night on the town, you run into him—literally run into him, I mean."

"I got nothing to say," said Winslow, drinking the last of his coffee and resealing the thermos. He was a big man, barrel chested, liver spots on his scalp and the back of his hands. He rolled down his shirt sleeves, straightened the cuffs.

Malloy shrugged out of his trench coat and sat down, tapped another smoke free from his rumpled cigarette package. He struck a match and lit the smoke. "Not true," said Malloy. "I think you got lots to say. And I got all the time in the world."

Hank Winslow pushed his chair back, leaned on the table, leveraged himself, about to stand. Malloy stated matter of fact, "You were in the merchant marines."

"How'd you know that?"

"Tattoo on the back of your arm—the anchor. You took an oath to faithfully and honestly perform your duties. And then you got a bum rap, fighting for King and country and yet none of you recognized as legitimate war veterans, denied veterans' benefits, the reason for this job."

Winslow said nothing. He sat there, fingers stained with nicotine, dandruff on his shirt collar, grey stubble on his chin. God only knew when he'd last had a decent four-bit shave and a haircut, a broken man who wore a perpetual scowl, most likely a consequence from the life he'd lived.

Malloy carried on, "Fourth Arm of the Fighting Services, and now, put out to pasture like an old warhorse, worthless. That's gotta hurt—make you mad. You look around, see these young bucks who have no idea what it's like to be in the thick of battle, acting as though it's a goddamn right, democracy, not something hard won with blood and guts and tears. And then, to see one of them consorting with the enemy—might as well have been the enemy."

Winslow said nothing.

Malloy tapped the table top. "Tell me what happened."

"Nothing to tell," said Winslow.

"Think of your oath. Guilt eats away at a man's good character, what little dignity he has left. You'll feel reborn once you get whatever it is off your chest."

Winslow pulled on his top lip, fiddled with the thermos. It was cold and damp in the shack, no heat. Had Winslow spent time in similar cramped spaces aboard a frigate during the war— hold up in some tightfitting place—mayhem and madness raining down around him? He was obviously wrestling with his demons. He glanced toward the tiny window adjacent to the door, the rain still pouring down. With a resigned sigh, he hung his head, looking a lot like little Petey Hughes after being busted for playing chicken in the middle of the road.

"That guy you're askin' after—he was at the Bull and Finch, same as me, on Robson—him with some of his fellow dock workers, all of 'em sitting at a corner table. I recognized him from the delivery I'd done at that Chinese place on Pender like you said. Turned my stomach the way him and his slanty-eyed pansy pal were friends, kibitzing with each other like a couple of fairies."

"And that gave you the right to kill him," said Malloy. He blew smoke into Winslow's face, not caring if the man liked it or not, he was done being mister nice guy.

"Didn't mean to kill him, just meant to scare him," said Winslow. "I'd had a few too many like I do most nights. I wanted to put a fright into him, make him think twice, he should be sticking to his own kind. He was crossing Robson, probably headed for a trolley. What with the dark and the rain, my car fishtailed on wet asphalt, no traction, brakes useless, and there he was, deer in the headlights. He hit the grill, flew upwards, past the windshield. When he hit the far curb on the sidewalk I could see he'd smashed his head. I figured him for dead. I took off, not my finest moment."

"No, not your finest moment," said Malloy, stubbing out the cigarette in a metal ashtray overflowing with butts. "How about we take a ride?"

Hank Winslow picked up his tweed cap, company jacket, lunch box and thermos, pocketed his own brand of cigarettes, Sweet Caporals, and followed Malloy outside. "I gotta tell the boss," he said.

Malloy grunted. "We'll do it together."

Once done, the boss, soaked to the gills, was extremely agitated he was losing his driver—who would make the next delivery? Time was money.

"Not my concern," said Malloy, his shoulders hunched against the wind and the rain. He and Winslow skirted the puddles as Malloy steered Winslow across the muddy yard toward his Chevy coupe. The two men didn't talk while driving to the precinct.

Malloy handed Winslow over to his old pal Detective Al Simms. He explained the story and Simms handed Winslow off to one of his fellow officers. "Book him, you know the drill." The officer nodded and led Hank Winslow toward the back of the precinct.

"Jesus, Malloy—sometimes you get all the luck. Finding the kid and now this."

"It's the year of the pig in the Chinese New Year," said Malloy. "I'm told pigs have a beautiful personality and are blessed with good fortune. What can I tell you, Simms—luck is my middle name."

Detective Al Simms smacked the back of Malloy's head with a meaty paw, stuck a clean toothpick in his mouth, waggled it side to side and told Malloy to leg it.

Malloy lit a cigarette, took Simms comment for an order and legged it.

Simms hollered, "Hey, Malloy—you still owe me two-bits for that shoeshine!"

Post-war Harvard—filled with war-weary GIs, kids fresh out of high school, and sinister intrigue at every strata of society.

The Tango Queen
by Albert Tucher

"Those two are strictly nose to the grindstone," LoSchiavo said.

"Beats talking to each other."

"Why's that?"

"Mrs. Gelb is a Viennese Jew," I said. "Got out just in time."

"Nineteen thirty-eight?"

"Give or take. Mrs. Kaposi left Budapest in a big hurry in 'forty-five."

"Meaning," he said, "people in the old country might have some scores to settle with her. Maybe including Mrs. Gelb. That could be fun."

We were breaking in place. There wasn't much to entertain us, other than the two women sitting back to back in the Catalogue Department with no more than six feet between their desks.

"Well," he said, "when hostilities resume, we'll have a ringside seat."

"I've lost my appetite for that kind of stuff."

We killed our cigarettes in the standing ashtray and went back to work as Widener Library's beasts of burden. Our job was delivering new books from the Order Department to the cataloguers. We spent our day pushing wheeled shelves that the librarians called "trucks." The name was apt, because it took a driver's skill to negotiate the turns between the tightly packed desks.

LoSchiavo had half-seriously asked me for a map of the huge room.

With the ten dollars a week that I earned, and my GI benefits, I could just about swing Harvard. But I was single. I wasn't sure how LoSchiavo planned to make do.

"What's with the Eastern European Mafia?" he said. "They seem to run the place."

"There is no Mafia. J. Edgar Hoover said so."

"If you believe anything he says."

I didn't answer. Lately he was saying too many things along those lines.

"Now that's more like it," he said.

A younger woman passed in front of us. She didn't acknowledge LoSchiavo's scrutiny, but he would take that as a challenge.

"Just don't say 'Hubba, hubba,' Joe."

"Who is she?"

"Anne Belwyn. She's a reference librarian. Married. Like you."

He didn't flinch.

"You know her?"

"I've been to her home and met her husband, so don't embarrass me."

"Wouldn't think of it."

Which meant he would.

LoSchiavo had brown bagged it for lunch. I went to the Freshman Union for a solitary tuna sandwich, if wedging myself into a crowd could count as solitary. Like everything at Harvard, the Union was jammed. The University ran straight semesters, without summers off. Demobilized GI's mixed with eighteen-year-olds, who looked like a different species.

LoSchiavo learned the job quickly. That was good, because it hadn't been easy to keep it open for him until his discharge came through. I was still waiting for us to settle back into our friendship, but it was different when we didn't depend on each other for survival.

I started to notice the things he said and did. He didn't seem to understand how two years of peace had changed everything.

He moved easily among the library staff. The various lunch and coffee cliques welcomed him whenever he chose to join them. That was why I noticed when he spent time talking with Mrs. Kaposi. It happened quite a bit, but I never picked up on any hostility between them. Maybe he had changed his first opinion of her.

I decided to keep watching.

It was Mrs. Gelb who first asked me if my friend was a Communist. Her tone was curious rather than horrified.

"You'll have to ask him. We've never had time to talk politics."

She nodded. Several times I saw the two of them spending a coffee break together. Mrs. Kaposi avoided Joe when Mrs. Gelb was with him, but I wouldn't have expected anything else.

I never saw him socializing with Anne Belwyn, which should have worried me.

One evening, as I was about to leave work, LoSchiavo found me at my staff locker.

"Want to get a beer?"

I didn't, but I also didn't want us to drift further apart.

"Sure."

In Cronin's bar on the Square we got dimies and looked for a place to sit. A quartet of seniors thought about racing us for the last table, but they sized LoSchiavo up and let us take it.

"So," he said, "how do you like the job?"

"It's a job."

"Pay is pretty bad," he said. "In fact, I'm not sure it's even legal."

"It just supplements my benefits."

"You're a veteran. You deserve better."

"What's your point?"

"Some of us are looking into getting organized."

"You mean, like a union?"

"Exactly. A real union. Not like the tame ones in this country."

I said nothing, but he must have read my lack of enthusiasm on my face.

"It's a basic right," he said.

"I've got nothing against unions, but that's not what I'm here for. I just want to get my degree and move on."

"Still aiming for the State Department?"

"That's right."

"You're diplomatic enough. But sometimes you have to chuck diplomacy and take a stand."

"Joe, enough people are already thinking you're a Red."

"That's always the first thing they think of. The first and the last."

"Are they wrong?"

"Let's just say that Dachau and Sachsenhausen opened my eyes."

"When you say, 'Some of us,' who is that, exactly?"

For a moment he lost his momentum. I knew I had guessed right. That made two reasons why he didn't want to be seen with Anne Belwyn.

"It was capitalism that made the war happen," said LoSchiavo. "No capitalism, no tyranny."

"I'd be careful about that," I told him. "The Soviets aren't allies anymore. A lot of people are working hard to forget they ever were. And a lot of other people are listening in on conversations like this one."

"There's time for you to see what's happening in this country. Not a lot, but there's some."

He drank the last of his beer and stood.

"Got to get home."

He hefted his battered briefcase, which looked heavy. He saw me noticing.

"I get most of my work done on the train."

"What is that, like an hour and a half?"

"Each way."

He started to move away.

"How is she?" I said.

I never wanted to ask, but I always broke down. I never said her name, though.

Katrina.

LoSchiavo always pretended that there were no depths to the question.

"Going a little crazy. Harvardevens is way out there. And she says the place makes her feel like a patient."

"Stands to reason."

The new married student housing had been a military hospital attached to the old Fort Devens, which the Army had turned over to Harvard.

"See you Monday."

On that Monday LoSchiavo and I worked eight to noon. He took his ten minutes with Mrs. Kaposi. I wasn't the only one who noticed that she didn't return from her break. No one could remember her missing a minute of work. In just one afternoon books in Hungarian, Romanian and Russian began to pile up noticeably on her shelves.

Back at the dorm I had intended to eat a sandwich at my desk as I studied before class. But someone knocked on my door. When I opened it, I found a timid freshman poised to try again.

"You're, uh, Sass?"

"That's right."

"Phone for you."

I went downstairs to the lobby. The voice I heard was unfamiliar.

"My name's Smithson. I handle security at Harvardevens. Joseph LoSchiavo has you down as an emergency contact."

"That figures."

"There's been trouble in his apartment. Gunshots, bullet holes in the living room wall."

"Anybody hurt?"

"Not that we can tell."

"Why are you calling me?"

"We can't find him. Can you come out here?"

"This sounds like police business."

"I'm not letting them in."

"What's going on, Mr. Smithson? Why wouldn't you let the police in?"

"It's a matter of principle. We're within the Shirley town limits, but we don't belong to them. I've told the local government that over and over. It's Federal property, leased to Harvard."

"Why do you care about that?"

"Have you seen the Shirley police?"

"That can't be the whole story."

"I don't want to make trouble for LoSchiavo. He's okay."

I thought it over. Sooner or later it would occur to Smithson to call the FBI.

"I'll be there as soon as I can."

Thirty minutes later I sat on the train to Shirley and restrained myself from getting out to walk. The train seemed to stop every three minutes. No wonder the trip took so long.

I disembarked and joined the crowd going to Harvardevens on foot. Soon we came to a gate and a guard hut. Beyond them I saw three one-story buildings that looked too much like an Army barracks to please a veteran like me. A loop road curved out of sight around the whole village and returned from the other direction. I waited at the gate for attention, while security men with pistols on their belts faced down four Shirley police officers. The local cops leaned against their patrol cars in poses that combined pugnacity with indecision.

A man in his forties verified identities, mostly by sight, and waved people into the village. When my turn came, he shook his head.

"Residents only."

"Smithson?"

"You're Sass."

I nodded toward the local law.

"Who called them?"

"Must have been a resident. I knew this would happen. Months ago I tried to get the FBI to admit it was their territory before anything serious happened, but they couldn't be bothered."

"Too busy hunting Communists."

"I guess." He studied me. "You and LoSchiavo were with the U.S. Constabulary?"

"That's right."

"I was an MP."

At his age he must have been the "Pops" of his unit. Every outfit had one.

"You know the wife?" he said.

"I knew her before he did."

That was true, if only by a few seconds. I was the one who had spotted her coming out of the Soviet zone.

"We don't know who was shooting at who," said Smithson.

"What does she say?"

"A whole lot of German."

Katrina spoke better English than some GI's I had known. That had been true even before she came to the United States. She was waiting for someone, and no one could find Joe. That left me.

"So you don't know if the shooter is still in there."

"My guess is no," he said. "A number of people left before we knew what was going on. We couldn't hear the shots from the gate."

I frowned. They really did need some law enforcement here.

Smithson saw my expression.

"I'll send one of my men in with you. I already have somebody with the wife."

Smithson left me and went to the guard hut, where he conferred with another security man. The second man came out and beckoned me to follow him. We said nothing as he led me into Harvardevens.

"This one," he said. "Twenty-six Eliot Street."

He left me and started back to the gate.

With my fist poised to knock, I froze. It was strange, but in my mind I saw Katrina grimy with road miles and emaciated from post-war privation. These days she had the plumpness that many German women develop at the first opportunity. It suited her, but apparently I preferred a time before she had chosen LoSchiavo over me.

I had no choice. I knocked, and the door opened. Another middle-aged Harvard man faced me. Again I identified myself.

He led me through the kitchen, which was small but newly painted. A lot of student wives bragged about the new two-burner stove and oven that came with each apartment.

I had seen enough bullet holes to recognize them. About three feet from the floor, two fresh ones marred the new paint job beside the door to the living room.

The living room was as small as the kitchen. Two huge radiators filled much of the available space. If they ever got going, even hospital patients would have found the heat too much. The furniture looked cheap and mismatched, but new. Katrina and Joe probably rented it from the University.

"Johann," she said. "Thank you for coming."

She said it in German. For the moment I decided to go along with her.

"You want to tell me what happened?"

"I heard a knock on the door. I asked who was there. A woman asked me to open up. I said again, who is there? She begged me, so I opened."

"Just like that?"

"Well, she spoke in German. I suppose that made me homesick. And careless."

"Anything noticeable about her German?"

"Viennese. Not dialect, but with the accent."

"Okay, you opened the door. Then what?"

"There was a woman in the hall. She pushed me, hard. I did not expect it, and I stumbled backwards and fell. She stood over me, and I saw a gun in her hand."

"What kind of gun?"

"Not one of ours, that's all I know. Not a Luger or anything like that."

"What did she want?"

"I still don't know. She kept saying, 'Who have you told? Who have you told?'"

"Then what?"

"I have faced guns before. I did not like how desperate she was. It could make her shoot without meaning to. Fortunately for me, she was too close. So I kicked her ankle. She fell on top of me, and we wrestled for the gun. I was younger and stronger, and I know how to fight. But while we were fighting, she pulled the trigger twice."

That agreed with what I had seen.

"Then she jumped up and ran back outside."

Katrina had survived the war in the east. For many displaced persons, the first days of peace had been even deadlier. If she knew how to handle an assailant with a gun, it didn't surprise me.

"You must have let her go."

"Yes. She wasn't a real killer. I know what they look like too."

"Do you have any idea what she meant?"

"None."

"Did you know her?"

"No."

"What did she look like?"

Katrina described half of the middle-aged women in Central and Eastern Europe. Brown hair, brown eyes, strong cheekbones.

A knock sounded on the front door. The middle-aged man asked who was there.

"FBI," I heard even in the living room.

They didn't need to show credentials. J. Edgar's boys travel in pairs, and they have to qualify their stern looks every year along with their marksmanship. These two were the real thing. One looked to be in his forties, while the other, trailing behind, was twenty years younger.

"We're looking for Joseph LoSchiavo," said the older one.

I glanced at Katrina. She was letting me handle it.

"Not here."

"Mind if we check?"

The younger partner was already heading for the bedroom and bathroom. He took a remarkable amount of time to search such a small range of possible hiding places.

"Where is he?"

"I don't know."

That was technically true.

"You are?"

"John Sass. A friend."

"Ma'am?"

Katrina shrugged.

"His wife," I said. "She's not speaking English."

If they concluded that she couldn't, that was their mistake.

"So you're taking jurisdiction after all," I said.

"What does that mean?"

"I assume this is about the shooting."

"What shooting?"

"Bullet holes in the kitchen."

"If LoSchiavo wasn't here, it's not our business. If you hear from him, we want to know."

The younger agent handed me a card. I glanced at the Boston address and phone number. They left without wasting more words.

Katrina and I sat without speaking. The Constabulary had taught me a cop's intimidating stare, but Katrina wasn't impressed. Nobody could intimidate her anymore, least of all a man who had wanted to marry her.

"I notice," she said, "that you're not asking me where he is."

"But you know. Or have an idea."

"It's that union business." She twisted her mouth. "Business. He has a habit of mixing business with pleasure. But you would know that."

"If the FBI is involved, it's about Communists. Joe has been talking like one lately. And I don't think the Federals get the difference between a labor agitator and a Communist."

"This is America. It's supposed to be different here."

I shrugged.

"Communists are the new Nazis. I suppose we need an enemy."

"And he married someone from the East. That makes him more suspect."

"That's probably part of it. But if Joe was already a Red in the Constabulary, he could have helped other people come out of the east. People the Soviets wanted to infiltrate into this country."

We looked at each other. We both remembered who had actually let her across the border with the Soviet zone. I had plucked her off the barbed wire, and I had wanted to care for her for the rest of my life.

"You're still his friend," she said.

"That's right."

"After… I made my choice. That's very European of you."

"I'm not a European. I'm a soldier. Joe and I served together. I had his back and he had mine."

"Johann, I can understand it if you lie to me, but tell yourself the truth."

"Oh, I do. Every day."

"There's some other reason why you protect him from everything he does."

"There you're right."

She could guess, but she would guess wrong.

I stood to go.

"You might as well start speaking English again. It doesn't look as if the local police will be coming."

Back at the checkpoint nothing had changed. I nodded at Smithson.

"The shooter is gone. She got out by hiding the gun and looking like somebody's mother."

"I figured something like that. What do we tell the Shirley boys?"

"Let's go talk to them."

Reluctantly, he came with me. As we approached the Shirley officers, I looked for a vet among them. Three were obvious 4F's, but the officer who seemed in charge had the hard, watchful look of a survivor.

I introduced myself, and we exchanged brief resumes. The Shirley officer had been at Guadalcanal with the Marines.

"I think we all want the same thing here," I said. "LoSchiavo is one of our own. I'm hoping we can work something out."

The Shirley cop looked as if he knew I had cornered him and didn't appreciate it.

"We could call it accidental discharge of a firearm," I said. "Nobody got hurt. My friend brought it back from Europe. Didn't we all do something like that?"

A slight nod from the Shirley cop.

"Any way you can let this slide?"

He and Smithson studied each other. I decided it was time to let them work things out.

Trains back to Porter Square ran infrequently, but I caught one just as the doors closed.

I knew what to expect, and I didn't want to be there for it. I had something more important to do. But the two FBI agents were quicker than I had expected. It had to be them at the door of my dormitory room. Even their knock sounded Federal. I stood aside for them to enter. Anything else would have aroused more suspicions.

"We're still looking for LoSchiavo."

"If he isn't home, I don't know where he is."

"I've heard about you Constabulary guys. Recruited from the cream of the Army. Encouraged to reenlist when everybody else was getting demobbed at top speed."

"Your point?"

"You're supposed to be incorruptible Texas Ranger types."

"I'm still waiting."

"We think LoSchiavo became a Communist convert while you were policing the eastern border of the American zone. He might have let some very bad people in."

"Not while I was watching."

"How did his wife get in?"

"She was trying to cross, and some Ivans were trying to drag her back. We made them stop. But after that we weren't just going to hand her over."

"Was that procedure?"

"Exercising our discretion was procedure."

"How about here at Harvard? Anyone he's especially friendly with?"

"Me."

"You wouldn't cover for him, would you?"

"He'd do it for me."

"Are you?"

"Any chance you can let it all be ancient history? That's what the war feels like to me, anyway."

"Maybe, but the Russians aren't. We know they have Harvard in their sights. People here advise the government on policy. Scientists work on classified projects. Students could become influential down the road. The Soviets want assets who can tell them what their targets are thinking and doing. We're appealing to your patriotism here."

"LoSchiavo talks a Red game, but that's all it is—talk."

"It would help if we could ask him ourselves."

"Now we're back where we started. I don't know where he is."

They exchanged stern Federal looks and left.

I didn't know for sure where Joe was, but I had a good idea where to look, in an apartment in North Boston. Anne Belwyn opened the door. She was dark where Katrina was fair, and slender where Katrina was buxom, but she would turn any male head. Trust LoSchiavo to go for the best.

"Oh," she said. "John."

"Anne, you need to get Joe for me."

"Why would he be here?"

"I don't have time, Anne. You're really digging yourself into some trouble here."

"What do you mean?"

"This isn't the time for talking like a Red. It's also a very bad time for humiliating your husband until he calls the FBI on you."

I didn't need to raise my voice, but I did anyway.

"Joe, I know you can hear me."

He came out of what I assumed was a bedroom.

"I'm serious, Joe. Go back to your wife. This is no time for amateurs."

"Amateurs didn't live to come home."

His remark reinforced my point. He and Anne didn't understand what they were involved in.

I left them to decide for themselves. I had another stop to make, and the FBI agents had already proved they were quick.

The address was only blocks away. The landlady claimed to speak only Italian, but I was getting tired of that tactic.

"She'll see me," I told her.

The landlady let me pass.

Mrs. Kaposi opened the apartment door as if she was expecting someone, but the sight of me surprised her. She recovered quickly and stepped aside for me.

She had a single room with a half kitchen. The bathroom would be down the hall. In the corner farthest from the kitchen sat a cot. A wooden table with two armless chairs completed her furnishings. I had seen it before among refugees. They had lost everything once and didn't plan to accumulate anything that they could lose all over again.

She and Mrs. Gelb might never exchange a word that wasn't library business, but the other woman probably lived in similar style.

My hostess indicated one of the chairs, but instead of joining me, she went and sat on the cot.

"Mr. Sass." She gave it the Hungarian pronunciation: Shahsh. "You speak Magyar?"

"Yes."

"How is that?"

"My parents spoke Hungarian with each other and German to my grandmother."

"Which is why you knew to come to me. Mrs. LoSchiavo told you I sounded Viennese."

Mrs. Kaposi smiled at something far away.

"Vienna and Budapest. I had so many friends in both cities, before the war. We used to go back and forth like sisters who live next door to each other."

She couldn't maintain the smile. I had seen similar listlessness among soldiers after a brutal battle, when they had spent the violence in them.

"But it still could have been Gelb. Or have you already spoken to her?"

"I didn't need to. I knew it was you."

"My husband was in the Hungarian Second Army."

"I know."

Her eyes had turned inward, and she missed my admission.

"Most of the men died at Stalingrad. Then their Soviet captivity killed most of the rest."

"But Joe LoSchiavo played a nasty trick on you. He said he had news about your husband. Is that it?"

"He told me his wife had traveled with some men who escaped from a Soviet camp. It was a cruel thing for him to do."

"He planned to give you hope that your husband was still alive. But it wasn't hope at all. You've known all along that the Soviets have him."

"Why did he do such a thing?"

"I think he planned to come back with more news, this time that your husband was dead. He would have expected it to crush you, but it actually would have given you hope of getting free of the Soviets."

"I ask you again, why?"

"He thinks you're a Nazi sympathizer."

"No more than I am a Communist. He has no idea how things were. We did what we had to do. Everybody did. We still do."

She controlled herself.

"As soon as I saw his wife, I understood he was lying. She knows nothing."

Mrs. Kaposi focused on me. My words had finally broken through.

"How is it that you know all this?" she said.

"Tango Queen," I said.

She sat back. Her expression reminded me of a German infiltrator I had once seen waiting to be executed by firing squad.

"Yes," she said.

She sounded like the infiltrator agreeing to a blindfold.

"The password is Tango Queen. It was an especially cruel choice on their part. My husband called me his Tango Queen, after my favorite operetta by Lehar. That is how I knew they had him. Or rather, that you have him."

I could have resisted the slightest hostility in her voice, but her tone stayed level, almost kind. In her place I could never have done as well.

"Not me," I said. "They."

I paused. There was still time for me to stop explaining. Even a particle of my old fervor would have allowed me to maintain my heartless façade, but I had none left.

"Suppose a young man had a brief period of idealism. What else are young men for?"

She listened.

"Suppose he met the wrong people, and suppose his idealism yielded to realism, and he tried to move on. And they said, 'Not so fast, pal. We own you now.' They never let go of anyone. And now our own government is saying the same thing—once a Red, always a Red."

I stood to go.

"We never had this conversation. I should never have had to reveal myself to you. Now you know I'm your handler, and I will have to pass you on to someone else."

I waited for her to nod.

"Do nothing. That's what you should have done in the first place. I hope I can keep us alive. And out of prison."

At the door I turned back to her.

"You were right about one thing. We all do what we have to do. Maybe you and I are better off than some."

"Because we know."

"Because we know."

And now a quick hop over to rural Connecticut where a cushy new job as Chief of Security for a water conservation district turns out be any but.

Trouble at Lunatic Lake
by DG Critchley

I didn't even have to check for a pulse. The bullet hole in Lou's forehead was a dead giveaway, if you'll pardon the expression. I walked back to my patrol car. By my count, I had one murdered security guard, a bulldozer currently in flames, and thousands of dollars in damage to the sluiceway. As Friday nights go, I've had better.

I walked back my patrol car, grabbed the radio mic, and changed the frequency to the sheriff's department.

"Sheriff? This is Dan up at Merritt Dam. I have a situation up here."

"Hi, Dan. More vandalism? You know I told you that it was your problem."

"I remember. But this time, I have a dead body." The static and silence told me that sheriff now agreed that this was officially out of my jurisdiction.

"Alright Dan, I'm on the way up there. Don't touch anything."

"Roger that. Thanks, Sheriff."

I decided to walk down the long dirt road to wait by the construction gate for Chief Mosley.

Three days after I got back from Korea, the two sides signed the armistice. As charming as I am, I don't think I had anything to do with it, but I can't help but also note Stalin chose to die on the very same day I started my discharge paperwork. You're welcome, President Eisenhower.

I had planned to serve just long enough to retire young on a military pension and join the Beat Generation as a poet. There were several problems with the plan. Getting sent to Korea definitely put a damper on my enthusiasm for Army green. My complete lack of talent as a poet was also a factor. I arrived stateside after one tour with no money, no prospects, and a skill set that was limited to shootings things and/or blowing things up. I thumbed my way down to Connecticut and moved in with my brother.

Finding a job suited to my skills, perhaps something in law enforcement or demolition, was proving difficult. My preference was security at the State College, since dealing with drunken frat boys was slightly safer than handling dynamite, but a year later, I was no closer to a job, security or demolition, and my brother's hints were getting a lot less subtle about moving out.

I don't know if it was my famed boyish charm or my 54th weekly visit to the unemployment office, but my case worker was eager to let me know that Fairfield County was looking for security officers at the prison and that military service counted toward seniority. I headed over to the County office and discovered something better than being a prison guard—the County Conservation District had openings for security for the water supply in their Western District. The pay was better and I had never heard of a lake shanking a guard with a shiv fashioned from a toothbrush.

Apparently, my résumé was stronger than I thought (or a grateful Ike finally made that call) but I was asked if I would consider the Chief of Security position for the Western District. Like I'd say no? The starting pay was a respectable $3000 a year, enough to live on and start looking for a house of my own. I got a county automobile and an office at the Water Department offices in the middle of Grassley. I even had a window in my office. Granted it looked out on the only traffic light in town, but it was a window office! More importantly, this had long-term employment potential. 1954 was starting to look up.

My first day at the job, I was introduced to the staff—a handful of conservation officers and a secretary/receptionist/dispatcher named Lissa (with a double s, as I was repeatedly reminded). Most of the guards were retired cops who couldn't afford to move to Florida. Then there were the two who weren't somebody's grandfather, Lou and Chuck.

Based on his personnel record, my first impression of Lou as a pig-eyed, little tub of ill-tempered lard had been overly optimistic. He had a stack of complaints against him by local fishermen, a stack of complaints from recreational boaters, and a handful of police reports about speeding in his patrol car or sleeping in it, and that was just the first manila folder of three.

Chuck looked like some sort of greaser in a uniform, with a pack of Camels rolled up in his sleeve and a carefully maintained DA. The old chief didn't trust him because he was a "motorcycle-driving punk." But his personnel file was full of letters from locals thanking him for his assistance.

The Conservation District welcomed me with gifts. They could have kept all of them. The first was eight months of unfinished paperwork, courtesy of my predecessor (mostly additional complaints against Lou for annoying fishermen). Problems with poachers in the watershed were on the increase, the County was asking for an audit of last year's expenses, and best of all, there had been a recent outbreak of vandalism at the construction site of the new Merritt Reservoir. I was beginning to see why my predecessor decided to retire.

After my interview, I never heard from the Conservation Commission again. Apparently, as long as I didn't poison the water supply or destroy the pumping plant, they were a hands-off commission, whose public meetings were once every six months, at the Grassley Tap House, booth 12.

I suspected part of the reason the Water Commission kept a low-profile was to avoid dealing with the County Commission, or more specifically, County Commissioner Byron Cunningham Dawes. Dawes was a local realtor, one of the few in an area that had not been embraced by suburbia. He apparently made a living at it, but he was covering a huge swathe of the county to do it. His sole contribution to local government was his overwhelming paranoia about the creeping Red Menace. Naturally, he was also the County's Civil Defense director.

I settled into my new office and tried to prioritize. The vandalism at the reservoir project was apparently a much bigger problem than I had realized when I took the job, mostly thanks to Commissioner Dawes. I knew better than to try and convince him the Russians had better things to do than vandalize a behind-schedule and over-budget construction project. Especially one, if the rumor was correct, was being reconsidered by the County Commission. Compared to that, other things looked fairly uneventful—Lou was investigating reports of drag racing on the access road at Perridas Pond and one of the grandfather officers had recently interrupted a vagrant roasting a duck behind the pump house on Curwen Street.

I decided I needed someone who knew the area who wasn't somebody's grandfather and wasn't Lou. I called Chuck into the office and had him sit down. "Chuck, I need some thoughts from a local, and you just volunteered."

He just sat there, looking faintly amused. "I don't suppose you are looking for advice on how best to fire Lou?"

I smiled. "You should be so lucky. What you know about the drag racing at Perridas Pond?"

Chuck broke into a smile. "It didn't take you long to figure out Lou, did it? Of course, there's no drag racing out there. Lou just likes to nap in the woods. The road is too narrow and it isn't paved. Nobody's going to risk their suspension. The dragsters are out at the old quarry off Capron Road."

I paused for a moment and digested that tidbit. Chuck saw the hesitation. "You did know Lou is slacking off on the payroll, didn't you?"

"I had my suspicions, but didn't have a location," I lied. "I've been more concerned about the vandalism at the reservoir."

Chuck looked relieved that he hadn't ratted out Lou, as far as he knew. He paused. Finally, he leaned in. "Boss, the story is that the land was an Indian burial ground. The whole project is cursed."

I looked at him. He was serious. I had to say something, but that question took me by surprise. "Cursed? Like zombies and ghosts?"

Chuck stood up and started pacing. "I don't know. I'm not even sure the story about the burial ground is real, but I've seen the damage up at Lunatic Lake—it's too much to be just bad luck and human error."

"Lunatic Lake?"

He relaxed a bit. "The local name for the reservoir. The official name of the project is the Merritt Dam at Ayerston, but when they painted the "no trespassing sign" on the gate blocking the access road along Sprague Stream, they messed up the abbreviation. Instead of MDA, the sign says "MAD access road." And the old chief wouldn't pay for a new sign. Considering the creepy reputation the area has, "Mad Lake" kind of fits. And Mad Lake became Lunatic Lake."

I kind of liked the name, which I'm sure the Conservation District would not adopt as the official name. "I don't suppose the name has anything to do with the damage to the sluiceway?"

Chuck went somber again. "With some of the weirdness in those woods, I wouldn't be surprised."

I pulled the files on the reservoir project. "I need to go over some of these reports, and I don't recognize all the names. Pull up a chair and walk me through some of this stuff."

My predecessor was not much of a note taker, but Chuck was able to supply who some of the players were. The papers on top showed an increasing amount of frustration with the vandalism. The FBI said it was probably shoddy construction. The contractor blamed union instigators. The unions blamed the sub-contractors. And Commissioner Byron Cunningham Dawes claimed it was commie sympathizers. No one believed him but they had appointed him head of Civil Defense in hopes it would shut him up. It didn't. The Conservation District's response was to "let the chief retire" and hire a younger man. That was where I came in.

The bottom line, as far as the County was concerned, was that if the vandalism couldn't be stopped, they'd cancel the project and move it to a designated alternative site upriver.

I let Chuck head home and tried to wade through the actual dam construction plans. From what little I could understand, the plan was to build the sluiceway first and then an earth levee would be built to dam the water temporarily while they poured the concrete footings for the permanent dam. When the water reached a certain depth behind the levee, they'd keep it stable with the sluiceway.

And that's as far as it got. The temporary dam was holding fine, but vandals kept hitting the sluiceway. Equipment was vandalized. Tools were stolen. The cement channel was damaged regularly. The sluiceway had to be completed before the autumn rains started upriver and overflowed the levee. If the construction didn't get back on schedule soon, the levee would have to be opened to let more water back into Sprague Stream, which would throw construction even further off schedule on the dam itself.

I decided to take a look at the construction site myself in the morning and perhaps increase the patrols up there. I suddenly had an idea of how to keep Lou out of trouble and shut up Dawes. I had Lissa contact Commissioner Dawes and ask for a meeting in the morning. Although she managed to tangle the phone cord around her desk lamp, the typewriter, and her autographed picture of William Holden, she actually managed to make the call.

I closed the door to my office and made a mental note to pull her personnel file and find out who she blackmailed to get this job. The way things were shaping up, it was probably Dawes.

I arrived early the next morning. If I played my cards right, I could get two monkeys off my back at the same time and figure out the vandalism problem in peace. But with Lou and Dawes in the same room at the same time, I wanted to make sure I had locked up my gun. Not that I thought either one would use it—I was more worried about me using it on them.

Lou showed up first. I had him sit down. He looked guilty, but then again, he always looked guilty. After a few moments of awkward silence, he couldn't stand it anymore. "Am I in trouble?"

I looked at him. "Of course not, Lou. You got a guilty conscience?"

"No." He said a little too quickly. "It's just that getting called in here is usually trouble."

I glanced over to the window to see Dawes pull up in the river barge on wheels he called a car. "Lou, I promise that you're not in trouble." I don't think he believed me, meaning he was smarter than I gave him credit.

Dawes burst into the office like he owned the place, which I suppose, as a commissioner, technically he did. I was already beginning to regret locking up my gun.

"Commissioner Dawes, how good to see you," I lied, trying to fake sincerity.

He just looked at me. "Well, I assume you called me here for a reason?"

I thought about getting the gun and then smiled. "Yes indeed. Thanks to Lou here, we have a lead on the vandalism up at the reservoir."

Lou looked at Dawes. Dawes looked at Lou. Both looked surprised. Then they looked at me. "I've been reviewing all the patrol logs and Lou here has single-handedly stopped all the drag racing up at Perridas Pond."

Dawes looked at Lou. Lou looked at me and went a little pale. "Don't be shy Lou, take credit where credit is due. We haven't had a complaint about car races out there since you starting your patrols."

Dawes looked at me with his eyes narrowing. "What does this have to do with the commies sabotaging the reservoir?"

I looked at Dawes while Lou stood there looking like a deer in the headlights. "Isn't it obvious, Commissioner? Hoodlums are communist sympathizers. Lou's heroism scared the punks away from Perridas Pond and now they're taking their revenge at the reservoir."

Lou looked downright queasy. Dawes thought about it. "It sounds possible."

I went in for the kill. "Since Lou is the only one who's dealt with the drag racers, he's the only one who knows what they look like. Right, Lou?"

For a split second, Lou looked like he was about to confess he'd been sleeping at the pond. Then he just gritted his teeth and nodded.

I looked a Dawes. Pointing to Lou, I said "That's why Lou is going on special assignment up at the reservoir. He can spot the perpetrators before they can commit more sabotage. All I need is one or two of your Civil Defense volunteers to randomly drive up to the construction site and make it look like we have more patrols than we can afford."

If he hadn't already, Lou would figure out my plan. Move him up to the reservoir but send CD patrols up just often enough that he couldn't risk taking a nap. He had two choices now, do the job he was paid to do and patrol the construction site or get fired by admitting he was slacking off.

Dawes agreed, looking forward to fighting the creeping scourge of the red menace. He hadn't figured out yet that if something else was damaged, it was Abbott and Costello taking the heat, not little old me. I was beginning to like this job.

It worked like a charm, at least at first. No new vandalism, and no one complaining about Lou. About a week later, Lou didn't check in on the radio for his 9 PM. Rather than deal with calling Dawes, I decided to head up myself. I assumed Lou had figured out the CD patrol timetable and figured out how to sneak in a nap. That assumption evaporated when I reached the access road and the gate was smashed open. I took the dirt road a little faster than advised. As I neared the dam site, I could see light. Considering the construction site had no outside lights installed, I immediately recognized that as a bad sign. I screeched to a stop and hit the ground running—a bulldozer had smashed through a retaining wall on the sluiceway and was now engulfed in flames.

There was no sign of Lou, and I doubted even he could sleep through a bulldozer crashing into a cement wall. I ran back to the car and grabbed my shotgun. The construction site was quiet, except for the bulldozer burning away. I followed the retaining wall to the foreman's shack. It was still padlocked. I headed toward the rest of the trucks. That's where I found Lou.

The sheriff showed up faster than I expected. Wordlessly he leaned over and opened the passenger door and I climbed in. I explained the situation as we headed back up the road. He parked beside me and looked around.

"Do we need to call the fire department?"

I shook my head. "It's mostly burned itself out. The impact where it rammed the wall is the real damage, a little more heat damage won't make a difference."

I led him to where Lou was laying. He squatted down with his flashlight.

"No exit wound, so small caliber. Entry wound is small enough to guess a .25 or .22. Minimal powder marks, so it's close range, but not face to face." He straightened up and glanced at my shotgun, then my service revolver, a .38.

I was mildly offended. "Chief, I'd fire him, not shoot him."

He looked around the construction site. "Just checking. I can think of a bunch of people who'd sooner shoot Lou than give him the time of day, but they'd use a deer rifle."

He straightened up and looked around. "I'll have Doc Haimer come and get Lou. I suppose we won't need an autopsy. No point looking around in the dark. I'll radio for a couple of deputies to secure the crime scene until it's light enough to search for evidence. Let's wait at the cars."

The next morning was a blur of examining the construction site with the sheriff, then dealing with an emergency meeting of the Conservation Commission in my office (the Tap House didn't open until noon). By the afternoon, I was tired. There was a knock at the door. Chuck quietly walked in with a box.

He placed it on my desk. "Lou's work equipment. The sheriff took the personal effects to find a relative. Doc Haimer thought we should hang on to it."

I stood up and walked around the desk. "Okay. Let's pretend this is relevant and take an official inventory. I doubt there's anything important but I don't feel like doing anything important."

I grabbed a clipboard and a blank piece of paper. Chuck opened the box.

He pulled out Lou's service belt. "One belt, with a billy club, which I might add is not county issue, a Conservation Office badge, and one clip-on flashlight. The first pouch has a whistle, which is county issue. The rest of the pouches are empty except for potato chip crumbs."

I skipped the part about the crumbs.

Chuck reached into the box again. "One Conservation Officer's cap." He gingerly placed it on the desk. "Might want to just burn that, unless you know how to remove Brylcreem stains."

I skipped the stain part too.

He pulled out Lou's citation book. "Conservation law violation citation book, mostly used." He stopped and looked at it. "This might be a list of suspects. Lou was not well-loved among the fishing community."

I nodded. "You can run it over to the sheriff."

Chuck smiled. "Good, I want to hear the latest updates on the fuss this morning."

"Fuss? A murder is a little more serious than a fuss."

Chuck shook his head. "It must have happened after you left. Your favorite County Commissioner nearly got himself arrested."

I sighed. "Of course. It was a matter of time before Dawes got involved. What did he do?"

Chuck smiled. "He showed up and insisted on inspecting the crime scene for evidence of the Red Menace. And the sheriff doesn't take kindly to people trying to push past his deputies into an active crime scene."

"Well, at least he's the sheriff's problem for a change." I nodded at the box. Is that it?

Chuck looked in the box. "Just one more item—Lou's camera case." He pulled a leather case out of the box by a strap. He put it on the desk. "It's not standard issue for a conservation officer, so I'm not sure why Lou had a camera. There's no sign of the camera, just the empty case. I don't ever remember seeing him with a camera either way."

I felt myself going pale. Chuck saw it too. I just stood there staring at the leather case, a familiar 4.5 inches by 3 & 3/8 inches with a half-moon window. And suddenly my bad situation was a worst-case scenario.

"Boss?" Chuck was still standing here, looking a little nervous.

I looked at him. "We got a problem."

Chuck looked at me. "That camera case?"

I collected my thoughts and licked my suddenly dry lips. "Chuck, that's not a camera case. It's a galvanometer carrying case." He looked at me blankly.

"I trained for demolition in the army. A galvanometer is used to test the circuit on blasting caps."

Chuck was starting to understand. "Blasting caps."

I nodded. "Chuck, I'm going to need to you to check something for me while I head up to the reservoir."

I opened the office door. "Lissa, get the sheriff on the phone. Tell him I need to see him immediately. Have him meet me at the reservoir."

I don't know if it was my tone or dumb luck, but she managed to dial the phone correctly. I grabbed my holster and headed to my patrol car.

Chuck followed me out to my car as I explained my suspicions. He hopped on his bike. I just hoped that his Indian Roadmaster was as fast as he claimed. I headed up to Lunatic Lake as fast as the ancient patrol car could go. I took the turn onto the access road too fast and hit a rock. I heard a noise under the DeSoto that told me it was making its final trip. The Club Coupe sputtered to a stop. I pulled to the side of the rutted path and start up the road as fast as I could.

There was no sign of the sheriff, but I had a thought. I went to the construction shed where they had a phone. I kicked open the door and dialed a number I knew by heart.

After we got back stateside from Korea, I took my honorable discharge and headed to Connecticut. My buddy Frank decided to make the army a career choice. He was now some bigshot up at Fort Devins in Massachusetts with the Army Air Defense Command.

I skipped the small talk. "Frank, this is Dan. I need a favor and I need it yesterday."

Frank knew me well enough to know the tone in my voice. "What's the problem?"

"Frank, I've been dealing with someone vandalizing a construction site. Now, I think someone has been playing up there with a military-issue galvanometer. Have you heard any rumors about the army misplacing explosives in the last few weeks?"

There was dead silence on the phone. "Dan, if there had been a theft, say down at Wellfleet, you know I couldn't confirm that to a civilian. And I certainly couldn't divulge details about how much military dynamite went missing, assuming half a crate was missing, which it isn't."

I paused. Half a crate meant twenty-five pounds of dynamite—enough to take out the whole town, never mind the construction site.

"Frank, can you let the MPs know I got a bad feeling where their dynamite is?"

"Dan, I can't send military police down there on a bad feeling from a civilian who officially doesn't know a problem exists."

I understood. "Okay, Frank. But if I find anything resembling military grade contraband, I'm calling back."

"Understood, and Dan, be careful. Wellfleet is nothing but reservists now and they are not teaching demolition. You know the only thing more dangerous than explosives are amateurs who think they know how to handle explosives."

I hung up the phone. I had two advantages. First, military dynamite didn't have nitroglycerin so it was less likely to blow up someone mishandling it. And more importantly, I knew demolitions at least as well as whoever planned to use them.

I stepped out of the shed and scanned the area. I knew where I would place the dynamite to do the most damage but that would involve attaching the dynamite about 4 feet up on the cement walls, which would be visible. I had to stop thinking like a soldier and think like an amateur. Put it in the ground along the base, attached the cap, run the wires, and then hide them under the dirt. Inefficient, but 25 pounds of dynamite would still leave a crater where the sluiceway used to be. An amateur would want to watch his handiwork, so they'd needed a vantage point, high enough for a view and far enough away to not get caught in the blast.

By the time the sheriff drove up, I knew where the vantage point was. I quickly explained the situation and we hurried up the side of the stream to a rock ledge. From the top, there was an uninterrupted view of the entire construction site.

The sheriff found the shunt wire first, buried in the leaves, the wire leading down the hill to connect all the firing wires. Assuming it was wired correctly, connecting that shunt wire to the blasting machine mean a simple push down on the plunger handle and the Merritt Dam at Ayerston was rubble. The debris would probably take out the levee as well, so the project would be back to square one. The good news was that all I had to do is cut any of the wires and the entire blast series would be inert until someone found and fixed the break.

A shot rang out and a bullet ricocheted between the two of us. We dove for the woods. Crouching in the brush, I pulled my .38. The sheriff already had his out.

He looked at me. "Rifle. Most locals use a Marlin," he whispered. "Lousy at long range, but if he gets closer…"

"Sheriff," I whispered back. "The phone in the shack is working. Your car radio works. Can you get down there and call for back up while I distract him?

The sheriff nodded and glanced at my gun. He took his gun and opened the chamber. He handed me four bullets. "If I need more than two, you did a lousy job of keeping him distracted. However, if he counts shots, you now have an advantage."

I nodded and put the bullets in my shirt pocket. The sheriff snapped the chamber shut and crawled off into the woods. Another bullet ricocheted off the ledge. I had a pretty good idea of the sniper's direction. I stood up, fired in that general direction, and dropped back down. The next shot was closer. He was getting a better idea where I was too. I stood up and ran back toward the ledge. There was a rather inviting boulder there. The next shot was between me and the boulder. I fired off two shots in a row as I ran back into the trees.

Suddenly, I remembered last week's episode of a radio detective show. Johnny Dollar was pinned down and out of bullets. The bad guy walked up to him and explained the entire plot. Then the detective shot him with the other gun he had in his pocket. I had three shots left. I ran toward the boulder again, firing the last three bullets. Shielded by the rock, I reloaded with the sheriff's bullets. I tucked it into my belt in the small of my back. And then I waited.

"I know your gun is empty." The voice was familiar. I stepped out to face Commissioner Dawes. He had slung his rifle over his shoulder and was holding a .25 Beretta Bantam in one hand and the blasting machine in the other. A Bantam was underpowered as pistols go, but at this range, I wouldn't survive to quibble the point.

"I assume that's the gun you killed Lou with?"

He nodded. "He called it a 'ladies gun.' Rather a poor choice for last words." He put the blasting machine down and pulled the shunt wire out of the brush with the gun carefully pointed at me. The gun never wavered as he attached the wire with one hand.

"Dawes, I'm impressed. There are soldiers who couldn't attach a shunt wire to a detonator with two hands. Have you considered surrendering and enlisting?"

He looked up and grinned. "I like you, Dan. I'm going to make sure you get a hero's funeral. After all, you died trying to prevent saboteurs from destroying the dam."

I needed to stall. "And the sheriff?"

Dawes smiled again. "The communist spies destroyed the squad car radio and cut the phone lines. By the time he walks back to town and comes back with help, you'll have died a tragic death protecting the construction site. I, of course, will have to insist his incompetence caused your death and have him fired."

"Not that I'm complaining, but why am I still alive then?"

Dawes stood up. "Simple. If I didn't follow the manual correctly, I need someone who knows explosives to fix it. Government documents are miserable to understand."

If he would drop his guard for a second, I might be able to get the drop on him. "Dawes, if I'm dead either way, why would I help you?"

He took a step closer. "Because you think there's still a chance you can survive this."

He had me there. He dropped to one knee and primed the detonator. He turned the key and nothing happened. He looked down and I ducked back behind the boulder.

"Seriously, Dan?"

I pulled out my revolver. I heard him coming toward the boulder. I came out firing. The first bullet blew the Baretta out of his hand. The second one hit him in the shoulder. He went running into the woods. I picked up the Baretta and threw it into

Sprague Stream. As I bent down to disconnect the shunt wire, I heard the bolt drop on a rifle and a shot roar out. The impact spun me around as I hit the ground. From the white burning agony in my ribs and the blood oozing out of my side, I was in trouble.

Dawes was standing there. Based on the blood soaking his shirt and the look on his face, I was not going to talk my way out of this. I pointed my gun at the detonator, which seemed to be getting a little blurry.

"Shoot me Dawes, and I'll still be able to destroy the detonator." Breathing seemed to be getting extremely painful.

Dawes took careful aim. "Go ahead. My idiot nephew stole a spare when he grabbed the dynamite." I waited for the shot. It rang out loud and clear. Surprisingly I felt no new pain.

I tried to focus and looked at Dawes. He had a surprised look on his face. Then he fell, face forward. Behind him was the Sheriff. The sheriff holstered his gun. "I told you I wouldn't need more than two bullets."

I waved my gun at the sheriff. "I have two left, so I guess I owe you two bullets." And then everything went black.

I woke up in Danbury Hospital with my side looking like a patchwork quilt gone horribly wrong. The nurses were not inclined to be chatty, but Chuck stopped by and filled me in. The bullet had shattered a couple of ribs which then punctured a lung. Two inches closer and I'd have bled out before they could get me down the hill. In addition to enough transfusions to make Count Dracula envious, they had rebuilt the ribs with metal plates.

"So," I said. "Dawes was the communist?"

Chuck shook his head. "Nope, just a greedy saboteur. You were right. If the Ayerston Dam was canceled because of all the vandalism, the backup site was upstream in Biglerville. And Dawes has been buying up property in Biglerville for a year or so."

I nodded. Even that hurt. "About the same time the vandalism started?"

Chuck nodded. "From what I could tell at the County Deed office, Dawes could build a planned suburban community of expensive but cozy little houses, all with waterfront access after the dam was completed."

Sheriff Moses walked in. "I was asked to stop by. The County Commissioners extend their gratitude for your assistance in my investigation."

"Your investigation? Nurse! Where are my painkillers?"

The sheriff smiled. "Relax. No one will care in another week. You're on medical leave indefinitely, and by the time you come back, the County Conservation District may even have a new car to replace the one you destroyed on the access road."

I was tiring fast. "What about the dynamite?"

The sheriff glanced at Chuck. "Under the supervision of the acting head of security, the Army recovered all the explosives. They also have Dawes's nephew in the brig up at Wellfleet."

The sheriff looked at Chuck and nodded at the door. "The doctor said to keep this visit short."

The two turned to leave. I shook my head to clear it. That hurt too. "Wait a minute—"acting head of security?""

Chuck pulled out his comb and straightened his pompadour. He just smiled.

I was having trouble focusing. "You?"

He followed the sheriff out the door. "Could be worse—could have been Lissa."

Now I really was ready for some painkillers.

In every high school there are stories about a teen who ran away to join a circus. In our last story, we tag along as Davy learns about...

Life and Death on the Road
by Kaye George

Davy lay awake, rigid, unable to relax. On his back on the thin mattress, his arms stiff at his sides, his shoulders tight, his eyes wide open in the darkness. The words of the Head Carny echoing through his young brain. He was just a boy, really, only fifteen. Not even old enough to drive. What was he doing here?

"Watch out for the Fat Man. He'll take your pay if you let him." The remembered words whispered to him, just above the night noises outside the trailer, people shuffling past, low conversations.

Watch out? How? What should he watch out for? The Fat Man slept in the bunk below his in the trailer. He wasn't there right now. The Fat Man hadn't come in yet. He would soon though. Any minute now. It was past one, maybe past two in the morning.

Davy had been glad to get paid this afternoon, the second time in the four long weeks of toil he'd put in for the traveling show. He tucked the wilted bills into the back pocket of his jeans at first. Then, after the Head Carny warned him, he changed them to a front pocket. In fact, he'd climbed into his bunk wearing his jeans. There was nowhere else to stash his pay besides his jeans pocket. Nowhere that the Fat Man, or anyone else, couldn't get to.

The first time they'd been paid, two weeks ago, he'd gone with Wolf Boy and some of the others into the eastern Iowa town, Cedar Rapids, where they were set up on the outskirts. Davy had been surprised he'd been able to walk into a bar with the others and even more surprised when he ordered a beer and no one asked him for ID.

Bart, a short wiry guy who ran the Ferris wheel, climbed onto the stool next to him. "After you finish that, I'll order you a real drink, sonny," he'd said, his smoker's voice raspy, ruined.

Bart growled the order to the bartender before Davy finished the beer. "Give the kid a real drink. He needs some whiskey."

Davy had choked on the first sip, but kept at it, trying to keep up with his fellow carnies. They were slugging down the whiskey like it was Kool Aid. After that, after some pleasant necking with a couple of pretty town girls, after stumbling back to the trailer, and after throwing up just before he went inside, he awakened the next morning to realize his money was gone. He never knew if he'd spent all of it, or if something else had happened to it. It was just gone. Every dollar, every dime.

This time, he'd resisted the invitations to join them. They were now in western Iowa, outside Council Bluffs, about to cross into Nebraska the next day. They'd broken the rides down and gotten them loaded before they got paid, and he was determined to keep this paycheck. He hadn't run away to join this carnival just to end up with no money.

He lay in the dark, trying to remember exactly why he had done it. He'd been mad at his dad, wanted to "show him." Dad had lit into him about not raking the leaves like he was supposed to.

"The grass'll die, son, if we don't get the leaves up. Look how thick they are." His dad bent down, grabbed a handful of dry, crumbling elm leaves and let them flutter to the ground. "The grass can't breathe." Their street, like most of the residential ones in Moline, was lined with majestic elms. They arched over the brick streets, making a cathedral ceiling for the whole town. But they sure shed leaves in the fall. They had to be raked up every week or so and piled at the curb.

He had to admit, he liked the smell of burning leaves. Nothing like it. When they burned them at night, he loved to watch the sparks fly and hear the popping. Tommy next door said that was insect bodies bursting. But what Tommy said wasn't always true.

Davy shut out the pleasant memories and returned to his dark thoughts about his dad—and that precious grass. The man seemed to care more for his lawn than he did for his four children. He gave them yard chores all year long, it felt like. Seed the lawn, fertilize it, mow it, pull the weeds, water it. The thought of the whirring of the push mower took him back again, but he tamped down that memory.

Davy's older brother, Jake, often joked that the blades of Kentucky blue had better not grow crooked if they knew what was good for them. Davy didn't think it was funny, though. He'd always rather be in his room reading.

When the carnival had come through town, he'd spent all his allowance on the rides, the Tilt O Whirl, Ferris wheel, Bumper Cars, all the time watching the guys who ran the rides. Tough-looking guys with their tee shirt sleeves rolled up and cigarettes dangling from their lips. What a life they must lead, he thought. Going all over the country, seeing everything. No family, no yard, no parents. Some of them looked almost as young as him.

He snuck out late that night and watched them tear down the rides. Then he summoned up more bravery than he ever had in his life. Walked up to a man who looked like he was in charge, barking orders and going from crew to crew. Asked him if he could work for him.

"Hey, kid, we just lost three men at the last stop. Good timing. Glad to have you. Get over there and give them a hand with the coin toss booth."

And, just like that, he was hired. Left town the next morning for a life of travel and adventure. Attracting the notice of the young girls was a heady experience. Girls had never given him a second look before. Or a first one.

Even the boss's daughter flirted with him. He knew to stay away from her, though. When he was at breakfast in the chow wagon the first morning, the Head Carny took him aside and pointed out his daughter. She was beautiful, about his age.

"See that girl over there?" he'd said. "That's Jori. She's off limits. She's my daughter and I'll tell you what I tell everyone who works for me. Stay the fuck away from her."

So he did. Ignored the fiery glances she gave him. She gave them to everyone, anyway. She wouldn't really want him. He was slight, pale, and loved to read. That's what he wanted to do with his money. Buy a pile of books and read at night in the trailer after they closed up.

So far, though, he hadn't had any money to spend. Life on the road wasn't like what he had pictured. Just about an hour ago, tonight, he'd heard gunshots. The sound bored a hole in the pit of his stomach. He missed his mom, his dad. Even the lawn.

⸻

He made up his mind. He had to get out of there. He needed to go home. Silently, he climbed down the ladder, slipped into his shoes, and grabbed his duffel. He always kept it packed, had never moved his things into the two drawers the Fat Man had said he could use. Had he always known he would leave like this? Sneaking out in the wee hours?

Without a creak, he edged the metal door open, just a crack, to get the lay of the land. Three other roughies, men like himself who broke down and put up the rides, stood in a circle about fifty yards away, smoking. The tips of their cigs glowed and the smell of the smoke drifted on the damp air, blended with the smell of the hay scattered on the ground, a sweet, exotic mixture. None of the three turned a head toward him.

He slunk away, keeping close to the trailer until he rounded the end of it, out of their sight. No one was in the alley between the rows of jungle buggies where all the carnival folk lived and slept. Once out of the passageway, he nearly stumbled over a couple of lushers passed out on the bare black Iowa dirt.

Looking down to step around them, something shiny caught his eye. The full moon overhead cast his own form as a short shadow before him. Next to his shadow, the moonbeam glinted off a pool of dark liquid beside the head of one of the passed out drunks. There was a neat little hole in the man's forehead, leaking slowly.

The back of Davy's neck prickled and his stomach clenched. His body knew, before his mind did, that he was seeing a pool of blood. It had to be coming from the man's head. The form on the ground was huge. It was the Fat Man.

Davy's heart hammered and his ears rang with alarm. He reached a trembling hand toward the glistening pool, black in the darkness. He drew his hand back just before he touched it, as the acrid stench hit his nostrils and made his eyes water. He squinted through the sudden tears to make himself look at the Fat Man's face. It was flaccid, his eyes half open and his mouth drooping to one side. He looked at the hairy man lying beside him, Wolf Boy. He lay on the other side of the Fat Man's bulk, his shaggy black head by the dead man's feet, his hairy arms flung out, one in front of him, the other above his head. Had he been fighting someone off? The Fat Man?

Or, was he dead, too? Davy stepped carefully to the other side of the misshapen pile the two figures made in the dirt and peered at him, leaning down and holding his hand over his mouth and nose for the smell. It was strong of alcohol and blood and… maybe the Fat Man had pooped his pants? Davy looked away.

A soft moan came from Wolf Boy. Davy looked again and saw the gun, clutched loosely in Wolf Boy's large hand. Blood dripped from a hole in his sleeve, but not much. Most of the bleeding was from the Fat Man. Had Wolf Boy shot him?

The gun lying in Wolf Boy's hand didn't look like the one he'd shown Davy once. This one was small, dwarfed by his huge mitt. The handle was plastic and—Davy squinted at it—pink. It had a pink, plastic handle. The handle wasn't in Wolf Boy's hand, the barrel was. What did that mean?

Wolf Boy raised his shaggy head from the ground, his eyes still closed. He was alive. Davy froze for a moment. Did they fight each other? Did someone else attack both of them? The Head Carny had warned him that the carnies often fought on payday, after they liquored up. He hadn't said they killed each other. Davy wouldn't have to worry about the Fat Man stealing his money.

Davy's first instinct was to holler for help, to try to save Wolf Boy's life. Davy straightened up, shocked that he would want to do that. He sorted out his thoughts. Wolf Boy looked like he was dying. But, if Davy were on the ground dying, Wolf Boy would never stop to help him. Or anyone else. Even though he was called "Boy," he was a grown man, and a big one. He had a snub nose and big brown eyes and his face looked young, innocent, faintly boyish. He was popular with the marks, but there was nothing innocent about him. He was a mean son of a bitch. He'd knocked Davy down more than once for not moving out of his way fast enough.

Just tonight, he'd grabbed Davy by the arm and shaken him for refusing to come out carousing with them.

"You too good for us, city boy? Maybe you don't belong here. Maybe you're a softie."

Davy hadn't looked at him, just stood there with his arm clamped in Wolf Boy's paw. "Don't feel too good," he mumbled.

Wolf Boy laughed, his signature howl. "I noticed you couldn't hold your liquor last time we went out." He'd let go with a shove and sent Davy sprawling on the ground. While Davy lay there, Wolf Boy had stepped close and opened the long coat he always wore, just enough so Davy could see the thick, black pistol.

"The boss's daughter is going to come with us. Does that interest you?"

Davy scrambled to his feet. Did Wolf Boy want to get shot by the boss? No one was supposed to mess with Jori. No way would he go with them tonight. He remembered thinking that someone might end up dead.

Now, looking at the two men on the ground, Davy wondered if Wolf Boy had shot the Fat Man in the head. Davy turned his back on them and hurried away, as fast as he could without making any noise. He wasn't going to help them. He didn't like either one of them and the Fat Man couldn't be helped. His mind spun, working out how he would get out of here and get home.

He passed the Head Carney's wagon at the end of the row. The boss man's '55 Chevy was parked beside it, as usual. Davy stopped to run his hands over the sleek, red front bumper. He loved that car. White top and white inset at the square back bumper. That car made a statement. It was new, this year's model. Davy loved it. He ducked his head to look in the window and saw that the keys weren't in the ignition. If they had been, he didn't know if he would have taken it or not.

A chill crept up his spine and he whirled around. Wolf Boy was ten feet from him. "Too good to stop and help a fella, kid?" he growled. "Where do you get off walkin' away like that?"

"I… I thought you were… I'm going to get help."

"Pettin' the boss's car ain't gonna help me."

He lunged at Davy.

Davy sidestepped and started running. When he looked back, Wolf Boy stood glaring after him. Maybe he was too injured to chase him down. Maybe he would try to shoot him. Davy didn't see any gun, and Wolf Boy wasn't coming after him, but Davy ran faster.

He left the grounds and stumbled onto the highway. There wasn't much traffic in either direction this time of night.

As he walked through the night, listening for an approaching automobile, serenaded by locusts in the trees by the road, he tried to figure out what had gone on. Had the two men messed with the Head Carney's daughter, Jori? Even though the boss threatened to shoot anyone who came near her? Had she really gone into town with the rough carnival men? Almost all the carnies were men. The women, the midget lady, the Bearded Lady, and the contortionist, never went out with the guys.

If the boss had caught the two men with Jori, he might have shot them. But he would have used his shotgun. And then Davy would probably have seen a lot more damage, the Fat Man's big head blown apart and brains all over. No, he hadn't been shot with the boss's shotgun.

If Wolf Boy had shot him, wouldn't he have used his own snub-nosed, black pistol? An evil looking thing. Why was he gripping that little pink-handled pistol? Looked like a toy. But it would make a little hole like the one in Fat Man's forehead. Why was he holding the barrel? And why was Wolf Boy shot, too?

Davy stuck his thumb out the first time a car came by. An older sedan, the skirts of its fenders rusted on the bottom from salted Midwestern winter roads, slowed and stopped in front of him. He ran to the driver's window. The man cranked it down and the smell of beer wafted out the window.

"Need a ride son? It's pretty late for you to be out here."

"Yes, I'd like a ride. Just to a payphone." There had to be a gas station somewhere with a payphone outside it.

"There's one just ahead. I'll drop you there." The man looked like he was a farmer coming home from a night at the local bar. His face was sun-ruined and smile lines had been etched into it, making Davy feel safe with him. Until he started driving.

The man's car wove from lane to lane, but there wasn't any other traffic, so they made it to the closed gas station without hitting anything. It was only a half mile down the road. Davy realized he could have walked there and that would have been safer.

He thanked the man and scrambled out of the car. As the taillights meandered down the road, he hoped the friendly man made it home safely.

The payphone was in a booth next to a pole. He opened the door and started to step inside. Something was on the floor.

It was a person, huddled, and shaking with soft sobs. A tear-streaked face looked up at him. It was Jori. The boss's daughter. The one everyone was supposed to stay away from. The one who flirted with everything in pants.

Davy's first instinct was to get away from her. That's what he'd done every time he found him anywhere near her, not wanting to get his head blown off. He stepped back and started to close the door. She grabbed the edge of it.

"No, don't go. Don't leave me." Her voice was thick with crying.

Did she know who he was? She seemed to. "Do you want me to call your dad?"

"No! Don't call him! He'll kill me."

Davy started breathing hard. He looked around for… what? There wasn't any help here.

What was he supposed to do? He had to stay away from her. But he couldn't leave her here on the floor of a phone booth. Could he? Anyway, he needed to use the phone. He had to get out of here. Get home. Call his own dad.

"Please stay here for a little bit, okay?" Jori turned her blue eyes, big as saucers, on him. She batted her eyelashes, wet with tears.

"What's the matter? What happened?" He held the door open. There wasn't room for both of them inside with her taking up the whole floor. "You want to come out of there?"

"I don't want my pa to find me." Her voice was hoarse. She must have been crying for a long time.

"Why not? He's probably worried about you."

"I wasn't supposed to go with them. I'm not supposed to do that."

Davy waited for the rest of it. He knew this part.

"I always thought Pa was being mean, never letting me do anything. I didn't know they were like that. Didn't know they would do that."

Davy tried to imagine what had happened. He wanted to know and he didn't want to know. Before he could make up his mind whether or not to ask, she supplied the details.

"I thought we were going into town, but we went to Wolf Boy's trailer. They both started drinking something from a bottle."

"Whiskey?" Davy asked.

"I guess. It smelled awful. But after the first couple of sips, it tasted okay. We sat around drinking for a long time. I don't know, maybe an hour. I thought I should go, so I tried to stand up, and I was trying to make it to the door, but I couldn't walk straight. Then the Fat Man came up behind me and held my arms and Wolf Boy started kissing me."

She wrinkled her mouth like she was tasting something bad. "He was all slobbery. Just like a dog. A wolf, I guess. It was gross. Then…" She was breathing fast, reliving the assault. "Then they both took off my tee shirt and started grabbing my breasts and… other places. I grabbed my shirt and ran out. All of a sudden I could run straight and wasn't dizzy any more."

New, fresh tears streamed down her soft face.

"I guess they chased you, huh?"

She nodded. "I had my little gun with me and…" Sobs shook her shoulders and she covered her face with her hands.

Davy could imagine what that had been like for her. "Are you okay?" That was probably a stupid question, he thought, as soon as he said it.

But she nodded. "I'll be all right. But I don't know what Pa will do."

"Your pa loves you. He wants you to be safe. I have some change. Do you want me to call him?"

She stopped sniffling and wiped her cheeks and nose with the back of her hand. Pushing herself up with the corner seat, she stood and straightened her shoulders. "I can't go back. You don't know what I've done."

In a flash Davy knew what had happened. The men had caught up to her. That little toy-looking thing was a lady's gun. It was Jori's. She had shot them. Wolf Boy must have grabbed the gun away from her by the barrel.

"The Fat Man is dead," Davy said.

She nodded. "And Wolf Boy?"

Yep, she'd shot them. Davy shook his head. "He's probably okay. Just a wound in his arm, from what I could see."

She stepped out of the booth and Davy backed up to give her room. "So, see? I can't go back. Wolf Boy knows I killed the Fat Man."

"I'm sure… I'm… you… but he was…"

"Yeah. He was. But I shot him."

"You were defending yourself, weren't you?" She was a killer. And he was here alone with her. At least Wolf Boy had her gun. Didn't he? "Did Wolf Boy take your gun from you?"

"They both ganged up on me. I couldn't fight them off. After he grabbed my pistol, I ran. I thought he might shoot me. I ran and ran, until I got here, and hid in the booth."

Davy didn't think Wolf Boy would do Jori any favors. Probably wouldn't tell anyone he and the Fat Man had attacked her. "I think everyone will believe you. That they went after you. Everyone knows what they're like."

"They do? I didn't. They've always been nice to me."

"That's because your pa was there. They wouldn't step out of line with him there. They weren't nice to everybody."

Jori frowned, thinking about that. Davy was getting the impression that she wasn't too smart. He'd always thought she was so cute, that he'd love to have a girlfriend like that. But maybe not quite like her.

"Really, I can call him. I can tell him what I saw."

She tilted her head at him in that flirty way she had. "What did you see?"

"That Wolf Boy had grabbed your gun. He was laying there, holding it by the barrel."

"But he's not dead?" She didn't sound like she would be upset if he was.

"No, he got up. He wasn't dead when I left."

She peered at him. "What are you doing out here? Did you shoot somebody?"

He almost laughed. "No, I just... I decided I need to leave the carnival and go back home. I came along because I was mad at my Dad. He'll be worried. Him and Mom."

"They don't know where you are?" Her mouth formed the prettiest little O.

"No. I need to call them."

"Yeah, you do." She stepped aside so he could get into the booth.

His dad wasn't mad. He was glad to hear from him. Relieved, and maybe crying a little, it sounded like. "Sit tight, son. Stay right there. I'll pick you up as soon as I can. Your mom and I are leaving now."

He stepped out of the phone booth feeling good about facing up to what he'd done. Running didn't solve anything.

It would be hours before his dad got to this side of Iowa. It had to be at least three by now. The gas station would open when it got light and Davy would be able to get something to eat. But what about Jori? What was he going to do about her?

"Jori," he said. She was sitting on the ground leaning against the phone booth. "You should call your dad. You can do it. You can own up to what you did. I guarantee it'll make you feel better."

She should go back to the carnival. "I'll bet your dad will drive here to get you."

"Could you come back with me? We can just walk. It isn't that far." That coquettish tilt of her head again.

"I can't." He could, but he wasn't going to. This was progress, though. She was agreeing to go back. "I have to stay here. My dad is coming to this station to get me." She didn't know how far away his family was. He hadn't told her where he lived.

"Maybe he could drive me back?"

Davy shrugged. This night was one problem after another. Was it ever going to be over?

Jori stood up. "You're right. He's probably worried about me. I'll call him."

Davy had to give her money for the coin slot. She called information first. The carnival set up a phone in every town for the few days they were there. She got the number and called. She had to hold the receiver away from her ear, the man shouted so loud. At first. Then he calmed down when she said she was okay.

After she hung up, she gave Davy a gentle kiss on the cheek. "He's going to meet me, so I'll leave now. I'll tell him you're not coming back." She smiled, turned, and started walking

Davy watched her walk away, glad to see the last of the carnival people.

Then, in case her father came looking for him, he hid in the phone booth until the station opened. He'd never been so glad to see the sun come up and the night end.

A Murder
of
Crows

Edited by Sandra Murphy

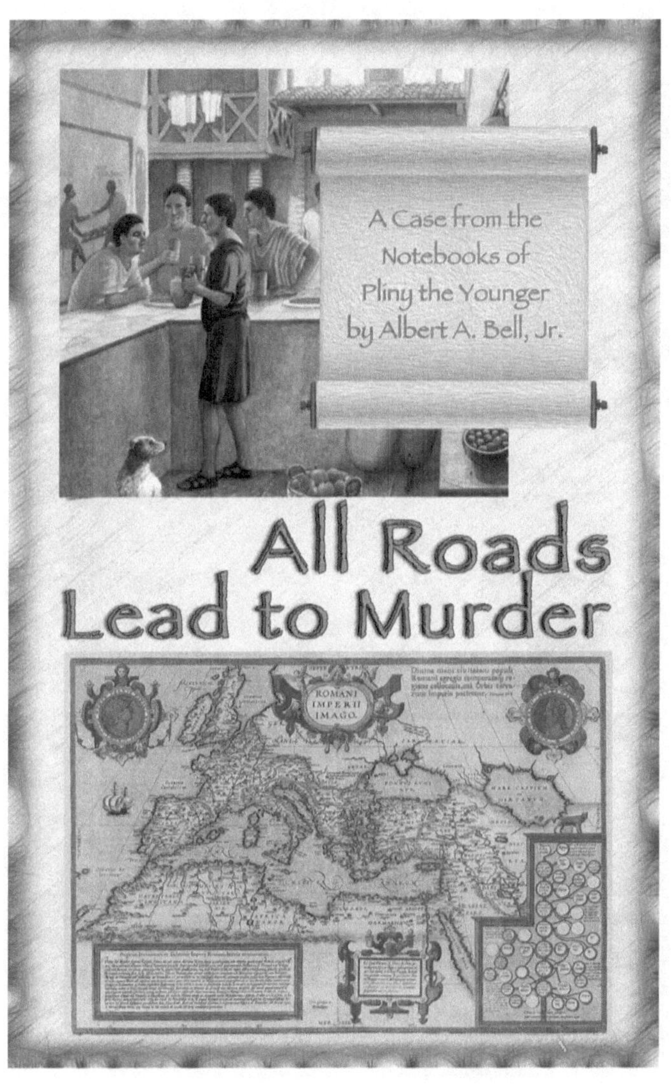
A Case from the
Notebooks of
Pliny the Younger
by Albert A. Bell, Jr.

All Roads
Lead to Murder

ROMANI
IMPERII
IMAGO.

Wilder
Rumors
A Lewis Wilder Mystery
MOLLY MacRAE

About This Book

The typeface in this book is 11.5 Garamond and Helvetica. The title font is Black Chancery. It was laid out using Adobe InDesign software and converted to PDF for uploading to the printing facility.

About Darkhouse Books

Darkhouse Books is dedicated to publishing literary, mystery, science-fiction, and horror.

Darkhouse Books is located in Niles, California, an inadvertently preserved, 120 year old, one-sided railtown, forty miles from San Francisco. Further information may be obtained by visiting our website at www.darkhousebooks.com.